NIGHTS ON, NIGHTS OFF

In a busy maternity unit there are inevitable tensions between modern technology and the demands by some mothers for a 'natural childbirth'. For widowed midwife, Shirley Pierce, there is no argument: the safety of the baby is always paramount, and her strongly held views are deepened when she meets a young man who has been brain-damaged since birth. Sister Pierce's defiant attitude towards a hospital manager and her refusal to heed the warnings of her friends lead to her involvement in a horrific tragedy, and she soon discovers that there is a heavy price to be paid for resisting authority...

NIGHTS ON, NIGHTS OFF

NIGHTS ON, NIGHTS OFF

by

Maggie Bennett

Magna Large Print Books
Long Preston, North Yorkshire,
BD23 4ND, England.

British Library Cataloguing in Publication Data.

Bennett, Maggie
    Nights on, nights off.

    A catalogue record of this book is
    available from the British Library

    ISBN   978-0-7505-2598-5

First published in Great Britain in 2006 by Century

Copyright © Maggie Bennett 2006

Cover illustration © Nigel Chamberlain by arrangement with
Alison Eldred

The right of Maggie Bennett to be identified as the author of this work
has been asserted by her in accordance with the Copyright, Designs
and Patents Act, 1988

Published in Large Print 2007 by arrangement with
Century, one of the publishers in the Random House Group Ltd.

Magna Large Print is an imprint of Library Magna Books Ltd.

Printed and bound in Great Britain by
T.J. (International) Ltd., Cornwall, PL28 8RW

Dedicated to
The Royal College of Midwives
And all Midwives working in
the National Health Service

Acknowledgements

To Detective Inspector Michael Lomas (retd.)
for his valuable information regarding police
procedures of arrest and custody.

To Mr Harry Monks, Prison Officer (retd.) at
HM Prison Manchester
(formerly Strangeways)
for his insights into prison life.

To Mr Leslie T. Mason
Who kindly took me on a tour of HM Prison
at Risley, Cheshire
(formerly Risley Remand Centre).

Chapter One

Band of Sisters

It's always easy to be wise with hindsight, though, when I look back now on that fatal sequence of events, I'm amazed at how totally unprepared I was for the tragedy waiting to break and touch so many lives. None of those involved in it emerged unscathed, but I hope I did more than just survive. Did I gain anything from it? Am I any wiser now? I've changed, of course – well, I'm ten years older for a start, with only another three to go to retirement, and that'll be another big change. Midwifery doesn't get any easier, what with the choice-in-childbirth brigade on the one hand and the ever-increasing technology on the other, and I'm finding it harder to keep up with it all. I tell myself that it will be nice to have more time to visit my grandchildren – there are four of them now, with Emma's two. And yet...

Some things stay the same, whatever happens. The permanent night staff on Maternity at Marston General Hospital are still as closely knit as they were then, and we still know everything about each other's lives, midwives and nursing auxiliaries alike; our individual circumstances are common knowledge.

For instance, we know whose marriage is going through a sticky patch; whose kids are playing up;

whose teenage daughter is pregnant, and whether she's having it or opting for a quiet abortion; whose elderly mother has gone dotty; and whether the family can cope or are sending her into The Willows Eventide Home, which is expensive, or the Marston Borough Council one, which is a bit overcrowded. We know whose husband has been made redundant, or if his small business has gone to the wall, whether he's actually facing bankruptcy.

And back at the time I'm talking about, we knew who had found a new meaning to her life at Shalom. More about Shalom later.

Then as now we were all local women, mostly forty-plus, and if the student midwives doing their three months on nights were sometimes indignant at having their pregnancies diagnosed before their periods even fell overdue, well, never mind about them; our collective consciousness was a comfort to us older ones, an emotional warm bath that meant we didn't have to cover up and pretend to each other. Goodness knows how I'd have coped without my colleagues during that dreadful week that Tom was in the Coronary Care Unit and they all turned out to the Requiem Mass at St Antony's, even those who'd been on duty all night. It was the same when Sister Grierson broke down and wept in the Postnatal Ward office on Christmas Eve, and discovered that we'd all known about her unhappy marriage for ages – how Howard Grierson's unyielding stance in the council chamber made him a tyrant at home, foul-tempered and stubborn. Our work provides a reassuring continuity, and when trouble strikes any one of us, everybody else weighs in with help and support. All for one and one for all!

And of course they all knew about me and Paul Meadows. More of him later, too. Much more.

This care for each other continued after retirement. When Dora Hayes developed bowel cancer and was admitted to Female Surgical, her former colleagues would go up to visit her before or after the night shift. She was only sixty-two, and we saw at once that she wasn't going to make it, though her husband and GP daughter insisted that she'd be all right once she got over the trauma of major surgery; She'd been a senior midwifery sister up to her retirement and was one of the old school, very conscientious but a bit brisk with mothers who had their own ideas about how and where and in what position they wanted to be delivered. I'd have gladly put my own daughters in Sister Hayes' care, knowing that their babies' safety would be her prime consideration, and it was very sad to see her laid so low. She was in a double room with another poor soul who wasn't long for this world, and her husband, Martin, sat beside her long after the other visitors had gone, because nobody had the heart to ask him to leave.

'Shouldn't you go home and get some rest, Martin?' I asked quietly, touching his shoulder as Dora opened her eyes and smiled in recognition.

'Shirley Pierce,' she murmured. 'How very kind of you, when you're so busy over there.'

'I'm just going on duty, Dora. How are you feeling now, love?'

'Laura says I'm making good progress, and of course it's such a relief not to have a colostomy.

Mr Jamieson was able to do an end-to-end anastomosis when he'd removed the – er – blockage. If only I didn't feel so tired–'

Martin entwined his fingers with hers and gave me an imploring look. 'She's doing very well, Mrs Pierce. Laura says she'll be up and about in another week or two. Thank God for a doctor in the family, eh?'

It was pitiful.

When I went into the Delivery Unit office, there was only one patient in labour, and she had just been sedated. Sister Linda Grierson was on with me, and we shared the auxiliary Sandra with Postnatal.

'The poor girl must *know* that her mother's dying,' Linda remarked when I told her what Laura had said. We all knew that Dr Laura Goodson was one of the most competent GPs in Marston, and it was she who'd sent her mother for X-rays and tests, then referred her to Mr Jamieson's gastro-enterology clinic.

'I don't know, Linda. It's funny how we can kid ourselves when it's somebody close to us. I think she ought to prepare her Dad, though.'

'She might have tried to, for all we know,' Linda said. 'Have you seen Bernie McCann yet? It's her first night back, and she's on Postnatal.'

'Oh, yes, of course, poor Bernie,' I sighed. 'Better not mention Dora unless she asks – you know, another mother dying.'

'Sssh!' hissed Linda as Sister Bernadette McCann joined us, a little pale and tired-looking, but smiling.

14

'Girls, girls! Are ye talkin' about me behind me back, now?'

Tall and slender, her pretty blonde hair turning white without intermediate greying, Bernie is an absolute sweetie from County Donegal, where she'd been for the past fortnight on compassionate leave to attend her mother's funeral. I poured out another cup of coffee.

'Great to have you back, Bernie,' I said as Linda kissed her. 'How was – er–?'

'Me dears, it was a marvellous send-off we gave her! And ye see, there was this old chimney-sweep gettin' married on the very same day at the very same church. We've all known Paddy Heneghan for years, and the whole village turned out for him and for Mother, the two Masses, like, the Requiem and the Nuptial. There were so many of us mourners, and it went on for ages, ye see, so Paddy and his bride had to wait until we came out o' the church before they could get into it – and it was so full o' flowers – oh, girls, it was a scream really, because we all ended up together, like, the weddin' and the wake!'

And there she stood, giggling with tears spilling down her cheeks. 'Sure and wouldn't she have loved every minute of it, God rest her soul – and such a beautiful, soft April day it was.'

Then the front door buzzer went.

'Yes? Can I help you?' I said to the electronic device on the wall.

'It's Mr – it's Martin Hayes, dear. Can I come in and talk to you for a minute, please?' I'd never heard a man sound so lost. We looked at each other and at the clock. It was nearly ten.

15

'Yes, of course, Martin – come in, come in,' I said, pressing the button that released the door.

'Right, let's leave Shirley to deal with poor Mr Hayes in here, and I'll come and give you a hand on Postnatal,' said Linda, leading Bernie away. That's the way we are on Maternity.

It was a good job we weren't busy just then. I brought him along to the D.U. office where he sat down with me, and after a few irrelevant remarks he broke down and expressed his inexpressible fears. When I stayed silent, his face went blank with terror. I put my arms around him – what else could I do? – and he laid his head on my shoulder and sobbed until my uniform dress was wet with his tears. Sandra looked in, and I mouthed to her over the top of his head: 'tea'. She nodded and mouthed silently back: 'sure thing', and retreated, closing the door quietly. It was nearly eleven when he left, just as an ambulance arrived with a patient in labour, and the telephone was ringing with news of another one on her way in. For the next few hours it was all go and, with two new lives beginning, I didn't have much chance to ponder on Martin Hayes' approaching bereavement.

One of the mothers was the single eighteen-year-old daughter of a couple who come to St Antony's – nice people, too. They both came in and sat one on each side of her throughout the whole of her labour. So much for that girl's A-levels, I thought; and knew who'd be getting up in the night for *her* baby boy. Once again I thanked my lucky stars that neither Ruth nor Emma had presented me with a too-early grandchild; so many of their con-temporaries had become single mothers, to the disruption of their parents' middle age, whether the girl had married the baby's father or not – and most of them marry *somebody*, sooner or later. My heart ached for this anxious couple, especially when the girl had to have a Ventouse vacuum extraction for failure to progress. Linda said she'd take the blood samples over to the Path Lab because Sandra was busy washing the other new mother who'd had a normal delivery. Usually an auxiliary goes over to the laboratory at night, accompanied by a porter, but Linda said she couldn't be bothered to wait for one.

'The lab technician's already in – he'll open the door to me,' she said.

'Be careful, Linda – you don't know who might be prowling around the grounds,' I cautioned. 'And if it's that deputy pathologist – what's his name – don't let him detain you with his hard-luck stories. Just remind him he gets twenty quid every time he comes in to do a cross-matching.'

Linda smiled. 'I'll give him your kindest regards, Sister.'

It was about that time that the Shalom movement was making a big impact on Marston, and I sometimes wonder how differently things might have turned out if I'd never gone along to that first meeting out of curiosity – though it's always futile to speculate, and doesn't alter anything. Not now.

When I'm asked what Shalom is all about, and what happens at the meetings, I can never really explain it, perhaps because I've never been quite sure myself – so let's listen to poor Dilly Fisher,

17

nursing auxiliary, deserted wife and mother of two, one of life's unfortunates. We'll go forward a couple of weeks to a night when she was sitting in the Postnatal Ward office with Bernie and me, nibbling a biscuit with her decaffeinated coffee.

'So what's it all about, Dilly? Do they go in for a lot of Hallelujahs? Tell us!' ordered Sister McCann.

'Ah, it's what we're all in need of, love,' Dilly answered seriously, her eyes lighting up. Her gentle face always made me think of a sheep. 'It's a united gathering of Christians from all denominations – Methodists like myself, Church of England, Roman Catholics, Baptists – and unbelievers are welcome if they're truly seeking faith. It was started by Philip Crowne, he's the lay preacher at my church, Moor End Methodist – and he's on the Marston Borough Council–'

'Labour or Tory?' asked Bernie.

'Independent, love. He doesn't believe in the party system. Anyway, Shalom's just gone on growing. We meet every month in different churches, and once you've been to one, you're never the same again. I've been changed, I mean really *changed*, since Philip laid his hands on me.'

I didn't dare look at Bernie. Dilly is such an innocent, and her life hadn't been easy since her husband left her for another woman, and Dilly had to agree to a divorce she never wanted. I suppose he just couldn't take poor Dilly's endless flow of nervous chatter any longer – and after a couple of nights on with Dilly I can understand, though nothing excuses the man for leaving her to cope with two difficult teenagers made even

18

worse by the upheaval. And of course she has spoiled them rotten.

'And how does this Philip character change people?' enquired Bernie. 'And why *Shalom?* What does it mean?'

'It's Hebrew for *Peace be with you,*' replied Dilly. 'At every Shalom meeting we go round and exchange the peace with each other – you know, we embrace in the name of the Lord.'

'Oh dear, I'm afraid I'm not very good at exchangin' the peace at Mass,' said Bernie. 'I never know how many I'm supposed to shake hands with.'

I knew what she meant, as I tend to run out of steam after about five or six handshakes at St Antony's.

'Oh, at Shalom we go all round the room, exchanging the peace with *everybody,*' Dilly enthused. 'Philip says it's important to affirm the brother and sisterhood of all believers, because we're all one in Christ.'

She paused, and an awkward silence fell, as it always does when God is brought into the conversation, even though Bernie and I are regular churchgoers. It was almost a relief when one of the post-natal mums rang the bell, and Bernie went to give assistance with changing and feeding the baby. It was two o'clock, the most deadly hour of the night, and I tried unsuccessfully to suppress an enormous yawn.

'Excuse me, Dilly, I didn't sleep much yesterday,' I apologised.

'That's all right, Shirley love, we'd all rather be in our beds,' she sighed. She stared at me for a moment, and her next words were quite un-expected.

'Don't you ever feel a bit lonely, love, now that both Ruth and – what's the other one's name? – now that they've both left home? You don't mind me asking, do you? Only we're rather in the same boat, us two, aren't we?'

I hesitated. I didn't think our situations were at all comparable, but I couldn't very well say so to poor Dilly. Whereas her teenage son and daughter give her constant headaches and throw her hard-earned cash around like confetti, I was so thankful for my own two girls. Ruth got married early to hard-working, ambitious Richard Butler, and at twenty-five she already had two children, Helen and Timothy. My darling Emma got a good degree and worked for a big publishing house in London, where she was buying her own flat. I missed her dreadfully, and at that time was hoping she wouldn't marry her current Italian partner and leave the country.

'It's not much of a life on your own, is it, Shirley?' Dilly had apparently forgotten how her life had been changed by Philip Crowne's hands at Shalom. 'Sometimes I'd give a lot to meet a nice, kind man who'd take all the worry off my shoulders so's I didn't have to go on slogging away here. I can say this to you, can't I, Shirley? I know you must feel the same, deep down.'

I looked into her sheep's face and tried to give an honest answer. And I couldn't.

'I just don't know, Dilly. Sometimes when I wake up in the cold light of dawn to go for a wee, I suppose I might feel a little shiver of loneliness run down my spine when there's nothing else to think about. But when I balance it against the advantages of my life – you know, the freedom and independence, my daughters, home, friends and the work which I really enjoy–' I smiled, shrugged and added, 'No, I don't think I'd want to marry again.'

Thinking it over later, I suppose what I'd meant to say was that at forty-seven I simply couldn't think of a good enough reason for tying myself down to a man's likes and dislikes again, having to defer to him in all decision-making. I suppose I'd become used to my own company, having my own way: perhaps I'd grown selfish.

And after the trouble I'd had with a stepdaughter in the past, I couldn't see Ruth and Emma accepting another man in Daddy's place, even though they're adult and their lives wouldn't really be affected. Yet Dilly's question had opened up a new train of thought: would I become a semi-recluse in my old age, an eccentric old woman with only cats for company?

Anyway, my curiosity about Shalom was aroused, and the upshot was that I agreed to accompany Dilly to the next meeting which was to be held at my own church, St Antony's, where Father O'Flynn had said he was willing to try anything once and would play host to the new movement.

Meanwhile there were two more nights to be worked through, and two more days of interrupted, insufficient sleep. I did three nights a week, four if there was a staff crisis, and being on my own was able to make a modest monthly saving, though there was always something extra to pay for, in addition to the regular bills; repairs, redecorating, rewiring, double-glazing, replacement of some appliance that had broken down – the list was endless. I'd given up the car, which I didn't really need, and told myself that cycling was healthier.

Enforced early retirement from the old soap-refinery had been a severe blow to Tom, and his loyal but ill-advised investment in the company's stock had wiped out three-quarters of his capital, though he died before he realised the full extent of the loss, for which I was thankful. Now three years later I lived modestly in a smaller house, and found that I'd become fond of it. It was so pleasant to cycle home on these lovely spring mornings, with no need to hurry: I'd feed the two cats their breakfast, have a shower and thankfully collapse into the matrimonial bed from our former home. The young tabby, Pussage, went out while old ginger Peppercorn stretched his limbs in unhygienic bliss on top of the duvet. Putting out a hand to stroke him, I reckoned that life as a widow was not all that bad; it was certainly preferable to poor Dilly's lot.

Remember, I'm going back to before that first encounter with Shalom. And Paul.

Chapter Two

A Religious Experience

The meeting started at eight, and St Antony's was filling up well by a quarter to. My usual place was already taken over by a whole row of visitors from Moor End Methodist, so Dilly and I sat in the pew behind them, which gave her the opportunity to greet her friends and introduce me as Sister Shirley Pierce, midwife from Marston General. I smiled across at Norma Daley and others I knew from St Christopher's (C of E) who were there, and noted that there was a couple from Our Lady of Sorrows, defying old Father Halloran's warning to stay away from Shalom and anything that smacked of the dreaded charismatic influence that had invaded even Holy Mother Church.

It was encouraging to see a few men, though the women outnumbered them by at least three to one; and there was a small sprinkling of the kind of young people who'd probably been brought up to go to church but had drifted away. (Neither Ruth nor Emma attend now, which saddens me, especially when I think of little Helen and Timothy, duly baptised but not followed up in the faith.) One of them was standing beside Norma Daley and smiling down at her from a height of at least six feet. He was not unattractive, even though his clothes were oddly assorted and his hair needed a good brush: a university student from Manchester, perhaps, who'd heard about Shalom and come out of curiosity – maybe looking for something more than the round of sex and swotting that made up the life of most undergraduates, or so I'd gathered from Emma. I felt myself warm towards him on sight.

The music was provided by three guitarists who clearly practised and performed together regularly; they provided a soft background sound as the church filled. When Dilly pointed out Philip Crowne, I remembered seeing his photograph in the *Manchester Evening News*; even before he began to speak his strong personality showed in every feature. Dilly had told us how his forceful preaching had changed lives at a stroke, releasing souls from all kinds of bondage and addiction; broken relationships had been mended and the wounds of the past healed. New lives for old!

'Wait till you hear him, Shirley love, it's like somebody opening a door to a new life,' she whispered, her pale blue eyes shining in anticipation. 'That's his wife Celia over there, talking to your priest – she's Philip's secretary, and supports him all the way.'

My first impression of Celia Crowne was of large, lustrous eyes behind horn-rimmed spectacles, and a heart-shaped face framed by dark, wavy hair cut unnecessarily short. She wore no make-up, and I judged her to be about thirty-five; she was in fact eleven years older, a beautiful woman who passed for a plain one, and Dilly was right, she was her husband's mainstay. She watched over his health, arranged all his engagements and discreetly shielded him from the lovelorn, as not a few women had already discovered.

When he got up to speak, power seemed to emanate from him. His voice was resonant, with a remaining trace of homely Lancashire vowels, and I was immediately riveted in a way I never experienced when listening to Father O'Flynn's little homilies. One could see how this man's personal magnetism attracted all sorts and conditions of men and women to hear his message. Dilly had not exaggerated: he was spellbinding.

At the start he might have been a politician on a moral crusade, sounding off against today's society.

'Our country is in a mess,' he said bluntly. 'We are faced with a failing economy, a rising crime rate and a general sense of hopelessness. Tens of thousands of children are growing up in our towns without any moral or spiritual guidance whatever. We are breeding a new underclass as this century draws to its close.'

He paused while a murmur of assent rippled over the church. 'Even the serving professions seem to have lost their sense of vocation,' he went on. 'We have a National Health Service chronically mismanaged, with incredible wastage of funds. We have teachers threatening to go on strike because of unacceptable conditions in the classrooms. We have the most appalling examples of immoral behaviour in high places, where we should be looking for an example to follow.'

Was he referring to the Tory Government or the Royal Family, I wondered as he held up an

25

accusing finger. 'And what are the churches doing? Are they showing the love of Christ to the world? Here and there we find a church that tries to follow His teaching to feed the spiritually hungry and heal the spiritually sick, but for the most part there is only an out-dated, inward-looking concern with their own organisations, their finances, their dwindling congregations – and no wonder! They are closing their doors to the needs of God's children!'

His voice had risen as he spoke, and filled the church. 'They don't reach out as our Lord reached out to the so-called dregs of society who fell at His feet. My friends, we turn to our churches and find them only half alive.'

A rustling sigh rose from his hearers, and when he spoke again he seemed to be addressing each individual personally. I felt that he was speaking to me alone.

'And what of *you?*' he challenged. 'Are you burdened by the need you see all around you? Or is your time taken up with your search for gain, for security, for advancement? Don't you want to hear what the Lord is saying to you?'

I can't remember his words exactly as spoken, but he had this power to make us look in upon our hearts and face the secrets contained there – the regrets, the guilts, the unforgiven hurts. There were sighs as memories were stirred, and a woman a few yards away from me began to sob. Immediately a couple of Shalom regulars, a man and a woman, got up to go to her side, laying hands upon her head and shoulders, whispering words of hope and comfort.

Crowne's persistent questions were having their effect on my own heart.

'Are you imprisoned by the pain of the past?' he demanded. 'Is your mind blocked by some old unhealed wound, some failed relationship, some other person you can't forgive or who has not forgiven you? I want you now to identify that area in your life that is holding you back – and then we shall break that barrier down!'

Another wave of sighs and murmurings passed over the congregation.

'In a little while we shall pray for ourselves and for each other – and if anybody here feels in need of special prayer, just raise your hand. Don't hold back. Don't feel that your particular problem is too bad or too trivial. We are all in need of heal-ing, my friends, and the Lord is waiting to receive us, to bind up our wounds and fill us with that peace which nothing in this world can offer us.'

I can only give a faint echo of the impact of his words. We no longer heard the sound of passing traffic, the shouts of a gang of youths spilling out of the Tradesman's Arms further up the road, the unceasing roar of the motorway half a mile away. Inside the church the atmosphere had become charged with expectancy: it was electrifying.

And then began that extraordinary experience I had, the one and only time that I 'passed out in the Spirit'. Bear with me while I try to remember how it felt at the time.

I bowed my head and tried to pray, but all that came to mind was a picture of myself, and not an attractive one. I shuddered as I faced what I'd so long tried to forget, the bitterness of my failed relationship with Tom's daughter, the shadow across our marriage, darkening the years that should have been a mellow and peaceful time for Tom – and all because I had been unable to get on with the girl. Only I could guess to what extent his coronary thrombosis had been the result of all that stress, all that unacknowledged tension. I thought I'd managed to expunge Joy Pierce from my memory for ever, yet here she still was, dredged up from the dark recesses of my psyche, unforgotten and still unforgiven...

A sense of utter desolation swept over me, and I began to tremble uncontrollably. Looking fearfully into the future, I saw nothing but a haunted old age, loneliness and failing powers. Panic rose in my throat, terror gripped my whole body, gasps turned to audible groans and rose to an inhuman shriek inside my head. Or was it out loud?

I felt my body falling into an abyss of total blackness.

And then... it seemed as if time had passed, and everything was quiet; the accusing voice had stopped, and I was resting in a place of peace and tranquillity. Then I realised that I was lying on the floor of the church, and gentle hands were lifting me, carrying me out of the cramped space between the pews to the central aisle where I lay on the mosaic tiles, looking up into a circle of faces. It was like being a road accident victim, surrounded by sympathetic bystanders, and there was a soft murmuring in the air all around, voices praying, repeating phrases over and over again. My hands were held, I was soothed and reassured as if I were a patient coming round from a general anaesthetic. I felt calm and contented lying there, even though tears were trickling from the corners of my eyes and running into my hair; the horror had left me, and a man's voice was speaking quietly, close to my ear. Crowne must have asked my name from Dilly, because he was saying, 'The spirit of fear has been banished, Shirley, and a spirit of peace has taken its place. Open your heart, my dear, the past is forgiven – you can leave it all behind you now, and be free!'

There was a murmur of assent, almost like congratulations. I sat up and caught sight of Father O'Flynn's face behind Crowne's, looking absolutely mystified at such goings-on in his church, and not too sure whether he approved. I immediately checked the level of my skirt, in case it had been pulled up when I was carried out into the aisle.

But it *was* a tremendous release, a turning-point, or so it seemed at the time. I revelled in the glow of relaxed contentment that enveloped me and stayed with me when I returned to my place beside an enraptured Dilly Fisher. That night and for the next twenty-four hours I experienced a blissful state of euphoria, as if I'd been drinking champagne but without any hangover. 'Passing out in the spirit' was a fairly common phenomenon at Shalom at that time, though much less frequent now that we've all grown older and wiser.

One of the faces in the circle above me had been that of the young man I'd noticed earlier, and I saw him looking at me and smiling as we sang hymns and listened to scripture readings. When the time came for us all to exchange the peace

29

with each other – 'Shalom!' – he made his way straight towards me, and I was touched by the way he put both arms around me in a big bear-hug, pressing his lips against my cheek. I willingly put my arms up on his broad shoulders, and there we stood, silently embracing for about half a minute. It seemed a pity to end the moment with intrusive words, so I waited for him to speak.

'Shalom, Shirley, Shalom!'

'Shalom, er–'

'My name's Paul Meadows, and I'm very pleased to meet you, Shirley,' he said, blue-grey eyes smiling down at me. 'Mrs Daley told me your name.'

'And I'm happy to meet *you*, Paul,' I replied, disengaging my arms and steering us clear of another Shalom greeting from two well-built middle-aged ladies heading our way. 'Let's sit down – tell me all about yourself!'

And he did just that: I had hardly expected such a torrent of words. When we'd seated ourselves at the end of a back pew, he told me how he'd been invited to Shalom by Mrs Norma Daley, mother of the boy he'd met in the fish-and-chip shop in Boreham Road. I tried to concentrate as he poured it all out, his eyes alight behind spectacles which had been inexpertly repaired with sticking-plaster across the bridge.

'I go to the Seagull's Nest most evenings when I haven't got anything else on,' he told me eagerly 'It's where Rod Daley goes with his friend Gareth – it was him who introduced me to Mr and Mrs Daley. She said I could go round there some-times, and it's nice for me to have somebody to talk to, somebody who respects my opinions and doesn't just ignore everything I say, or worse still make so-called jokes about it, especially when the subject of politics comes up – and I've got strong views where that's concerned, Shirley, based on my own experience, as it were.'

I smiled. 'So you agree with Philip Crowne's views, I take it?'

'Oh, yes!' Enthusiasm gleamed behind his smeary glasses. 'He spoke to Mr Moss in the Housing Department for me, and got me this flat in Boreham Road. The Crownes helped me to move in, and Celia, that's his wife, she brought some furniture along, and the music centre, though even with that I still get very lonely if I'm there on my own for days at a time. I feel the need to make contact with other people on a friendly basis, as it were, but there are too many of the other sort about, Shirley, louts who've got nothing better to do than follow me down Boreham Road to the shops and back, yelling out words I'd rather not repeat to you. It's getting to be no joke, I can tell you, and Philip says he's going to get on to the Marston police headquarters to sort them out, and all I can say is, the sooner the better!'

His voice had been steadily rising as he talked, and he now paused to take a breath; I found that we were still holding hands as the stream of words flowed over me. Slowly and with a sense of dismay I began to realise that all was not right with this young man: that he was - what do we say? Not the full shilling? An older generation would have said not quite right in the head. He was retarded.

And straightway I willingly accepted him as a

31

fellow human being, and it was the beginning of our friendship, with instant and genuine affection on both sides. The Shalom movement inevitably attracts the lonely and marginalised, who come in out of the cold world for the brief warmth of a human embrace, and I felt myself to be an outsider, too. There and then I took Philip Crowne's words to heart, and opened my door to Paul Meadows.

'Would you like to visit me at home one day, Paul?' I asked him. 'I live alone, too, and I enjoy cooking meals for my friends.'

'Oh, that'd be *great*, Shirley – can I come tomorrow?' And that was how it all began.

On being told of the invitation, Philip Crowne spoke with approval and possibly a certain relief. 'How very kind of you, Shirley – and I hope you'll make yourself useful to Mrs Pierce, Paul, and give her some help in the house and garden. Keep him occupied, Shirley – make him pay for your hospitality!'

Paul came round for tea the very next day, and stayed for a good dinner, after which we talked and watched a couple of television programmes. From then on he was a regular visitor, and the amount of pleasure I got from his company surprised me, not least being the satisfaction of cooking man-sized meals again; I found out his favourite dishes, and set them in front of him with a flourish, to be rewarded by his healthy appetite.

He enjoyed listening to all kinds of music on tapes and CDs, and had a passable singing voice with perfect pitch, so we'd join in with *Songs of Praise* on Sunday evenings, or sit together on the settee and do the easy crossword puzzle in the *Marston Messenger*. I soon learned to keep off the subject of party politics, or at least the Conservative Government under John Major. To hear Paul speak of them you'd have thought they were a pack of evil fiends out to ruin the country and prevent the dawn of a socialist Utopia led by the Labour Party, when unemployment and every other social evil would be removed. When he could bring himself even to mention the name of former Prime Minister Margaret Thatcher, it was clear that he held her personally responsible for his failure to find a job, his struggle to live on a disability pension, and his consequent social isolation and frustration. I learned never to argue with him, but to steer the conversation into safer channels.

Such was Shalom, and of course we went to all the meetings, though I never 'passed out in the spirit' again. I sometimes witnessed others doing so, and have concluded that it's a form of auto-hypnosis brought on by a strong emotional appeal to the subconscious, like Crowne's highly charged preaching, and the heightened atmosphere that accompanies it. I was never convinced about the Holy Spirit's involvement, though one tries to keep an open mind. Not that it makes any difference now.

Dilly Fisher lost no time in telling the night staff that Shirley Pierce had found a new meaning to her life at Shalom, and wasn't it wonderful? Bernie McCann wasn't so sure.

'I couldn't be doin' with all them Hallelujahs, Shirley,' she said, adding quickly, 'though of course if it does somethin' good for ye, dear, that's fine. We've all been a bit worried about ye since–' She hesitated, and I felt that she was not only thinking of Tom's death, but of Emma's departure, which had left me on my own. 'D'ye think it'll last? And how much is it to do with this Philip Crowne? Did he lay his hands on ye, like he did on Dilly?'

'He's a most remarkable man, Bernie, and his wife's very nice, too,' I told her firmly. 'She's his secretary, and totally supportive of his ministry – they're a perfect team.'

'Thank God for that! A man like that without a wife is nothing but a menace to poor, unattached women.'

Needless to say, my colleagues were far more interested in Paul Meadows than in Shalom, and some were highly dubious about this new relationship. They warned me to be careful about who I let into the house, but of course I took not the slightest notice, and listened eagerly for his ring at the doorbell.

'Who is it?' I'd call out, and he'd answer, 'A lonesome stranger!' Then I'd open up and he'd step inside, where we would at once exchange the Shalom greeting and embrace.

'Shalom! Peace and joy, Shirley!'

'Peace and joy – lovely to see you, Paul!'

And I'd start preparing supper while listening to his latest news, and if it was a fine evening we'd eat in the conservatory and switch on the table-lamp when it grew dark. In the afternoons I'd get him working in the garden on jobs like digging dandelions out of the lawn, or painting the fence with wood-preserver; he'd even help tie in the young tomato plants to bamboo stakes, under supervision. He worked quite well, though his concentration span was short, and he needed constant encouragement to finish jobs.

There used to be a system of labels by which the mentally retarded were graded, from educationally subnormal to severely subnormal, with specific types of subnormality like *cretin* for congenital thyroid deficiency and *mongol* for the chromosomatic defect now known as Down's syndrome. In these days of political correctness they're all lumped together under the clumsy and misleading label of 'people with learning disabilities' – I mean aren't we all, in certain subjects? Why not just say mentally retarded or handicapped? And Paul Meadows' tragedy was all the more heartrending because it was caused by human error. For I gradually came to realise that my young friend had been brain-damaged at birth, and was now thirty-two years old and unemployable.

My colleagues know that I have little time for the natural childbirth brigade with all their talk of birth plans, a woman's right to choose, and so on, as if anybody's crackbrained ideas were of more importance than a baby's safety. Maternal death is now mercifully rare in this country, but babies can be damaged all too easily, and is any risk ever worth taking? I wasn't there when Paul's forty-plus mother gave birth to her third child; all I can be sure of is that *something* occurred to deprive him of oxygen for a significant period of time, not long enough to render him mindless

35

and helpless, but enough to separate him from the common herd, the acceptable average. His life was ruined at its onset because somebody failed to notice a falling foetal heart-rate, or mismanaged the mechanics of delivery, or did not know how to resuscitate a limp, silent, blue-tinged newborn baby. Where was God in that fatal hour? Not even Philip Crowne has been able to give me a satisfactory answer to that one.

Paul told me that he had lived at home with his parents until his late twenties, when his mother had died and his father, then well into his seventies, had not been able to cope with him and had gone to live with an older married daughter. It was Philip Crowne who had eventually persuaded the housing department of Marston Borough Council to allocate Paul a flat in Boreham Road, and the social services had awarded him a disability allowance which paid the rent and theoretically kept him in the basic necessities of life; but he had no idea of how to budget from week to week, and lurched from crisis to crisis.

I was not the only person to over-estimate Paul's mental ability. Even Philip and Celia Crowne were taken in at first by his deceptively wide vocabulary, which gave the impression that he was less retarded than he actually was. Various assessments and reassessments had been made by clinical psychologists, educationalists and psychiatric social workers, and he had been given a mental age ranging from ten to twelve years; so here was a boy in a man's body, with all of a man's needs for love and friendship, for normal sexuality, for acceptance as a man. And through no fault of his own he was denied these basic rights from the hour of his birth, and lay imprisoned under the dead hand of retardation.

He had been sent on any number of training programmes and courses in this and that, from O-level English, through yoga for beginners, to music and drama as a means of self-expression, all with little benefit beyond the social contact it brought him. He was not handicapped enough to be committed to an institution, where he would have at least been safe from the cruel disillusionments that waited for him in the so-called normal world. And yes, I know that I must take my share of responsibility for what happened.

But at that time I had no thoughts of possible consequences, let alone dangers, in opening my door and my heart to one who was so eager to accept the friendship I had to offer.

Looking back on that glorious spring, I suppose that the Crownes, like the Daleys, hoped that our association would fulfil a mutual need, the solitary widow and the lonely misfit who had found a welcome at her table. And it was true that as the days and weeks went by, my spirits lifted; I was like a hibernating animal awakening, stretching its limbs and rejoicing at feeling the warmth of the sun on its skin once again.

Chapter Three

Breaking Point

The sound of the Tippett children playing in next door's back garden woke me just after seven, and I switched on the radio to listen to *The Archers*. Most neighbours can be noisy when you're trying to sleep in the daytime, but the Tippetts were easy to get on with, and were planning to move to a bigger house after their expected third child was born. On the other side were the Newhouses, a mother and the adult son she dotes on, quite decent people. These small semis have long, narrow back gardens, and I've always enjoyed growing flowers; at the end of June the Madonna lilies come into bloom, and their heavenly scent wafts up on the warm air in the evenings. They had been Tom's favourites, and I'd brought the bulbs from our former home; for me they were his memorial, there being no headstone after a cremation.

I lay there wondering whether to get up and brew a pot of tea or stay put for another half hour; the ring at the doorbell made up my mind for me. From the top of the stairs I looked down to the glass-panelled front door, and saw Paul Meadows on the step. Down I padded.

'Paul! What brings you here? You know I'm working tonight, don't you? Oh, my God, what have you done to your face?'

'Let me in, Shirley, I've got to speak to you.'

He had a purple bruise across his forehead, and the skin of his nose was broken. He was also in a highly emotional state, so I took him straight through to the kitchen where I sat him down, put the kettle on and bathed his face with weak antiseptic solution.

'Don't try to talk, Paul, we'll have a cup of tea first.'

'All right, Shirley, if you say so.' There was suppressed anger in his voice, and I knew not to question him until he had calmed a little.

'D'ye fancy something to eat? A sandwich?'

'I might as well.'

He sat watching me as I cut two cheese and tomato sandwiches, and I realised I was wearing only a thin cotton nightie. When I'd made tea in a couple of mugs I put the lot on a tray. 'Right-o, Paul, come up and tell me what happened.'

He followed me upstairs and into my room at the back. I put down the tray on the bedside table, heaved myself back under the duvet and indicated the chair beside the dressing-table.

'Bring that over and sit down here, Paul,' I told him, sipping tea while he set to work on the sandwiches, speaking between mouthfuls.

'I'm afraid it's trouble, Shirley, and I hope you're not going to blame me out of hand as everybody else seems to do.'

He sounded aggressive, and I smiled, reaching out to pat his hand.

'I can't blame anybody at all until I've hear what it's about, can I?'

'Well, *I* never started it, Shirley. I was in the White Hart having a pint of lager, minding my own business, as it were, when in comes this load of loud-mouths, four or five of them–'

'Did you know them?' I asked.

'They're not exactly friends of mine, but I've seen them standing around looking for somebody to pick on. That's their idea of fun and I might add that it's their level of intelligence. There were a couple of girls with them, which always makes matters worse, because the girls egg them on and think it's clever to made snide remarks in a voice loud enough for everybody to hear!'

His own voice was rising, and I cut in quietly, 'What sort of remarks, love?'

'The usual stuff, Shirley, like "See old Simple Simon over there," and "Had any luck with the birds yet, mate?" – that sort of thing. It seems to amuse a certain type of mentality, and these girls started to giggle – thought it was *very* funny!'

'That's too bad, Paul. What did the barman say?'

'That's just it, Shirley, nobody said a word. There was nobody around with the guts to tell them to stuff it. They went on horsing about, putting on stupid voices, but as soon as I started to answer them back, the chap behind the bar said, "Watch it, mate, we don't want any trouble in here!"'

'That really is disgraceful,' I said indignantly. 'I hope you just finished your drink and went out.'

'No, I *didn't*, Shirley, and why the hell should I? It wasn't *me* that started it all, was it?'

By now he was shouting, and I leaned forward to touch his shoulder. 'All right, Paul dear, don't get upset. So what did you do?'

'There was this girl, laughing and pointing at me, so I told her to shut her face, and then all hell broke loose. They bawled at me, it was fucking this and fucking that, till I threw my glass at them!'

'Paul!'

'So then they all came at me, and I lowered my head and charged. I knocked one of them over on to his back, and then I went for this horrible girl–'

'*Paul!* You didn't hit a girl?'

'Why not? She'd made fun of me and worked me up into a rage – why should she get away with it, Shirley? I head-butted her, and she yelled blue murder – and the next thing I knew was a couple of these thugs were holding my arms behind my back, and then they dragged me to the door and threw me out. I hit my nose on the step and my spectacles were smashed to bits. They've told me not to show my face in the White Hart again – but it wasn't my fault, Shirley, I didn't start the rough stuff, I never opened my mouth until those bastards started on me!'

It wasn't the first time that Paul had come to tell me about a brawl he'd unwittingly become involved in, but this sounded worse than usual. His violent retaliations always put him in the wrong and lost him sympathy; nobody made allowance for his brain-damaged state. Looking back now, it seems so obvious that what happened eventually was inevitable, yet nobody raised a finger to prevent it.

Anyway, I did what I could at the time. It was useless to say that he should have ignored the taunts and kept his fists to himself, especially where the wretched girl was concerned.

'Drink your tea, Paul, and let's just be quiet for a while. I know, let's have some music.'

I turned the radio over to Classic FM and got a string quartet playing a violin sonata, pleasantly repetitive and soothing. I took hold of Paul's hand and he gazed at me like a sad, bewildered child. My heart ached, and I was close to tears.

'Come and lay on top of the duvet,' I said.

He unlaced his trainers and did as he was told. And so we lay there, side by side, together yet apart, his head on my shoulder and our hands entwined. I turned down the volume of the radio, and through the open window came the sounds of a summer evening – the muted birdsong, the Tippett children's voices, a dog barking in the distance and the ever-present hum of the motorway.

And drifting in on the breeze came the scent of the Madonna lilies, a sweet and heady fragrance, the very essence of summer. I looked at Paul's face: his eyes were closed, his breathing had slowed and a little smile lifted the corners of his mouth. Every feature was childlike and peaceful, the horrors of the White Hart and its clientele forgotten for a while.

I glanced at the bedside clock: ten minutes to eight. All too soon I'd have to stir myself and get ready for another night on duty. My companion gave a sigh, one of those long-drawn-out exhalations that rise up from a deep well of contentment; his long body lay warm and relaxed against mine on the other side of the duvet. A great wave of tenderness and yearning swept over me, and the sudden secret stirrings of my own body took me so completely by surprise that I drew a quick intake of breath and rolled over to look at the clock again; in an instant, it seemed, time had leapt forward to ten minutes past eight. With enormous reluctance I had to disturb him.

'Paul dear, it's time to move – I have to go to work,' I apologised.

He grunted and half-opened his eyes. 'Oh, *no*, Shirley! Not when we're so happy – must you really go?'

'Yes, of course I must, love. Come on, put your shoes on!'

He sat up and swung his legs on to the floor. 'My mother used to say that all good things come to an end,' he said sadly. 'But we can be together again, can't we, Shirley?'

We parted with the Shalom embrace: *Peace be with you.*

And his touch stayed with me, and kept returning throughout the hours of that night.

The day sister on Delivery Unit was anxious to get home to her husband and three-month-old baby. She rolled up her eyes in rueful apology when I went into the office.

'Fun and games for you tonight, Shirley – that music teacher's in, the one who plays the violin for the Marston Choral Society.'

'Constance Blair? I thought she must be about due,' I replied. 'She was head of the music department at the Girls' Grammar School when my daughters were there. She must be in her late thirties by now.'

'Nearly thirty-seven, first baby and a birth-plan as long as your arm. Husband's a lecturer, and thinks he's going to conduct the labour.' She turned down the corners of her mouth. 'Came in at six with spontaneous rupture of membranes and not much else doing. They weren't at all happy when I said I'd have to do a vaginal examination to exclude cord prolapse, because she's requested no internals without their permission.'

'Oh, Lord.' It was my turn to roll my eyes heavenward. I picked up the carefully typed birth-plan. 'Request no pubic shave – no enema – no drugs by any route except for gas-and-air – no continuous electronic monitoring – no deliberate breaking of the waters – well, that's no problem, they've already gone – no intravenous fluids – no episiotomy – so what do we do, wait until she's climbing up the wall before we tentatively suggest an epidural? Why didn't she book a home confinement?'

'Couldn't find a GP to take her on. Anyway, she's not in established labour yet, just backache that she's had since early morning, and the odd tightening now and again. I could hardly reach the cervix, the head's so high above the brim. She's in Room One, and he's playing classical tapes.'

I sighed. 'I'd better go and have a word – try to persuade her to take a sedative and get a few hours' rest before she really gets going.'

'Yes, let her wait and find out what real labour pains are like.' She set aside the Blair case-notes, and picked up another set. 'And now for something completely different, as they say. In Room Three you've got Tracy Wiseman, nineteen, single, had a spontaneous abortion at sixteen, due in three weeks, admitted in labour. Contractions commenced at two this afternoon, now one in five, fair to moderate. On palpation, vertex presenting and engaged, left occipito-anterior. On vaginal examination, three centimetres dilated, vertex at level of ischial spines. Temp, pulse and blood pressure normal, urine NAD.'

'Who's she got with her? Boyfriend? Mother?'

'No, poor kid, there only seems to be a younger sister who spends half her time sitting in the waiting room smoking. They've been living in a women's hostel, and she was admitted from there.'

'Baby for adoption?'

'No, she's keeping it, she says, and moving into a council flat with her sister. Well, they all keep them these days, don't they? That's all you've got for the present, but there are five for induction on Antenatal, so you could get some transfers over if their prostin pessaries do the trick. Right, I'm off to see how Matt's coping with Jamie – shall we check the drugs?'

The other midwives on duty were Bernie McCann on Antenatal and two young staff-midwives, Sue Weldon who was on D.U. with me, and Carol Parsons on Postnatal. Two student midwives and an auxiliary completed the team. Bernie came over to discuss the allocation of the students.

'Ye'd better take one o' them to look after the Wiseman girl,' she said. 'What's this Mrs Blair doin'?'

'Nothing much. Could be a long night's journey into day. Nice woman, used to teach at the Girls' Grammar–'

'Have ye heard about Dora Hayes, Shirley, the way she got up and walked out o' that ward?

45

When I think o' that poor man, the night I came back from Mother's funeral – I never thought she'd leave that bed at all.'

'I dare say Mr Jamieson's as surprised as we are, but I wonder how long it can last,' I replied cautiously. 'You get these inexplicable remissions sometimes, but secondaries in the liver don't go away.'

'Dilly thinks it's all due to the prayers she's been sendin' up at Shalom,' Bernie said, giving me a sideways look. I shook my head.

'I'm afraid I don't believe in miracles, Bernie – not that sort, anyway. I wish I could. You could say that Dora's been given an unexpected reprieve for a time – it's happened before.'

'God love her,' murmured Bernie, her blue eyes softening, and I had a sudden vivid recollection of Martin Hayes's head on my shoulder in the D.U. office, the damp warmth of his tears, and the way his nose had dripped.

I went to see my patients.

In Room Three a pasty-faced girl with lifeless hair dyed red was sitting up on a bank of pillows. I smiled brightly at her.

'Hi, Tracy! I'm Sister Pierce – Shirley – your midwife tonight, right through to eight o'clock in the morning, so I'll be there when you have your baby. How's it going?'

She made no reply, and I studied the graph-paper spilling from the cardiotocograph monitor. 'Ah, I see your contractions are getting stronger, that's good!'

'Yeah, it's dead painful.' She winced. 'I'd be bet-ter if I could 'ave a cigarette, though. Any chance o' goin' out to the waitin' room for a smoke?'

'No, Tracy, I'm afraid not. Sorry,' I said, noticing her nicotine-stained fingers. 'You'll be able to have one after you're delivered. Is your sister around?'

'Yeah,' she said glumly. 'Keeps goin' off for a smoke. An' I'm dyin' for a pee.'

I undid the straps which fastened the monitoring sensors to her abdomen, and helped her into the en suite toilet; when she'd finished I led her back to bed and reconnected the monitor.

'By the way, Tracy, would you mind if a nice young student midwife delivers your baby? I'll be here with her, of course. Her name's Carol.'

'Don't care 'oo's around as long as I can get this lot over and 'ave a smoke.'

'Good. I'll introduce you to her, and we'll get you something to ease your pain, OK?'

I handed her a women's magazine and patted her shoulder. I didn't know who I pitied the most, the undernourished, uncared-for girl or her baby soon to be born into deprivation. With no father, no anxious grandparents awaiting its arrival, this child would be solely dependent upon a young mother and aunt, with a succession of social workers in the background.

Then I went to face the Blairs in Room One.

A dark-haired, intense-looking woman was seated in the obstetric rocking-chair, determinedly rocking herself backwards and forwards in time to *Eine Kleine Nachtmusik*, while her husband stood sentinel over her. He was tall and thin, with receding hair and rimless spectacles; he eyed me speculatively as I entered with a routine smile.

'I don't believe it – Miss Constance Brindley!

47

Oh, I do beg your pardon, I mean Mrs Blair, don't I? What a lovely surprise,' I enthused, deliberately aiming for a light, informal atmosphere. 'Remember Ruth and Emma Pierce, my daughters and your pupils?'

She stopped rocking and looked up in unfeigned pleasure. 'Mrs Pierce – oh, I *am* glad to see you! Do turn the sound down for a minute, Piers, please – of course I remember your girls, especially Emma. Have they kept up with their music?'

Her husband cut in abruptly. 'The fact is, we've been left rather high and dry here, er, nurse. The midwife who admitted Constance didn't give us any idea about what was to happen next. Are you on duty for the rest of the evening?'

'Until eight tomorrow morning,' I smiled. 'Sister Shirley Pierce, midwife for twenty-two years and mother of two, at your service. Now, Mrs Blair, normally we'd put you on the monitor for an hour or so to see what your contractions are like – are they getting stronger?'

'It's the backache, Mrs Pierce – do I call you Sister? I just can't get comfortable in any position. The uterus is beginning to contract now, but the backache is there all the time.'

I noted her flushed face and recognised the look in her eyes: fear.

'We've been timing the contractions ever since Constance began to feel them,' said the husband. 'The last three intervals have been of twelve and a half minutes' duration. Ah, you're getting another one now, darling – that was only–' he looked at his watch – 'just over ten minutes.'

I addressed myself to her. 'May I ask you to get

up on the bed and let me feel your tummy, Mrs Blair? I'd like to find out what position your baby's in.'

'Oh, heavens, it's not a breech, the head's been down in the pelvis for weeks,' the man cut in with a condescending air.

I counted up to ten as I helped her up on to the bed. 'Nobody said anything about a breech, Mr Blair. I'm talking about the position, not the presentation. Right, Mrs Blair, arms by your sides and try to relax – good girl!'

I felt what I'd hoped not to feel: a direct occipito-posterior position, with the head still above the pelvic brim and not well flexed. I tried to explain to them that the baby was facing towards the front instead of the back, which meant that it would have to rotate round to an occipito-anterior position in its descent through the birth canal, which made for a longer labour, especially as Mrs Blair was a first-time mother and older than average. And the baby was a good size.

'Are you absolutely sure of that, Mrs – er, Pierce?' asked Blair.

'Nobody can be absolutely sure of anything in midwifery; and I've learned not to make predictions,' I said evenly. 'What I'd suggest now is a cup of tea and a couple of paracetamol tablets. It'll ease your backache for a while. Later we can discuss further pain relief.'

'Actually we were planning not to use too many drugs – not to use drugs at all, in fact,' she said doubtfully, and Blair added, 'Connie and I are natural childbirth enthusiasts, and we deplore all this modern interference with a natural process.'

He spoke with the lofty authority of one who had read extensively in a subject on which he had no personal experience whatever. I looked him straight in the eye.

'So I understand, Mr Blair, but I'm sure you won't wish to see your wife suffering unnecessary pain. And these pains are going to get much stronger, believe me.'

'These *contractions* are a natural physiological process, and my wife is well trained to control the – er – pain level by breathing and relaxation exercises,' he countered. 'I shall be at her side throughout her labour to assist her at every stage. Who knows, you might even learn something from us!'

I resisted the temptation to make a sharp retort, and smiled at Mrs Blair.

'So how about that cup of tea, love?'

'That would be very nice, Sister Pierce.'

'Call me Shirley.'

'Thank you, and I'm Connie. And my husband's Piers. I'll accept those two paracetamol, but nothing else, thanks.'

'My wife's here to give birth to a child, Sister Pierce, not to be put to sleep,' added Piers with a superior smile.

I picked up the Sonicaid, the portable electronic stethoscope for listening to the foetal heart; placing the lubricated sensor on her abdomen, I switched it on and the room was filled with the familiar pit-a-pat-a-pit-a-pat-a, a reassuring hundred and forty beats per minute.

'Oh, Piers, just listen to that wonderful sound!' she said, turning to him with shining eyes.

'Handy gadget, that – a much better idea than

tethering the poor women to those great inhuman machines,' he sniffed.

I smiled at her again. 'Right, Connie, I'll see about that cup of tea.'

'I'll put another tape on, darling,' he said.

Carol Parsons was a sensible young woman. She set about befriending the Wiseman sisters, getting them to chat about their experiences and plans for the future. She got on much better with them than I did, being closer in age and genuinely interested in their lives.

'Honestly, Sister, what a life that poor girl's had! She never knew her father, and the mother's an alcoholic. She and her sister Kerry – only sixteen – have been in and out of care, and for the last three months they've been living in this Manchester hostel with all sorts of peculiar women. Tracy's supposed to be getting a council flat, and I feel I'd like to keep in touch and see how she copes – know what I mean?'

I said she might like to take up health visiting later on. Who was I to dampen such youthful ideas with the cynicism that comes from age and experience?

Over coffee in the D.U. office I confessed to Bernie and Dr Stephens, the house officer on call, that I'd had bad vibes about Mrs Blair from the moment I set eyes on her. And him.

'Yeah, I think we ought to ask Lance to have a look at her,' agreed Chris Stephens. 'He'll be up anyway to see if there's anything brewing.'

'D'ye think any o' the prostin ladies'll go into

labour tonight?' Bernie asked him.

'Two of them might, possibly three. Ripe and ready to drop!' He poured out a cup of coffee and added two teaspoons of sugar. 'How's that poor kid from the hostel?'

'Getting undivided personal attention from one of our best student midwives.'

'Great. Probably the last time she'll ever get that sort of care. Poor Tracy.' He shook his head, then picked up Constance Blair's carefully typed birth-plan. 'Good God! It says here that this woman wants to be delivered in a squatting position – supported by her husband – and the baby's to be handed to her for a first breast-feed before the umbilical cord's cut – by the husband. Wow, he's going to be a busy lad. What's their line?' He turned back the pages of the ante-natal notes. 'She's a musician, and he's a physicist – God save us from academics. Who encourages women to write this stuff?'

'What stuff?' came the unmistakably Australian tones of Dr Lance Penrose, obstetric registrar, who now strolled into the office, poured himself coffee and took the birth-plan from Chris Stephens.

'Bloody hell,' he muttered as he read. 'Women like her ought to be sent back thirty or forty years to see the kind of labours their mothers and grandmothers had.' He lit a cigarette, and I pointed to the notice, *This is a non-smoking area.* He ignored it.

'So how's she doing, Sis?'

'Early yet, doctor – but I think it's a posterior position.'

52

'Hell, that's all she needs. Could go on all night, then. Membranes?'

'Spontaneously ruptured. And I'd like you to see her, please. And the husband.'

'Why, is he pregnant?'

'I think he may be putting pressure on her.'

'Didn't he do that nine months ago?'

'Oh, if you're just going to be facetious, Dr Penrose–' I began, and of course the others tittered. He put down his cigarette and accompanied me to Room One.

As he carefully palpated Mrs Blair's abdomen, he addressed his remarks directly to her, acknowledging the husband's presence with a brief nod.

'What I want to make absolutely clear to you, my dear, is that you are in no way bound to stick to your self-imposed rules. Going by past experience I'd guess that this labour is going to be longer rather than shorter, OK? And these pains are going to get a lot stronger. When you feel that you need pain relief, ask for it. Tell Sister Pierce here how you feel, and go by her advice. My own recommendation would be to start an epidural anaesthetic when the cervix reaches three centimetres dilatation, right?'

'Er – yes, Dr Penrose, but I'm not to have an epidural,' replied poor Constance, glancing at her husband.

'No way!' emphasised Piers. 'My wife and I happen to–'

'Suit yourself, Mrs Blair,' cut in Penrose. 'This is a free country, and you have the right to suffer severe pain and to refuse relief for it. Only remember that you can change your mind at any time, right? Sister will check your baby's heart-beat every quarter of an hour or so, and we'll see how you get on. Good luck!'

I'm sure he gave her a barely perceptible wink. Piers looked daggers at his retreating white coat, but back in the office Penrose shook his head.

'I'm not happy about this one, Chris. That kid's head could get well and truly stuck in the trans-verse diameter. Might be an idea to take blood now for cross-matching a coupla units. Save time if we have to move quickly.'

'There's no way that those two are going to let anybody take blood from her,' I declared.

Penrose shrugged. 'Don't some people make life bloody difficult? My guess is that the poor woman will be only too happy to have an epidural in another couple of hours – and that means a drip and continuous monitoring anyway.' He yawned widely. 'I'm off to get my head down while I can. Call me if she gets to full dilatation. See ya!'

I sipped my coffee and all at once thought of Paul Meadows.

We'll be together again like this, won't we, Shirley?

And for a full minute I forgot all about Constance Blair and her birth-plan. And her husband Piers.

'It's the way Chris puts 'em in!' grinned Bernie as she transferred two of the prostin ladies from the Antenatal ward to the Delivery Unit soon after midnight. Elsie the auxiliary had answered a frantic call to find a patient standing by her bed in a large pool of water from her ruptured membranes, and at the same time another patient tearfully confided that she'd been getting pains ever since eleven o'clock but hadn't liked to say anything because she'd been told that you get pains after prostin pessaries anyway. In both cases the cervices were dilating up well, so into Room Two and Room Four they went, and their partners were hastily sent for. (The word *husband* is out of date these days, but I always give a proper husband his proper title.)

I asked Sue Weldon to take over the patient in Room Four, a primigravida with mild toxaemia, while I took charge of the one in Room Two who was having her second baby and cracking on in labour. We called the other student midwife, an Asian girl, to help on D.U., and hopefully get a delivery; I didn't want to take Carol away from Tracy, now progressing well, and beginning to give the characteristic grunts that warn of a fully dilated cervix.

Bernie had temporarily taken over the Blairs while I saw to the two transfers, and by a quarter to one poor Constance was writhing around on the bed while Piers tried to make her sit up and use the force of gravity to aid the baby's descent. He also had other natural remedies for stimulating and relieving contractions, as Bernie reported.

'Oh, Shirley, didn't I barge in there with the Sonicaid, and found him kissin' her in all sorts o' rude places – somethin' to do with releasin' endorphins from the pituitary gland. I apologised for interruptin', and said I was sorry but could I listen to the baby's heart – and I don't think the endorphins are havin' much effect, if the noise comin' from there is anythin' to go by.'

I had a mental picture of thin-lipped, sarcastic Piers Blair kissing Constance's nipples and putting his long hand between her thighs: I imagined his quickening breath, his half-closed eyes – and his erection. (Other people's lives, oh, *God.*) I hurried to Room One and found her in agony, which reflected badly on me as her midwife, responsible for her well-being in labour. She wrung my hand as another contraction seized her, tightening her abdomen to board-like hardness.

'Sister – Shirley – please, pethidine, something, anything to help me,' she pleaded, between sobs.

'I can give you pethidine, love, only I'd have to examine you first,' I said.

'Oh, my God, must you? All right, then, only please get on with it, I can't take much more – no, Piers, I'm sorry, but this – this is worse than anything I ever dreamed of.'

Blair stood over me and watched every move as I passed two gloved, lubricated fingers into the vagina. The baby's head was still quite high.

'All right, my dear, you're progressing. The cervix is three centimetres dilated.'

'Is that all? Oh, however much longer?' she wailed.

'Take my advice, love, and let me send for Dr Okoje the anaesthetist to commence an epidural for you. It's the only thing that will really take this pain away.'

'*No!* She's not going to be browbeaten, I won't allow it,' broke in the insufferable Blair. 'We are *not* going to be talked into a potentially dangerous procedure. I happen to know something about the damage that can be done by these epidurals. My wife and I are going to stay in control of our child's birth – oh, all right, then, Constance, if you insist on this injection of pethidine, but remember that it crosses the placental barrier and affects the baby.'

I didn't rise to the bait, but if looks could have killed, he and I would both have been dead on the floor. I checked a hundred milligrams of pethidine with Sue Weldon, together with an anti-emetic which I decided not to mention. Into her left buttock it went, and it helped to keep her partially sedated over the next two hours, for which I was thankful, for we had two deliveries in that time.

Tracy was mercifully straightforward, as is often the way with these young girls. A few short, sharp pushes and an assortment of obscenities led swiftly to the emergence of a baby boy, a scraggy little fellow weighing 2.353 kilograms, or five pounds, three ounces. The placenta was small and unhealthy-looking, the cord thin and stringy.

'Well done, Tracy! You've got a beautiful little son,' breathed Carol, and I heard the break in her voice as she guided the slippery little body over her hand and on to the sterile towel. Good for her, I thought, may she never lose that sense of wonder.

'Now can I go for a smoke?' These were the new mother's first words, and I took her to the waiting room in a wheelchair while the baby was handed to his young aunt who had no idea how to cuddle him. Struck dumb by his ear-splitting yells, she simply gazed down at him in bewilderment.

I left them in Carol's capable hands to go to

Room Two where one of my two prostin ladies was now in the advanced second stage of labour. The Asian student midwife was very unsure of herself, and I felt like a sort of cheer-leader, encouraging the mother to push down hard with contractions, and in a lower voice instructing the student at every step. The woman groaned and her partner sat silent and horrified by it all, having been woken from a deep sleep and bundled into a taxi called by his mother.

Another boy was born, and although the perineum was torn, I was able to put in three deep synthetic sutures, sufficient to pull the edges together. As soon as I'd finished Bernie appeared at the door. It was nearly three.

'Shirley, we *have* to do somethin' with Mrs Blair.'

I found Constance kneeling on the floor beside the delivery bed as if in prayer. Blair was telling her to take deep breaths and use the force of gravity to aid her in labour. When she saw me her voice rose hysterically

'Get me an epidural, please – *please*, an epidural, or I shall die!'

If a woman in labour is out of control, the midwife has failed to do her work well. I've let this woman down, I thought, and was anxious to make amends.

'No, Connie, you're all right, don't worry, I'll get Dr Okoje up right away – don't panic, there's a good girl. Here, let's get you back up on the bed.'

But Blair was not ready to concede defeat.

'*No*, darling, you know about the danger of a dural tap, and the effects of injecting fluid into the spinal cord – listen, we're going to do this Nature's way. Take another long, slow, deep breath and open your mouth–'

Constance duly opened her mouth, and neither Bernie nor I will ever forget what she said.

'*Fuck* Nature's way, *fuck* the force of gravity, fuck, fuck, *fuck!* This pain is *hell*, and I need an epidural, you stupid bugger!'

The expression on that man's face was something that still affords me comfort to this day, but of course my priority then was to relieve the woman's misery. Dr Okoje was summoned, and Chris Stephens came to put up the necessary intravenous drip. When he inserted the needle into the vein on the back of Connie's hand, I held a blood sample bottle at the ready while he let ten millilitres of blood run into it, and Elsie was despatched to the Path Lab with it for cross-matching two pints of blood, just in case.

The tired-eyed Nigerian anaesthetist set about his task in silence. Strictly speaking he should have recited the routine information about possible side-effects of a dural tap, but Mr Blair had already done it for him, and all Connie wanted was relief from pain. Within seven minutes the epidural space below the fourth lumbar vertebra was bathed in a solution of marcain, bringing instant loss of sensation to all parts of the body below that level.

Blessed relief of pain without loss of consciousness: the epidural anaesthetic has been the greatest advance in pain control for women in childbirth during the last three decades of the twentieth century. The technique has been much improved, so that side-effects are now seldom seen, though the patient should always be warned. Freed from the vicious circle of pain, fear and tension, we all felt a sense of release, and even Piers closed his eyes and shut up. For a couple of hours there was peace of a kind: the monitor showed that the contractions were continuing, but they were not felt as pain, only a hardening of the uterine muscles.

But ... the monitor also showed the foetal heart-rate, its slowing-down during contractions and acceleration in the intervals. As the hours of a long labour go by, the baby is under increasing pressure; the dips in its heart-rate last longer, and are slower to pick up speed, so deprivation of oxygen can occur. By five-thirty, as the sunrise shone in through the windows, the decelerations were getting longer and falling lower. I called Bernie to take a look at the graph.

'Not very happy, is it?' she mouthed. I shook my head and went to ask switchboard to bleep Dr Penrose. At that very moment Carol came to tell me that my other prostin lady in Room Four had a fully dilated cervix and an urge to push; she was to have a short second stage because of her toxaemia, and I asked Sue Weldon to supervise Carol for the delivery.

'Wait for the head to come right down on the perineum before you encourage her to push, and do an episiotomy if there's any hold-up,' I told her.

Back to Constance Blair: Lance Penrose took one look at the graph and nodded. Foetal distress. Anoxia. The need to cut a long story short and get the baby out.

'Your baby's showing signs of getting tired, Mrs Blair, and the best thing we can do for it is to operate – we'll do a Caesarean section right away, OK?'

Dr Okoje was recalled, and the paediatrician on call was summoned. A consent form had to be signed by the patient and if possible by her husband as well. Piers refused to sign.

'All this hurry to cut a woman's body open and yank the child out, without her even being seen by her consultant – no prior explanation given to us–'

Penrose left me to cope with Blair, and I simply ignored him, guiding Connie's hand to scrawl her signature on the form; then I went into the theatre to scrub up and don a sterile gown and gloves. Lance did likewise, with Chris Stephens assisting – 'good job we took that blood for cross-matching, eh, Shirley?' – and the paediatrician, a nice girl doing her six month's housemanship, came running up the corridor and shot into the changing-room.

From the moment of decision to the first incision, nineteen minutes elapsed. In cases of a grave emergency, I've known it to be done in ten; our team-work is fantastic.

Baby Cecilia Blair was extracted from her mother's body at seventeen minutes past six. She weighed 3.515 kilograms or seven pounds and twelve ounces, and Connie, being conscious, was able to see her and touch her briefly before she was handed to the paediatrician. The first piercing cry of the newborn filled the theatre and a collective sigh went up from us all.

When it was all over and the mother ready to be

transferred to Postnatal with her baby, Chris Stephens went to repair the episiotomy in Room Four, where a baby boy had been safely delivered by a jubilant Carol. As I was pushing a trolley loaded with bowls and instruments from the theatre to the sluice, Blair approached me in the theatre annexe.

'I'm letting you know, Sister Pierce, that I'm not satisfied with the way I've been treated in this matter of rushing my wife into the theatre without my consent – without even having been consulted, in fact.'

I stopped, my hands on the trolley with its pile of stainless steelware.

'What?' I made no pretence of politeness.

'I think you heard what I said. I intend to ask some rather pointed questions about the way this case has been conducted.'

His cold eyes glinted behind his spectacles, hollowed by a sleepless night; a defiant flush pinked his cheeks in an otherwise muddily pale face. He smelled of stale sweat, as I suppose I did. Well, we all did. I stared at him, and he continued his bleating.

'From the start you have opposed every point of a carefully thought out birth-plan. Never once was the consultant brought in to see my wife, and our friend from the outback decided to submit her to this ordeal on the strength of a few variations on a graph-paper. I know the way you doctors and nurses panic over these damned machines. My wife was coping well with the help of the epidural, and another two or three hours could have seen her through to the natural delivery we'd planned.'

'Are you complaining because you have a live, healthy baby?' I demanded, and heard the edge to my voice.

'No, of course not, I'm merely pointing out that my wife has become one more statistic, one more hasty Caesarean section that wasn't necessary.'

I felt anger rising up inside me like bile, fuelled by a night of anxiety and my dislike of this know-all who knew nothing. When I spoke it was quietly at first.

'I'd have thought that even a fool like you could see that a *hundred* unnecessary Caesarean sections are to be preferred to *one* that should have been done and wasn't – and your wife's could have been that *one*.'

The flush disappeared, leaving his face chalk-white. His mouth opened but no sound came out, like a dying codfish. Leaning on the trolley I heard my voice rising higher and higher.

'You'd have something to complain about if your baby was damaged, wouldn't you? If her life had been ruined at the outset by being starved of oxygen – if she grew up mentally retarded – educationally subnormal – unable to take her proper place in the community – ah, *that* would be a real tragedy, and one to weep over, wouldn't it? Eh? Well, *wouldn't* it?'

He stammered and spluttered in shocked incredulity.

'Look here, I'm not standing for this kind of abuse–'

He laid his hand on the trolley, and I began to push it roughly towards the sluice; a couple of bowls fell off with a noisy clatter.

63

'Get out of my way!' I shouted.

When I reached the steel sinks I was weeping bitterly, and it was nothing to do with Blair.

Sue, Carol and I sat in the D.U. office with a mountain of paperwork to complete and a tray of tepid coffee. Bernie appeared in the doorway and raised her eyebrows at me.

'Shirley dear–' She glanced at the other two. 'Could ye ever spare me a couple o' minutes now, before Mrs Gresham gets here?'

Mrs Gresham was the Supervisor of Midwives for the Department, and we were all accountable to her. I got to my feet and followed Bernie to the linen cupboard where she closed the door and faced me with a certain embarrassment.

'Don't tell me, let me guess,' I said wearily. 'Our friend Blair has been sounding off to you.'

'Well, he's certainly not a happy camper, Shirley, and we haven't heard the last of him, that's for sure. That was some mouthful ye gave him, wasn't it?'

'Bernie, if you're suggesting I apologise to that – that–'

'All right, all right, Shirley, I'm only tellin' ye that he's goin' to make a complaint to the management, and it's yeself who'll be up in front o' Mr Hawke–'

'I don't give a shit for Hawke or for Blair, Bernie – and I've got an hour of writing up to do before I get away from this place, so if that's all you've got to say–'

'Shirley! Don't be talkin' to me as if I were against ye. We're *friends*, for heaven's sake!'

And then she said, very softly, 'It's your young friend Paul, isn't it, love?'

I tried to speak, but all that came out was a choking sound, and dear old Bernie gathered me close in a silent bear-hug. After that I had to go and splash my face with cold water over the washbasin in the staff toilet before going back to the office and the tactfully averted eyes of Sue and Carol, nice girls, both young enough to be my daughters.

It was half past nine by the time I got home to Pussage and Peppercorn on that lovely summer morning.

Chapter Four

Complications and a Farewell

Two more nights on duty followed that one, and then I was off; it was a Friday morning, and I wasn't on again until Monday night. Only those who have worked on night shifts can appreciate the holiday sensation I felt as I poured a glass of wine and went to sit in the garden, stretching out my weary legs and relaxing in the sunshine.

Mine was the best-kept garden in Chatsworth Road. The Madonna lilies with their thick, creamy petals still filled the air with fragrance, blending with the lighter scent of the sweet peas, a pastel rainbow of colours. Delicate pink-and-white blooms were appearing on the lemon-scented

65

geraniums, and the old-fashioned climbing roses on the trellis would outlast them all. In the little conservatory old Peppercorn stretched himself out on the table I used for seed-trays and potting-up, while Pussage basked on the coconut matting below him, surrounded by young tomato plants whose pale yellow flowers promised a good autumn crop. It was idyllic, my own almost private paradise; I waved to June Tippett who was just taking five-year-old Mandy to school, accompanied by the toddler in his trolley; on the other side Mrs Newhouse was bustling around in her kitchen; she gave me a smile through the open window, and called out, 'Another nice day, love!'

I closed my eyes and sighed with satisfaction. Bliss!

Until the powerful scent of the lilies began to disturb my thoughts with memories of Tom. He had so loved and tended them in our garden at Wellington Avenue, usually working alone while I slept or caught up with jobs after being on duty. Did he see my care of his lilies now? Did he know how much I regretted everything that had gone wrong? *Do* the departed in fact continue to watch over those left behind, or have they done with the troubles of the world, its disappointments and disillusionments?

I finished the wine and rose abruptly. Time for bed and a few hours' sleep before rejoining the world of daytime living: there were three nights off to enjoy!

The persistent ringing of the doorbell eventually filtered down through the layers of consciousness. I raised my head and squinted at the bed-side clock: ten past four.

Of course it was Paul. I'd asked him to stay away until Friday evening, and he'd lasted till tea-time.

'Just go round to the back, will you, Paul, and I'll be down in a minute,' I called from a front window and, after dashing to the toilet and hastily throwing on my full-length cotton kaftan that's so comfortable in hot weather, I went down to the kitchen and put on the kettle to make tea. I took a couple of cans of coke from the fridge, and got out the chocolate cake I'd made earlier in the week. Then, putting it all on a tray, I carried it out to where Paul was sitting beside the garden table. We kissed and exchanged the Shalom peace, but I immediately sensed his unease, though his bruise was fading and the scab on his nose looked clean.

Lilian and Brian Newhouse were in their garden, and she looked at us with barely concealed curiosity.

'I hope we didn't wake you up, love,' she said, eyeing the kaftan admiringly. 'Mm, that's a nice, cool-looking whatsit you're wearing.'

I smiled, and she called out over her shoulder, 'All right, son, you can mow the grass now, Mrs Pierce is up, so we haven't got to keep quiet!'

Brian Newhouse, thirty-something and not bad-looking, went to get the lawnmower out of their shed, giving us a grin. He's one of those easy-going, uncomplicated men who never seem to worry about anything, and I liked the way the Newhouses seemed to accept Paul. The Tippetts were inclined to look askance at him, and June

Tippett hadn't been too happy when he got into an argument with little Mandy over the merits of spiders and their right to life; but Lilian treated him much as she treated her son, which was rather like an indulged teenager. She was divorced and had been living on her own for some years when Brian came home after the break-up of his marriage, much to her satisfaction; she had a married daughter and grandchildren living in Bury, but her son was the apple of her eye. He worked unsocial hours doing something mechanical at the airport, and she always waited up for him with a freshly cooked meal.

I poured out tea, and pushed a can of coke towards Paul. 'Cup of tea, Lilian? And Brian?'

I cut slices of cake for the four of us. Oh, the joy of a glorious July afternoon, and not having to go to work that night! But Paul's agitation broke in on my contentment, and I sensed his impatience to talk. When the noise of Brian's lawnmower began, it allowed us more privacy, and I knew I was in for another long story. I expected a follow-up to the White Hart saga, but as was so often the way with Paul, he had been overtaken by a new grievance which turned everything else into yesterday's news. Today's bitter tidings were soon told.

I knew that Paul had been sent on yet another training course, this time in computer technology for beginners at the Marston College of Further Education, and now the six weeks were up and he had not been given a certificate as all of his fellow students had.

'You'll find this hard to believe, Shirley, what Graham Paxton said to me this morning – "Sorry, mate, it's been good to have you with us, but I can't award you a certificate of proficiency!" Those were his exact words, Shirley.'

A cloud descended on the brightness of the afternoon; I looked at the hurt and resentment on his face as he sat with shoulders hunched. I felt annoyed, too, and my indignation was directed not so much towards this Graham Paxton as the social services department that had sent Paul on this unsuitable course, paid for by the local education authority and filling the poor boy's head with hopes of a career in computing. Surely they should have foreseen that with his short concentration span he'd be doomed to disappointment once again! I bit my lip and desperately tried to think of something positive to say while not offering too much sympathy; in fact I blundered in and said the wrong thing.

'Oh, Paul dear, I'm so sorry – but to be honest, I never thought that course was a good idea for you.'

'Why not? Tell me why you thought that, Shirley, will you?' he demanded loudly. 'You never said so at the time!'

'No, but – well, somehow I can see you working in a – a rather different kind of job, Paul, easier perhaps, where you could proceed at your own pace.' I hesitated. 'You may have heard of "sheltered employment", it's where manufacturing firms have special schemes for – er–' I floundered to a stop, unable to find the right words.

'Yes, Shirley? Special schemes, did you say? Go on, I'm listening!'

He was getting angry, and I flushed as if I'd said

something indecent. 'What I mean, Paul, is that there are lots of firms around Manchester who employ people to – to assemble and pack their products, people with various difficulties, you know, like – er–'

He broke in furiously. 'Look here, Shirley, if you're suggesting that I go and work on an assembly line with a load of half-wits and epileptics, I can tell you it's already been tried and was a complete disaster!'

I saw Lilian glance in our direction. Brian had taken off his shirt, revealing his broad, bare back as he pushed the lawnmower across the grass.

'An absolute *disaster*, and whoever sent me there must have had a very strange idea of making the best use of available manpower,' Paul continued hotly. 'Surely *you* can see that I need to do something where I can meet people, talk things over with them, share problems and points of view – damn it, Shirley, I'm capable of something better than filling cardboard boxes with plastic bottles, for God's sake! And I didn't like the attitude of some of those jokers on the assembly line, either!'

He turned down the corners of his mouth and fixed me with a belligerent glare. I had touched on another painful memory, one more in a line of failed attempts to find the right niche.

So I smiled. 'Tell me about it, then, Paul.'

And he did. It had been six years ago when he lived with his parents, but it was still sore in his memory. He'd been sent to work at the packing station of a company that used by-products from oil refining. They'd had a special section where selected disabled men and women performed simple repetitive work under supervision, and Paul was put on this assembly line under the eye of a big, bossy woman who had complained that he spent too much time talking – 'making daft remarks,' as she'd put it – and not enough time packing bottles of shampoo or whatever it was into the passing boxes. His defiant retorts had upset some of the female workers, and the supervisor had made a big fuss and refused to work with him. Paul had been denounced as a trouble-maker and cautioned, but needless to say there had soon been another bust-up, and dismissal had followed.

My poor friend would never be able to understand that he was unemployable and, being somewhat obsessed with party politics, he blamed his blighted job prospects on the long-running Conservative Government, and now once again he began to call down curses on the name of Margaret Thatcher, Prime Minister at the time of that fiasco. I couldn't have this tirade within earshot of the neighbours.

'Now, Paul, this isn't very sensible, is it? You can't blame the Conservatives just because you didn't get a certificate today!'

I drew back sharply as he turned on me with a snarl.

'Oh, Mrs Pierce, I *do* beg your pardon, I'm *sure!*' he squeaked in what was supposed to be a take-off of my tone. 'I didn't realise that you and the honourable Margaret were such *friends*, you see. I thought you were too intelligent to be a – a *Conservative!*'

If he'd called me a Satanist, he could hardly have conveyed more venom. Lilian was openly

71

staring and Brian paused in his mowing, his chest and back glistening with his exertions.

'Don't be daft, Paul,' I replied, keeping my voice low. 'I don't give a toss one way or the other about party politics. Let's just change the subject, shall we? What about another slice of cake? I baked it specially for you.'

But he refused to be side-tracked. He got up from his chair and stood glowering at me with fists clenched. I too stood up and looked straight into his eyes, keeping my voice steady.

'Paul, this is so ridiculous.'

'Hey! You all right there, Mrs Pierce?' It was Brian Newhouse calling to me over the fence. I nodded to him and smiled. 'Yes, thanks, Brian, we're fine.'

The brief interruption with its note of warning was just what Paul had needed, and his shoulders suddenly sagged. His blue-grey eyes met mine with a look that went to my heart. He held out his hand.

'All right, Shirley, I'll leave it there, then. If it was anybody else I'd argue it through, but I love you too much to–' His voice broke, and I took hold of his outstretched hand, at which he pulled me towards him so violently that I nearly fell against his chest. His arms tightened around me, his hands gripped the flesh under the folds of the kaftan, and his lips pressed my forehead; he gave a choking sob.

'Oh, Shirley, Shirley!'

He was so tall. And so strong. I twisted my head round to see the faces of Lilian and Brian watching us, she with amazement, he with amusement.

72

'All right, Paul, all right, don't worry,' I soothed, gently extricating myself, and smiling reassuringly at my neighbours. 'Now what about that cake?' He sat down to eat his third slice, and I put my hand on his shoulder. I was so sure that I understood him and never doubted that I could manage him: such arrogance!

But I was in for a big shock. And soon. Later that evening when we were at supper, the telephone rang.

'Hallo, Mrs Pierce – Shirley – this is Philip. How are you?' said a pleasant male voice.

'Oh, hal*lo*, Philip, how nice to hear you. I'm fine, thanks.' I glanced at Paul and put my hand over the receiver, whispering, 'Your friend Philip Crowne'.

'What can I do for you, Philip?' I asked, but Crowne's voice had become wary. 'Ah, you're not alone, then?'

'No, I've got a mutual friend of ours with me, Philip,' I said brightly. 'Paul Meadows.'

'Ah.' He cleared his throat. 'In that case I'll phone you again some time over the weekend. What I have to say is private.'

'Oh, I see. All right, then, Philip,' I replied, though I didn't see and it didn't sound all right. 'I'm not on duty this weekend, so we can have a talk whenever it's convenient.'

'Bless you, Shirley.'

'Can I speak to him while he's on?' asked Paul.

'Paul says he'd like to have a word with you, Philip.'

'Oh, dear. All right, then, you'd better put him on. Thanks.'

Paul took the receiver and began to unburden himself again. 'Hallo, Philip! You'll never believe what Graham Paxton said to me this morning, after I've slogged my way though six weeks of computer studies!'

I rolled my eyes and went to put the kettle on again. This would take some time.

On Saturday morning I returned Crowne's call as soon as I'd finished breakfast. Celia answered, and I picked up the ever-so-slight hesitation in her voice when she heard mine.

'Ah, yes, Shirley. Philip felt that he should have a word with you. He's around somewhere – just a minute, I'll call him for you.'

I waited, conscious that my heartbeat was a little faster than usual.

'Hallo, Shirley my dear, sorry to keep you waiting.' Philip sounded apologetic. 'Just a little word in your ear – I couldn't speak to you last night with young Paul around, because it's about him, you see.'

'Ah, I thought it might be, Philip. I understand only too well.'

'Bless you. The thing is, you see, Shirley, we've been a little worried lately about you. Perhaps we should say that our consciences are not quite clear!'

'Whatever do you mean, Philip?'

'You've taken him on in a very generous way, Shirley, and Celia and I don't see so much of him now. Quite frankly that's something of a relief, as he always seemed to be on our doorstep at one time. And now I hear that Alfred Daley has put his foot down and said that Paul is not to visit Norma unless he or Rod is there. You are a woman living alone, Shirley, and you really ought not to allow Paul to visit you without a third person present.'

'Oh, Philip!' I actually laughed. 'There's no need to worry about *me!* I can manage Paul, in fact I understand him better than some of the social workers he's had, and he trusts me.'

'No, listen to me, Shirley. He can be very difficult to deal with if he's in one of those defiant moods, in fact he's potentially dangerous if not very carefully handled.'

'And I can handle him,' I insisted. 'You needn't worry, honestly, Philip.'

'You're very kind, and I only wish that more people shared your understanding attitude towards the poor lad–'

'I'm very fond of him, actually,' I said, smiling modestly to myself at his compliment.

'Yes, Shirley, I know you are. Only – you may not have realised how he passes on details of other people's private business.'

I laughed again. 'Don't worry, Philip. I'd never pass on anything I heard from Paul.'

'That's not quite what I meant, my dear. It's *you* I'm concerned about – things that Paul might pass on to others about you.'

'Whatever do you mean?' I spoke sharply, but my heart gave a sudden lurch.

'Paul called here on Tuesday evening after you had gone to work, and he told us a very strange story indeed. We know he often gets facts distorted, and puts wrong interpretations on what he hears, but I've never known him to tell a

75

deliberate untruth. And we feel that you ought to know, Shirley, that he told us he had been up in your bedroom.'

I gave an involuntary gasp. 'Oh!'

'Yes. And he said that you had asked him to come to you there, and that he'd actually lain on the bed. With you.'

Philip said the words in a light, matter-of-fact way, as if he was remarking that Paul had sat on the garden table, but of course I went rigid with shock and embarrassment, feeling that I'd been caught in some shameful act. I felt my face flush crimson.

'Oh, Philip, is – is that what he said? Oh, heavens, er, I mean – whatever must you think?' I stammered, gripping the receiver so tightly that my knuckles showed white.

'Naturally, Celia and I know that there must have been a reason for – that you must have had a reason, Shirley, for allowing him into your room, and–'

'I'd been on night duty, and had only just woken up, the doorbell went on and on, I was fast asleep,' I heard myself babbling in my anxiety to explain, and he answered kindly.

'Yes, of course, Shirley, we know that you have to sleep during the day. My dear, I'm not questioning you, in fact I can very well see how the situation must have arisen.' He was clearly doing his best to let me off the hook of any suggested impropriety. 'I just thought I'd better tell you what he told us – and to warn you that he is likely to repeat it to other people he sees.'

'Oh, my *God*,' I groaned, though I know that

Philip hates hearing the name of God used as an exclamation.

'You've been very kind to the boy, we all know that, Shirley, in fact Celia and I have been more than grateful. But perhaps it's time for you to step back a little, and let somebody else take him over. Don't have him round quite so often. You do have to realise the need to be very careful where that young man is concerned.'

Be careful. I had ignored my colleagues' warnings, but if anything made me stop and review my whole attitude towards Paul Meadows, it was that caution from Philip, so kindly expressed. My hand was still shaking as I replaced the receiver.

How much had Paul said to Philip and Celia, and how many others would he tell about our peaceful, innocent twenty minutes last Tuesday evening, before I went to work? Innocent, but ... on the *bed.* I could picture the raised eyebrows, the exchanged glances, and I squirmed inwardly. Such stupid indiscretion, such lack of foresight! I knew I should be grateful for Crowne's friendly warning, but I continued to go hot and cold every time I thought about it, and blushed at the memory of those secret stirrings that only I knew about – thank God!

Philip was right, it was time for some back-pedalling. Paul's visits would have to be cut. But *how?*

While I was debating this point, the phone rang again. It was Martin Hayes, asking a favour. 'I was wondering if you were free tomorrow, Shirley,' he said tentatively.

'At your service, Martin,' I replied at once.

'How's Dora?'

'I'm afraid she's going through a bad patch at present, the heat's getting her down a bit.' He sounded anxious. 'The fact is, I'd like to take her out for an afternoon drive to see a bit of country, she's always loved Cheshire. We've got a wheel-chair, and I can get it into the boot, but if there was somebody – an extra pair of hands to help Dora – Laura says it's too big a job for me on my own, and she's on call this weekend.'

'Oh, Martin, of *course* I'll come out with you! Why don't you and Dora come to Sunday lunch beforehand?'

'You're so kind, Shirley dear, but actually she hasn't got much appetite, and we usually have something light at midday. But if you could come out with us in the car to help with Dora, it would be a God-send. Would two o'clock be all right for you?'

'No problem, Martin. I'll be over at two. Give Dora my love – see you soon!'

I hung up the phone with a sense of gratitude. Had Martin realised it, he was doing me a favour in providing an excuse for saying I was engaged for the weekend, and after the usual phone calls to Ruth in Solihull, Emma in London and my parents in Shrewsbury, I threw myself into an orgy of housecleaning for the rest of that day, washing chair-covers and curtains. It was perfect weather for drying, and helped me to stop brooding over Crowne's phone call.

Sunday was another fine, sunny day with a fresh-ening breeze that made it ideal for a trip into the

78

country. I was shocked when I saw how thin and weak Dora had become after her initial recovery from surgery, but she spoke eagerly of seeing woods and fields, and Martin had decided on Tatton Park with its extensive grounds and gardens.

I eased her into the passenger seat, carefully lifting first one leg in and then the other, and fastened the belt across her chest. She looked as if a puff of wind might blow her away, and her once needle-sharp eyes were sunken in their sockets.

'It will do us both a world of good, Shirley – nothing like country air for restoring the spirits. Martin needs to relax as well, he's worn himself out waiting on me. So kind, so kind.'

She laid her head back and closed her eyes. I got into the back seat, and Martin turned round to smile at me.

'You don't know how much this means to us, Shirley.'

'It's my pleasure,' I said, and meant it.

We avoided the usual hordes of Sunday visitors to Tatton, and Martin stopped the car in the drive so that we could get the chair out of the boot. While I helped Dora to settle in it, he drove off to the car park, and caught up with us later as I pushed the chair up to the top of a grassy incline that gave a magnificent view of the estate, including the lake below. Dora's little face lit up.

'Ah, this is what I wanted to see again, Shirley,' she whispered. 'This green and pleasant land.'

Martin put his arm around her shoulders. 'Are you happy now, dearest?' he asked her, and she mutely reached for his hand. No further words were necessary; time was running out for her, and they both knew it. I felt their need to be left alone together.

'If you'll excuse me, Martin, I'll just take a stroll down to the lake,' I murmured. 'Back in twenty minutes, OK?'

They scarcely heard me, and I started to make my way down the track.

And it was then that I caught sight of the other couple, a man and a woman walking some distance ahead of me, deep in conversation, as oblivious as Martin and Dora to everything but each other. The man was stockily built, and gestured forcefully with his hands, speaking rapidly. His profile showed horn-rimmed spectacles perched on a largish, thrusting nose: a strong face. They were too far away for me to hear what he was saying, or whether she replied, but they seemed surrounded by an aura of strong emotion. Her shoulder-length hair hung loose, just touching the collar of the plain short-sleeved blouse she wore with a long skirt; he was casually dressed in an open-necked shirt with light trousers, rather creased. They both carried jackets, hers folded over her left arm, his slung across his right shoulder.

Suddenly he stopped and swung her round to face him. She drew back a little, and when I saw her profile I too stopped walking, and watched as he looked intently into her face. He said something, and then she flung her arms around his neck, and he gathered her close against him, kissing her hair, her forehead, her mouth in an overwhelming release of tension. His spectacles

80

slipped off one ear, and he made a grab at them, pushing them into his trouser pocket. She dropped her jacket and bag on the path and clung to him, throwing back her head to look into his eyes and tell him – though I couldn't hear the words – that she loved him. Oh, yes, there was no doubt that she loved him.

And I had to turn back and retrace my steps, hoping that they wouldn't see me.

Because she was my colleague and friend, Linda Grierson. And whoever *he* was, he certainly wasn't Councillor Howard Grierson.

Dora was woefully tired by the time we reached home, and went straight to bed. I helped her undress and put on the beautiful silk nightie Laura had bought her. I found a plastic washing-bowl in the bath room, and brought it to her bedside to give her a face-and-hands, as we say at work, followed by a puff of talcum powder and a light spray of her lily-of-the-valley scent. Her little waxen face looked calm and peaceful against the pillow when I kissed her goodbye.

Martin was waiting at the foot of the stairs, his eyes dark and shadowed by grief.

'Help me, Shirley dear.'

What could I do but put my arms around him and draw his head down on to my shoulder as I had done before in the Delivery Unit office?

He wept. I stroked his thinning hair.

We kissed: it was unavoidable, inevitable. We stood there, wordlessly kissing.

Just before eight o'clock the following morning

Dr Laura Goodson rang to tell me that her mother had died peacefully in her sleep. Martin had woken to find her dead beside him, and was in a state of shock, she said, adding that he would be staying with her and her husband for the time being. She thanked me for all I had done for Dora, especially for the visit to Tatton Park, and I murmured my condolences, the things one says on these occasions, the usual platitudes.

Life has to go on, and I was back on duty at nine on Monday evening. It was Bernie's last night on, and she looked whacked out after working over the weekend with the family at home. She was on Antenatal, I was on D.U., and we shared Dilly Fisher between us.

The news of Dora's death affected us all. She had been a well-respected senior midwife at Marston General for a quarter of a century, and our sense of loss was shared by medical staff and the thousands of Marston women who had been Sister Hayes's patients.

But as I said, life goes on. There was a thin brown envelope waiting for me when I went into the D.U. office, containing a note from Mrs Gresham, asking me to see her in the morning at ten past eight. It was rather like being asked to report at the headmistress's study, and I wondered what was up.

'Know anything about this, Bernie?' I asked, slapping it on the desk. She grimaced.

'I'm sorry, Shirley, but she did mention it to me the other mornin'. There's been a complaint, y'see.'

'Complaint? What about?'

She shrugged helplessly, and the penny dropped. 'Blair!'

'That's right, Shirley. Our friend Piers feels that he wasn't consulted enough, in fact he says he was *insulted* by the midwife in charge o' the case, and he wants an apology, so Mrs Gresham says.'

'Oh, does he, now? Well, Bernadette McCann, he can whistle for his apology. Pompous idiot! God, when I think how I sweated and stewed over her labour–'

'All right, Shirley, save the dramatics for Mrs Gresham. Meanwhile Constance Blair's been asking for ye – she and the baby are doin' very well.'

I was pleased to hear that, but in view of the complaint, I *didn't* go to see the mother and baby in the Postnatal ward. Thus may a midwife's relationship with her patient be spoiled.

At half past eleven Bernie, Dilly and I were talking over coffee in the Antenatal ward office, and I was telling them about Dora's last day.

'She must have had a premonition,' said Dilly. 'And you made it possible for her to get her last wish, Shirley – isn't that wonderful?'

Somehow I couldn't think of a reply. I had my own memories of that visit to Tatton.

'The funeral's to be on Friday at St Christopher's at eleven,' said Bernie. 'Mrs Gresham's goin' to alter the off-duty roster so that senior night staff can go. D'ye want a lift, Shirley? I'll pick ye up if ye like.'

Before I could reply the telephone rang, and I answered it.

'Maternity Unit, Sister Pierce speaking. Hallo?

Oh, Mr – *who* did ye say? Mr *Grierson?*'

Bernie looked very hard at me as I went on speaking.

'Yes, well now, I'm afraid she's in the theatre at the moment, you see, Mr Grierson. Yes, scrubbed up for a Caesarean section – yes – no, there's no way that she can come to the phone right now. Shall I ask her to ring you back as soon as she's free? No trouble at all, Mr Grierson. I'll let her know you called.'

I put down the phone, and the other two looked at me in total amazement.

'Why did you say that, Shirley?' asked Dilly. 'Sister Grierson's not on duty.'

How true that was. I'd thought very quickly, and taken a chance by reassuring Grierson that his wife was on duty that night. In reply to me telling him that I'd ask Linda to ring him back, he'd said that there was no need, which seemed to indicate that he'd been checking on Linda's movements, rather than actually needing to speak to her.

'Just pray that he doesn't ring again, girls.'

He didn't. But it showed that Grierson was on the warpath and, when I got Bernie alone, away from Dilly's innocent ears, I told her what I'd seen at Tatton. She whistled.

'Jesus, Mary and holy St Joseph! I thought she'd been actin' strange lately, Shirley, stars in her eyes and sort o' bubblin' inside – haven't ye noticed? So is it love, then?'

'It's happiness, Bernie, and after all these years with that miserable sod, I can't really blame her, in fact I'm glad for her,' I replied with a certain relish.

'But she's got them two boys comin' up to their GCSEs in the next couple o' years, and that little girl who's the spittin' image of her Daddy,' said Irish Catholic Bernie with a frown. 'And where is she tonight? By what ye've just said, she'll be in bed with this other guy, whoever he is.'

I could imagine it, too.

'I'll have it out with Linda tomorrow when she's back on duty,' I promised. 'She'll have one hell of a shock when she hears about Howard ringing up, and how I fobbed him off.'

'He couldn't be fobbed off again, Shirley, and I wouldn't even try. She's playin' with fire, that's for sure.' Bernie shook her head with a doom-laden sigh.

My interview with Mrs Gresham was predictably stormy. She's a nice woman with a thankless job that I wouldn't want myself, having to smooth things over between staff and management, deal with complaints and pacify the aggrieved, some-times at the expense of fairness, or so some of us thought.

'I have every sympathy with you, Sister Pierce, and I know you gave Mrs Blair first-class care, but you just can't go around calling patients' relatives bloody fools. You simply must watch that tongue of yours, it will get you into real trouble one day.'

I didn't recollect that I'd actually said *bloody*, but didn't argue on that point.

'For heaven's sake, Mrs Gresham, that man has got a healthy, normal baby. What more does he want? If I ever felt that I hadn't done my job properly, and was responsible for harming a mother or baby, I'd do more than apologise. I'd resign. It's my worst nightmare.'

'My dear Sister Pierce – Shirley – can't you get it into your head that your competence is not in question. It's your professional attitude, the way you lay down the law to people like Mr Blair, who is after all a University lecturer–'

'And knows absolutely nothing about obstetrics!' I retorted. 'If it hadn't been for that ridiculous birth-plan, Mrs Blair would have had an easier labour and might – just *might*, mark you – have dilated up more quickly and had a normal delivery. And what's more–'

'Shirley, will you *please* try to look at this calmly and sensibly?' she pleaded. 'All that's needed here is an apology for what you said to this man. My secretary will draft a standard letter, and all you'll have to do is sign it. That's not asking too much, is it?'

'No way! I'm *not* apologising to that man, Mrs Gresham, so don't waste your breath asking,' I said with cold anger. 'If there's any apologising to be done, it's on his side.'

She sighed deeply. 'In that case I shall have to write a letter from the Marston Health Authority, and sign it myself.'

I gathered up my jacket and bag. 'You can do what you like, Mrs Gresham – crawl to the man on all fours if it makes you feel better. Only leave my name out of it, will you?'

And I swept out of her office, ignoring her demand for me to come back.

Chapter Five

Warnings Disregarded

I couldn't get off to sleep that day, and in desperation took a sedative at eleven with a couple of aspirins for the headache that raged behind my eyes; the result was a surrealistic dream in which Dora Hayes in a white gown floated downstairs towards me, her face dissolving into a skull with empty eye-sockets. Breathless with terror, I reared up in bed, shouting, *Help!* Then came a sound of thudding boots on the stairs, and a huge, unkempt man with burning eyes burst into the room. *Help! Help me!* You can get spectacular nightmares with mogadon.

I awoke with a cry, and Peppercorn opened a reproachful eye at the disturbance. Muttering, I pulled on the kaftan and went downstairs to plug in the kettle. It was half past three, and I took my mug of tea out to the garden, silently cursing when June Tippett appeared with two pregnant friends she'd met at the ante-natal clinic. She called to me over the fence.

'Excuse me, Shirley, but is that black sister still on Maternity, the one who comes round squeezing your nipples to see if there's any milk coming through?'

'That's right, June,' added one of the others. 'She did it to a girl I know who wasn't even feeding it herself, it was on the bottle!'

Their shrieks of laughter gave me the chance to disappear discreetly without answering. Back in bed I dozed for a couple of hours, and when the doorbell rang I knew it was Paul. Sighing, I pulled on the kaftan again and went down to let him in.

'Hi, Shirley! I forgot what nights you're on this week.' He grinned broadly, and I frowned.

'I told you, Paul – Monday, Tuesday and Wednesday.'

'Oh. And today's Tuesday, so you won't be off till Thursday, then?'

Now was as good as any time to tackle it. 'Look, Paul, come in and have a cup of tea – would you prefer coke? There's something I have to say to you, love.'

He marched in eagerly and sat down at his usual place at the kitchen table.

'Paul dear, I'm going to be very busy for a while, and I shan't have so many free evenings to spare.' I tried to sound firm, but felt awkward. 'So I'm asking you not to call quite so often – say once a week – is that all right?'

The grin disappeared as if wiped off, to be replaced by perplexity.

'Why, Shirley? What's happened? You're always so pleased to see me – you said we help each other!'

'Yes, Paul, but a friend of mine has just died, and I have to give some help and support to her – her family. And I'll have to go to see my parents again soon.'

'They live in Shrewsbury, don't they?'

'Yes, and it takes quite a time to get there and

back. I'm really sorry, but I won't be able to see you so often, Paul,' I continued lamely. 'And besides, you ought to be seeing more people of your own age – somebody like Rod Daley – instead of a middle-aged housewife like me.'

'I don't agree, Shirley! I've been happier than ever before, since we've been friends,' he retorted, raising his voice as he always did when his emotions were roused. 'I told Philip and Celia last week how close we were–'

I winced, and he went on, 'And you said the same, Shirley, in fact you said it had made a big difference.'

'I *do* appreciate your friendship, Paul, really I do, but there just isn't going to be as much time for it,' I said, flushing at my own perfidy. It was like telling a child that his best friend was going away and didn't want to see him, no longer loved him.

His blue-grey eyes searched mine, bewildered, uncomprehending. 'So when *can* I see you again, Shirley? Can I come round on Thursday evening?'

'No, Paul, I shall be too tired. And I've got a funeral to go to on Friday.'

'Is that your friend who died?'

'Yes. And now, Paul, I really must get some more rest before I go to work.'

'So when can I see you, Shirley? Friday evening? Saturday?'

'*No*, Paul, this week's out, I'm afraid. It just isn't convenient. And I'll have to ask you to leave now, please.'

'Will you kiss me, Shirley?'

'Yes, of course. Bye-bye for now, Paul.'

He put out his arms to give me a bear-hug, and pressed his lips to my cheek. 'Shalom, Shirley, Shalom. Peace be with you. Peace and joy.'

'Peace be with you, too, Paul. Bye-bye.'

I cycled to work that evening feeling – as they unpleasantly say – a shit.

'Shirley, how are you? It's ages since we were on together!' Linda beamed at me. 'Terribly sad about Dora, isn't it? Have you seen her poor old husband?'

'No, he's staying with Laura this week,' I told her. 'His grandchildren will probably do him more good than a stream of visitors.'

She nodded. 'I've heard the son-in-law's very helpful, I mean at dealing with the formalities, registrar and all the rest.'

In spite of her respectful gravity there was a vibrancy in her, an inner glow that I'd never noticed in all the years we'd been colleagues. Remembering the strained eyes and compressed lips that had become all too familiar, she seemed to have, come alive, after being only half-alive, living under the shadow of Grierson's petty tyranny. How could I not rejoice at the change?

We studied the duty roster. 'I'm down for D.U. tonight, with a couple of students,' she said. 'You're on Antenatal, and we share Sandra. Dilly's on Postnatal with Staff Weldon.'

Thank heaven for sensible nursing auxiliary Sandra. Dilly was a dear, of course, but rather uphill work.

I pushed the trolley into the Antenatal ward to

do the four-hourly blood pressures and have a word with each of the fifteen patients who were in with a variety of conditions, like pre-eclamptic toxaemia, 'small for dates' and urinary tract infections, the sort of problems commonly associated with poor social conditions – plus the occasional diabetic, asthmatic or epileptic patient in for observation and adjustment of medication in pregnancy. A fair percentage of them came from Cockshott, an overspill estate which had become a byword: there's rough and there's very rough and there's Cockshott. It was well represented that night.

'Good evening, ladies! I'm Sister Pierce and I'll be looking after you tonight, so if you have any worries on your mind, don't hesitate to let me know, OK? And I'll do what I can to sort things out for you.'

They gaped at me as if I had two heads.

'I was 'opin' that nice Irish one'd be on tonight,' muttered a girl to her neighbour in the next bed.

'My boyfriend says 'e'd pack all the bloody Irish back to the bogs,' was the surly reply.

I raised my eyebrows and looked straight at her. 'Really? Then your boyfriend would get rid of some of the best midwives we've got.'

She stuck out her bottom lip. 'Christ, some people got bloody good 'earin'.'

There were some giggles and a sharp 'Shut up!' from somewhere, and I deliberately went deaf, which is often the best policy. What was the good of trying to reason with the likes of these, I thought wearily.

I stopped at a bedside. 'Ah, Mrs Thompson, you're for a prostin pessary tonight, aren't you? Dr Stephens will be coming up soon to pop it in for you. And where's the other lady for a prostin – Melanie Sayers – is she around?'

'Gorn out for a smoke, nurse,' said a woman sitting on the next bed. 'Dreadin' the bloody thing, she is, poor kid.'

I tried to remind myself that these women and girls were underprivileged in every way, socially and educationally, but I was still sometimes inclined to dismiss Cockshott as an irredeemable dump – though Philip Crowne had pointed out that the same had once been said of Nazareth: could any good thing come out of it?

Chris Stephens arrived with the case-notes of the two prostin inductions under his arm, and I drew the curtains around Mrs Thompson's bed.

'Could you start taking her history, doctor, while I go to fetch the other one?'

Melanie sat glumly in the day room beneath a poster that showed a smiling couple and the caption, 'Baby care started on the day we both stopped smoking!' Somebody had drawn a cigarette drooping from the, mouth of each. The air reeked of stale tobacco smoke.

'Come on now, Melanie, Dr Stephens is here to see you,' I smiled, trying to look reassuring. 'Will you go to the toilet first, and then get on your bed, please?'

Back behind the bed-curtains Chris was checking Mrs Thompson's obstetric history, and she looked startled when he murmured, 'I see you had a termination at seventeen, and a normal

92

delivery at twenty.' Record-keeping can be a problem to patients who would rather forget the past and, when a woman wants her partner to be beside her throughout labour, it has been known for a man to glance at the case-notes and see things he has never been told.

'Right, Mrs Thompson, you're a week overdue now, and I'm just going to examine you internally and put a little tablet inside your vagina, to make the neck of the womb ready for you to go into labour, OK?'

'Knickers off, love,' I whispered, helping her to lie back with her knees drawn up. 'Hold my hand if you like. Doctor will be very gentle.'

I winked at her over the top of his head as he probed the cervix, closing his eyes for a procedure that relied entirely on the sense of touch. She gasped and grimaced as he thrust the prostin pessary well in.

'No getting out of bed for an hour, Mrs Thompson, we don't want it to fall out,' he warned. 'Sister will put you on the monitor for an hour, and we'll see how you go, OK?'

Melanie was an eighteen-year-old whose parents were both with new partners and had new families. The father of her child was on remand, and she lived with a grandmother who worked as a cleaner by day and parted with her earnings at bingo every night. Melanie's blood pressure had begun to rise, and although she had two weeks to go to the delivery date, it had been decided to induce labour. Chris launched into the usual spiel about the risks to the baby due to toxaemia, and the need to start her off. Her only response was another spout of tears, and Chris looked at me helplessly, reluctant to go ahead with an invasive procedure without the patient's full consent. Even then we were becoming more aware of the looming shadow of litigation.

'Come on now, be a sensible girlie,' I urged, taking her hand and smoothing the tangle of hair from her eyes. 'You want to be delivered, don't you, and get out of here and back to your Nana's with the baby?'

This was a line of argument that appealed to her more, and she reluctantly agreed. Chris was very good with her, though she gripped my hand painfully and gave a shriek as the pessary went in. We heard murmurs beyond the curtains of 'Bloody 'ell!' and 'Christ, what's 'e doin' to 'er?' We ignored them, and I attached the cardiotocograph to Melanie's abdomen, giving her the call-bell.

Back in the office I poured out coffee for Chris and myself. 'Honestly, the things we do to these women.'

'Yeah – poor little kid, eh? But they brought themselves in here, Shirley – we had nothing to do with that bit.'

Linda joined us, and I asked what she had on D.U.

'A girl who could end up having a section – Lance has just taken blood from her. Then there's a possible concealed antepartum haemorrhage, but she's in good shape, so it's probably another urinary tract infection, so she's for full blood count and the usual urine culture. That's it for the time being.'

'Has Sandra taken them over?' I asked.

'No, she's still trying to get the midstream specimen. No rush. Lance has phoned the technician.'

Melanie rang her call-bell before her hour on the monitor was up and, by the time I'd settled both her and Janet Thompson down to await events, if any, Sandra was tying up the laundry bags.

'There are some specimens to take over, aren't there, Sandra?'

'Sister's just taken them.'

'Has she? But you're free, aren't you?' It was the normal practice for auxiliaries to go on these errands, as midwives were not supposed to leave the unit.

Sandra gave me a look. 'Sister Grierson always likes to take the lab specimens when a certain deputy chief pathologist is on call. Don't tell me you didn't know, Shirley! He comes in specially when she's on.'

For a moment I stared at her, then quickly lowered my eyes to the case-notes on the desk, taken aback by this new light on Linda's extra-marital liaison, already hospital gossip.

'I thought everybody knew, Shirley,' said the auxiliary in surprise. 'Charles King comes in regularly when Sister Grierson's on – they call him King Charles over there.'

So *that's* who he was – the gloomy technician, presumably a happier man these days. Trust the auxiliaries to know. Trivial little incidents now fell into place, and I remembered how Linda always seemed to be available to go to the lab. I busied myself with the case folders.

'There are too many tales going round this unit, and really it's hardly our business, is it?' I tried to give the impression that I'd known all along but hadn't cared to indulge in idle gossip, though I don't think Sandra was fooled. She said, 'Very well, Sister,' and dragged the bags to the end of the corridor. I was back to Sister after being Shirley for a while, though when Lance Penrose appeared on the ward full of Australian bonhomie, and I called him *doctor*, he asked if he'd said anything to upset me. When Linda returned he was still on the Unit, and I didn't get a chance to speak privately to her until about two o'clock.

'Did you know that Dora went for a drive on Sunday afternoon, just hours before she died?' I asked her.

'Yes, somebody was saying – I heard that he took her out. It's heartbreaking, isn't it? He was so devoted to her. If only more marriages were like theirs, eh?'

'I went with them.'

She looked up in surprise. '*You* went with them? How come?'

'Martin asked me. He felt he couldn't cope on his own, what with the wheelchair and everything, and her being so frail.'

'Oh, my dear, what a marvellous memory for you to keep! And how strange you must have felt when you heard that she'd gone, so soon afterwards. Oh, Shirley, I didn't know – has it upset you, love?'

I had to get to the point. 'We went to Tatton Park.' I saw the immediate tension of her neck muscles. 'You were at Tatton – on Sunday afternoon, Shirley?'

'Yes.' We looked at each other.

'Oh.'

'Yes, Linda, I saw you. I left the Hayeses to let them have a little time on their own, and I walked down towards the lake. Except that I turned back when I saw you.'

She swallowed, and faced me. 'You mean you didn't want us to see you?'

'I didn't want to intrude on something that wasn't my business – but I saw enough.'

'So why are you telling me now, Shirley?'

'Because I thought – well, Bernie and I both thought you should know that you're heading for trouble, Linda. Your meetings in the Path Lab are fairly common knowledge–'

'Oh, heck! I might have known that'd be sniffed out. But as for you and Bernie being so bothered, you needn't be. I'm happier than I've been since – oh, I can't remember!'

She suddenly smiled, a delightful little up-curving of her lips, ever so slightly saucy. I felt a rush of affection for her, and of pity. I wanted to hug her, but she had to be told.

'Oh, Linda, if you only knew how desperately sorry I am – it's been a joy, a real *joy* to see you looking so happy, but Howard's on to you, love.'

All sauciness was gone at a stroke. 'What do you mean?'

I told her about Grierson's phone call the previous night, and my downright lie.

'Oh, God. Oh, my God.' She leaned over the desk and covered her face. 'He never mentioned it when I saw him –you'd have thought he'd have been waiting for me to ask why he rang. Oh, thanks, Shirley love!'

'I couldn't bluff him again, and Bernie certainly wouldn't try. But he's on to you, love, and knowing him–' I left the rest to her intimate knowledge of the man.

'No, of course not.' She sat up straight, clasping her hands together in resolution. 'All right, then, so he's on to me. It only means that the balloon goes up sooner rather than later. I've put up with his damnable moods all these years, his bullying of the boys, his foul language when he's been drinking – if I hadn't had my job to go to, and all of you here, I'd have gone crazy. But now I've had a taste of something better, Shirley, and I'm not going back to the way things were. Thanks for telling, me, love, it's better to know in advance. Let battle commence!'

This was a new Sister Grierson indeed.

'And your – your friend in the lab?' I prompted curiously, 'what exactly is his – er – is he married?'

'Yes. Wife's been in and out of Carrowbridge for years.'

'Oh, Lord, a nut-case?'

'Yes. Never really got over puerperal psychosis after having their only child, Jonathan. He's going through University now, seems to be doing all right – got the usual live-in girl.'

'It can't have been easy, I mean with her being that way,' I said cautiously.

'Charles has had his moments with her, like when she set the bed on fire – and she's tried that at Carrowbridge, too. Suicide attempts and the most awful scenes in public – but of course she's to be pitied. You can't compare it to Howard taking out his spite on me and the children.

Anyway, it won't be for much longer, Shirley, because I'm leaving him. We'll have to sort out the details, but I'm not going on as we are. And I won't give up Charles. Not now. Or ever.'

There was a finality in her words that left me with nothing to say. To start pointing out such objections as the effect on her children or the financial minefield would have been a waste of breath, because she wouldn't have listened.

After a moment or two she said in a much softer tone, 'Charles is so different, so kind and understanding, Shirley. It makes such a change to be able to hold an intelligent conversation with a man on an equal footing, and to be able to disagree without a lot of shouting and abuse. It's heaven, sheer heaven.'

'Excuse me, Sister, but are you by any chance talking about Philip Crowne?'

Dilly Fisher stood in the doorway with her tapestry bag containing her decaffeinated coffee and copy of *Here I am, Lord.*

I had to smile. 'No, Dilly, Linda's never been to Shalom, so she hasn't had the pleasure of meeting Philip!'

'But her husband sits in the same Council Chamber,' Dilly pointed out. 'So she must hear about him from Howard – don't you, Sister Grierson?'

Linda's mouth tightened. 'Yes, Dilly, I do. Things like "That sanctimonious hypocrite Crowne mouthing away again about kids in moral danger in Marston, the usual bullshit."'

Dilly gasped, but Linda added kindly, 'And that's as good a recommendation for your Mr

99

Crowne as any praise, as far as I'm concerned. Anybody who can enrage Councillor Grierson that much can't be all bad!'

As she walked out of the office to return to D.U., Dilly shook her head sadly.

'Poor Sister Grierson's going through a time of temptation, and we'll have to pray for her, Shirley. Which reminds me, the July Shalom meeting is at Moor End Methodist on Friday week. Will you be coming along?'

I hesitated. 'I'm not quite sure yet, Dilly – I've got rather a lot on just now.' I looked at the clock. 'Isn't it time you went back to Postnatal? Sue will be needing you to help with the night feeds.'

But Dilly stood her ground. 'It's the children who suffer when marriages go wrong, Shirley. I know what my two went through when Reg and I were divorced. My Mark especially, he's fourteen now, and he hasn't done as well as he should have done at the Comprehensive. He was getting on so well, but it's really put him back, poor lad.'

I looked at the clock again, but she was clearly nerving herself for some kind of confrontation. 'And there's another thing I feel I should say to you, Shirley.'

'Go on, then.'

'That – er – friend of yours, the big lad who lives on Boreham Road – the one you met at Shalom.'

'Yes, Paul Meadows. What about him?'

'Only to warn you again to be very careful, love. He's not safe. He's been terrorising some of the children as they come out of school.'

'Oh, I find that hard to believe, Dilly,' I said,

100

shaking my head. 'It's more likely to be the other way round. Paul's as gentle as a lamb towards anybody who treats him properly, though he's often pestered by young hooligans who tease him and try to wind him up.'

'Well, I'm sorry, Shirley, but Mark's seen him turn on kids for no reason at all, and they're afraid to walk home along Boreham Road when they know he's about. If I were you, I wouldn't have him at your house when you're alone. Right, that's it, I've said my piece and I'll go now.'

She gathered up her cardigan and bag and trotted back to Postnatal, leaving me to ponder.

Janet Thompson and Melanie Sayers both rang their bells at the same time, and there were no opportunities for further confidences that night.

As I went off duty Mrs Gresham handed me a memo from Mr Hawke, manager of the Department of Obstetrics and Gynaecology. I was asked to make an appointment to see him in his office. I guessed it would be about apologising to Blair, and so I tore it up.

Dora's funeral was very well attended, in fact St Christopher's was packed, making a change from their usual meagre congregations. Bernie and I sat a couple of rows behind the mourners with Mrs Gresham and other senior midwifery staff.

'Look, there's Mr Horsfield,' someone whispered as a slightly stooping figure in an expensive dark suit took a seat in a side row.

'If only Dora could see him at her funeral, wouldn't she be thrilled?' I murmured.

'Ah, 'twould have made her day, for sure,'

Bernie agreed, and we lowered our heads to hide our smiles. Dear old Dora, how she'd relished those emergencies when the consultant had to be brought in at night. It had been Sir this and Sir that, and fetch Mr Horsfield an ashtray for his cigar, nurse. It was nice to see him paying his last respects to her: he and she were of the same vintage, trained just after the end of the war. No first-name familiarities for them, but great mutual respect.

I couldn't see Linda anywhere. 'I thought she said she'd be coming, but with all this other business going on–' I looked at Bernie, who shrugged.

'She's been a different woman, it's true, but how can it possibly work out, I ask ye?'

There was a stir at the entrance, and we all stood as the coffin was carried in and up the aisle, followed by Martin flanked by his daughter and son-in-law. A number of relatives walked behind them, a drab medley of blacks, greys and navys. The coffin was completely covered with floral tributes, including the one from the Maternity Unit, and they filled the air with the indefinable churchy smell of Anglicanism. I reflected that Roman Catholic churches have a darker, more pungent odour compounded of incense and candle-grease, while the non-conformist places tend to be lighter, though Moor End Methodist always brings to mind old well-thumbed hymn-books on dusty shelves.

The organ note halted these wandering thoughts, and as the first hymn began I saw Martin lower his head. Laura put an arm around him, and her husband passed a large white handkerchief over, but Martin already had one. The service proceeded, so much shorter than a Requiem Mass, and in no time at all, it seemed, the coffin was being carried out to the singing of 'Now Thank We All Our God', the mourners got into the waiting cars for the drive to the crematorium, a private family affair, and the rest of us dispersed.

'I'll walk home, Bernie – no, honestly, I feel like a breath of air,' I told her, though I soon felt rather conspicuous in my slim, dark suit topped with a navy straw hat, in contrast to the usual informal cycling gear. When a heel caught in a paving crevice, I nearly lost my balance, and righted myself with an involuntary, *'Shit!'*

A car drew up at the roadside, and Linda's laughing face appeared at the open passenger window. 'Go on, get in the back, you're not safe on the streets!'

It wasn't the Griersons' Cavalier but a Sierra with a registration from five years back. I thankfully got in and sat on the back seat, pulling off my hat. I recognised the driver, a stockily built man with horn-rimmed glasses and a prominent nose. He briefly turned his head and nodded when Linda introduced us.

'Friend and colleague Shirley Pierce, meet Charles King of the blood bank!'

She made it sound like Charles, King of the blood bank, and I bowed my head. 'Do I say Your Majesty?'

Linda giggled. 'Only on ceremonial occasions. We're going for coffee at La Gondola if you'd like to join us.'

'Well–' I hesitated. Gondolas are meant for two.

103

'Go on, we could all use a cappuccino after that ordeal. Poor old Hayes, I nearly wept for him.'

'Didn't see you at the church,' I remarked.

'No, we came in late and sat at the back to make a quick getaway,' she explained. 'I felt I should go, and Charles had no objection, so–' She turned her shining eyes towards him, and he returned her look, a look between lovers, as was every word, every lightest touch between them; their love was as visible as if they were enveloped in a rainbow soap-bubble. Yet I was not excluded; Linda clearly wanted to share her love, to show it off like a prized possession.

Can't you see how happy we are, how right this is? Her eyes said it all and more. She had the boldness, the recklessness, even, of a woman passionately in love, and I felt myself being drawn in to see King not as a middle-aged pathologist with a big nose, but as a prince who had restored her to vibrant life with his kiss. Don't forget I'd seen her distraught with the misery of a habitually unhappy marriage: how could I possibly be sorry for this change?

Charles gradually lowered the guard he had put up when I joined them, and at La Gondola we sat at a pavement table and talked, laughing at silly jokes with that sense of relief and lightening which often follows a funeral, and was no disrespect to Dora.

They dropped me off at Chatsworth Road where I got out of my funeral outfit and put on a blue cotton sundress. Two letters had been delivered: one was a buff envelope franked with the Marston Health Authority logo, first-class, and it contained a note from Mr Hawke, repeating his request to see me in his office 'at a time convenient to you', all very polite and placatory, and signed by himself, William Hawke. I tore it up and opened the other letter which was from Emma. Another woman in love.

'I know this is the real thing, Mumsie,' she wrote, 'and I do so want you and Danilo to be friends. I'm sure you *will* when you get to know each other. Actually he's a teeny bit nervous about meeting my formidable mother! So I'd like to bring him up to Marston for a weekend – and don't get into a tizzy over the sleeping arrangements, he'll be quite happy to kip down in the small bedroom in deference to propriety! What nights are you off during the next couple of weeks? I'll phone on Sunday, when you've had a chance to think about it. Oh, Mumsie, I'm just so happy!'

Of course I was thrilled at the prospect of seeing Emma again soon, less so about Danilo. He was from Milan, and they'd met through the Italian publishers of the magazine she worked on. Emma was rapidly on her way up, and too young to end her career by marrying an Italian who would inevitably take her away from her own country.

I got out my diary and writing-pad to begin a letter, and took it out to the garden table.

'Hallo, Shirley.'

I looked up at a picture of misery. Creased and stained trousers, scuffed trainers, a downright filthy T-shirt that I'd given him, the Greenpeace logo obscured by black daubs; unruly hair, stubbled chin and troubled eyes. Everything about him looked uncared-for. And he smelled – a rank blend of perspiration and unwashed clothes.

'Paul!'

'I know you said not to come again this week, Shirley, but I just have to talk to somebody. Philip and Celia have gone down to London to meet some MP, and Norma Daley–'

He sat down at the garden table and put his head in his hands.

'Yes, Paul? What about Norma?'

'She was in, but I didn't see her. Mr Daley said she was busy, so I said could Norma just come to the door for me to say something to her, but he said that she was Mrs Daley to me, and she couldn't.'

'Oh, dear.' I remembered what Philip had said about Alf Daley putting his foot down.

'It's no joke when your friends turn against you for no good reason, Shirley. I told him that you'd told me not to come here again this week, and he said it was about time that Pierce woman showed a bit of sense. And when I asked him to please explain what he meant by that, he shut the door in my face, which I thought was uncalled-for. Don't you think it's a bit much when a man can forbid his wife to speak to a friend on her own doorstep, Shirley?'

I could just picture Alf Daley, normally a rather retiring man who supported Manchester United and was happy for Norma and Rod to pursue their activities at St Christopher's and Shalom. There were those who said that he actually encouraged his wife's evangelical zeal, which got her out of the house, so he could relax and watch his favourite programmes in peace. But now it seemed that he had decided enough was enough, and I suspected that Norma was in agreement on this matter of Paul; his visits had become an inconvenience.

'And I hope you're not going to turn me away as well, Shirley, because I'm just about up to here. There's this little weasel from Marston Comprehensive who's been getting at me, in fact that's what I was going to see Norma about, or rather Rod, to ask if he'd do something about it. He's supposed to be a youth leader, so he should be able to sort out an objectionable school kid!'

'Sssh, ssh, Paul, don't shout, love.' I laid a hand lightly on his shoulder. 'Tell you what, I think you could do with a shower. Then I'll get you something to eat, and maybe we could talk after you've calmed down a bit. Only I've had a bit of a heavy day, too, you see.'

His eyes brightened and his mouth curved upwards in a smile of pure joy. 'So we can comfort each other again, Shirley, can we?'

I hesitated. A thought had suddenly occurred to me, and although I was anxious to get his mind on to safer topics, I had to ask a question.

'Paul dear, this – er – weaselly type you mentioned – how old would he be?'

'Fifteen or maybe fourteen, I don't know. He comes up to me holding his nose and saying things like, "Phoo, anybody got a bar of carbolic soap?" and "ever seen a poo with a face before?" But if there's a teacher about, he's all smirks and what-a-good-boy-am-I, a right Little Lord Fauntleroy!'

'You don't know his name?'

'I think I heard somebody call out, "Hey,

107

Fisher!" – but they could have meant somebody else. All I know is that I'm made to feel like a criminal just for walking down Boreham Road, and it's *wrong*, Shirley! I'm sick and tired of it, I can tell you!'

'All right, Paul, let's leave it there. You go and take a shower now, and shampoo your hair at the same time.'

Whether his young tormentor was Mark Fisher or not, I made up my mind to speak very firmly to Dilly.

While he showered in the bathroom – the trouble was that he had to put on the same clothes afterwards, and the thought came to me that I could do something really useful for him in providing a free laundry service – I prepared a salad with tinned salmon and bread and butter. When Paul appeared again, scrubbed and smiling, I felt a rush of indignation towards Alf Daley and his arrogant remark about myself. And as for those damned kids...

'Feeling better now?'

He nodded happily, and sat down to consume every morsel of the salad, followed by ice cream and cake.

'Come on, Paul, let's sit down on the settee and listen to some music.'

I put on a compilation tape which included the Adagio in G Minor attributed to Albinoni, and settled down beside him, taking his hand. The yearning strings, at once mournful and romantic, rose on the air like the scent of the lilies drifting through the open patio door on the evening breeze. My thoughts strayed to Linda and

Charles, and hoped that they would find happiness in spite of all the odds stacked against them, and then I remembered Martin in his lonely grief, and wondered when he would return to his empty home. Ought I try to keep in touch, at least for the first few weeks of his widowerhood?

Paul's painful indrawing of breath recalled me to the present moment, and his exhalation was a long, shuddering groan. With a despairing gesture he turned towards me and hid his face against the bodice of the sundress.

'What is it, Paul? Oh, my poor boy, what's the matter?'

I stopped speaking and held him close as he wept his heart out in great wrenching sobs. There was nothing else to do but wait until the convulsive heavings gave way to shallower breaths and the storm passed over.

'All right, Paul, all right, all right,' I repeated, stroking the soft, newly-washed hair as he buried his face deeper. I don't think I have ever heard anything so heart-rending as the sound of that boy in a man's body mourning for his lost life, the mind that should have been lively and perceptive, the artist's or musician's intellect that had been taken away from him with his first breath. Such meaningless waste, such a cruel tragedy, not like a road accident or a gunshot wound, but a silent disaster that went unnoticed at the time it happened. Oh, God, where were You in that black hour, what were You doing when this baby's lack of oxygen deprived him for ever of a normal life? *Where were You?* What good is his manhood to him now, O Lord? Nothing but an additional torment, through no fault of his own. WHERE THE HELL WERE YOU?

For this was the question that Paul was wordlessly asking. Why had he been set apart, irreversibly different from other men, in a way he could never understand? Unlocked by the mysterious power of the music, his tears flowed in grief and rage.

I felt my own tears welling up, but I checked them. What good would crying do? None whatsoever. What, then, could I do at this moment? Only follow the dictates of my heart.

When he finally lay passive in my arms I kissed his stubbly cheek and put on a cassette of Taizé chants; I always find their repetitive phrases soothing. I told him to take off his trainers and lie down on the settee. I put a *Manchester Evening News* under his feet and sat beside him, taking his head on my lap and gently stroking his forehead – a soft, slow caressing to comfort him, as a woman comforts a baby at the breast.

'Aaaah.' His sigh was one of pure pleasure, like Peppercorn's purr of contentment when he settled down on the duvet. The music played on quietly, the Latin words coolly flowing like a mountain stream.

Ubi caritas, et amor
Ubi caritas, Deus ibi est.

'Aaah. Thank you, Shirley.' He lay back and closed his eyes. The stresses of the day drained away, leaving his face untroubled and trusting. The little weasel was banished along with all the

110

other anxieties and uncertainties of his life. How quickly satisfied he was with just a little human kindness!

To hell with being careful.

Chapter Six

Yes, my Darling Daughter

'Is er – very good, Shirley, and pleases me very much – er – is real Italian lasagne!'

Danilo's wide smile revealed even white teeth. Tall and athletic, he was almost a stereotype of a Latin Romeo, dark-eyed and dark-haired; at thirty he had so far evaded the net of matrimony, and I reckoned that he must have bedded a fair number of girls in the past dozen years or so. Why should he now let himself be caught by my Emma?

Her bright eyes danced at hearing his compliments, and of course I *had* been brave to serve an Italian dish to our Milanese visitor. I'd prepared it in the morning and put it in the fridge with the gooseberry tart, ready to cook in the evening. Real Italian coffee lay waiting in the cafetiere, a jug of cream at hand, and I asked Danilo to uncork the bottle of Valpolicella I'd bought at the off-licence. We ate out of doors, and although the lilies were over, the garden made a good setting; we could imagine ourselves a long way from Chatsworth Road on that Friday evening in late July.

Emma looked utterly charming with her fair hair

cut in a simple shoulder-length bob, and her eyes were alight with happiness; they were neither blue nor green, but something subtly between the two, with golden flecks, a most unusual colour. Like Pussage's, I thought, as she leaned down to stroke the fine sleek cat she'd brought with her as a four-month-old kitten when she left University. Her hair fell forward in two shining wings – ah, was it any wonder that men were attracted to her like bees to a honeypot? There had been a fair number of admirers before Danilo, and I hoped there would be more after him; she was still so young.

'Why do you call him Pussage?' he asked.

'I called him Sausage when I first had him, but Mum called him Pussy, so he ended up as Pussage,' she explained, putting down a saucer with a spoonful of cream. 'Yes, you's my darling boy,' she crooned to the pampered creature. 'And you's coming to bed with your mamma tonight, aren't you?'

'He comes to bed with his mamma?' Danilo raised symmetrical black eyebrows in a question, and murmured, 'Then we shall call him Nero, yes?'

I caught his eye over the top of Emma's lowered head, and he grinned boldly at me, clearly convinced of his own charm.

'Who's for some more wine?' I asked, picking up the bottle. 'And what are your plans for tomorrow, Emma? Are you taking Danilo to see the sights of Manchester?'

'Yes, we want to do some shopping, and get him an English cap!' she answered. 'I thought we'd have lunch in town, and in the evening we're taking *you* out, Mumsie, to something you'll really enjoy. We didn't want you to be slaving in the kitchen all the time, did we, Danilo?'

'*Che? Si – si, e vero*,' he smiled.

'No, you work much too hard with all those mamas and babas,' she went on. 'How are things at that place? Any new scandals I haven't heard about?'

'Mm, yes, as a matter of fact there *is* one going on, and it'll be more than just a nine days' wonder,' I replied. 'You remember Linda Grierson who works with me? She lives – lived – up on Marston Park, overlooking the golf course.'

'Grierson? Isn't he a big noise on the council? The one who saved the old railway station?'

'That's the one. Well, she's left him.'

'Really? Why?'

'He's been impossible, Emma, a real domestic tyrant – and a drinker. She's had a wretched life with him, and so have the kids. We've all known about it at the Maternity Unit for years. Anyway, she's taken the three children and gone to her sister's in Altrincham. And she's got a solicitor–'

'Coo! So is she going to divorce him for cruelty or unreasonable behaviour or whatever they call it?'

'Yes – only it isn't going to be straightforward, because *he's* got a solicitor to bring a counter-accusation of adultery against Linda.'

'Wow, that thickens the plot a bit. Who's the other bloke?'

I cleared my throat. 'He's the deputy chief pathologist at Marston General. They're looking for somewhere to rent.'

'Can't she just move in with him?'

'Well, no. The trouble is that he's got a wife who's in and out of Carrowbridge – she's in there now, a long-term psychosis, goes completely off the rails every so often. And of course there are Linda's children, the twin boys are thirteen and at the Grammar School, and little Cathy's eight. They've all broken up for the summer holidays this week, so Linda won't have to ferry them to and from school, and by September she hopes that they – she and Charles, I mean – will have found somewhere to live.'

'With the kids as well? Gosh, it sounds complicated. I bet the old solicitors are rubbing their hands together in anticipation. Now, let me clear away these things, and then we'll – oh, my God, what the–'

She stared open-mouthed as Paul Meadows appeared around the corner of the house, carrying a large plastic bag.

'Hallo, Shirley – oh, I say, you've got people to supper.'

'Yes, Paul, I *told* you that my daughter was coming home this weekend,' I said, wondering how quickly I could get rid of him without appearing to do so.

'Oh, yes, so you did. Ah, this must be her Italian boyfriend, then – very pleased to meet you. I enjoy meeting new friends!'

'Emma, this is Paul Meadows, a friend of mine from Shalom,' I said quickly. 'I must have told you about–'

Emma has always been able to convey disapproval without actually saying anything. Even

114

as a baby in her pram she could fend off unwelcome endearments like 'Who's a pretty little girlie, then?' with a long, hard stare in the opposite direction. Now she withdrew from Paul's outstretched hand, though Danilo rose, smiling politely, and took it.

'Good evening, Paul. Yes, I am happy to be the friend of Emma.'

Paul eyed the table. 'Oooh, that looks good, Shirley. Is that some sort of a pie, what's left of it?'

Emma's jaw dropped in unbelief, and I quickly replied. 'Yes, it's gooseberry tart, and you're welcome to finish it. I'll just go and get a plastic container to–'

But he had already pulled up the fourth chair and sat down at the table. 'Oh, great, thanks.' I poured the last of the cream over the portion as he dug in with a spoon.

'And how long are you staying, Emma?' he asked conversationally.

'We're visiting my mother for the weekend.' Her voice was cold as she rose and began to clear the table. 'Come on, Danilo, we'll wash up together while Mother deals with – er–'

But Danilo was not inclined to cooperate, and said he had not yet finished his coffee. Emma carried a tray of used plates and cutlery indoors without another word.

'Actually, Shirley, the reason I've called is to see if you've got any clean underpants and socks,' said Paul between mouthfuls. 'I seem to have run out of stock, as it were. And you *did* say they needed changing every day, didn't you?'

'They certainly do, Paul. And yes, I've got some

clean stuff, enough to see you over the weekend, anyway. I'll pop them into a bag.'

'Thanks. I've got another lot here for you. Mm, this is good.' When I rejoined him after exchanging the soiled underwear for clean, he chatted to me in his usual eager fashion. 'The schools are out now, thank goodness, Shirley, which means that ordinary decent people can walk past Marston Comprehensive at four o'clock in the afternoon without fear of abuse from Weasel and friends!'

'You *must* try to ignore those silly kids, Paul,' I told him for the umpteenth time. 'If they see that you don't take any notice of them, they'll lose interest.'

'That's all very well, Shirley, but you can take it from me that it's easier for you to talk than it is for me to keep quiet when I'm followed by a gang of young thugs that nobody seems to be able to do anything about! The police don't want to know, the teachers are no use at all, and even the lollipop lady told me to get off the road. In short, to put it in a nutshell, nobody cares a bloody toss!'

As usual his voice got louder as he listed his grievances.

'Ssh, ssh, Paul, don't get yourself so worked up, love.'

'I can't help it, Shirley! I could murder that bloody Weasel! I'd like to—'

Danilo had discreetly taken himself off indoors, and I was suddenly aware of Brian Newhouse standing at the fence and looking straight at Paul and me.

'You all right, Mrs Pierce?'

'Yes, we're fine, thanks, er, Brian. Paul's leaving

now,' I said hurriedly, adding, 'My daughter's home this weekend, with a friend.'

Brian nodded, and continued to potter around his garden while Paul finished his coffee – 'A bit strong for me, actually, Shirley' – and gave me the usual unrestrained embrace.

'Shalom, Shirley, Shalom.'

'Peace, Paul.' I was conscious of Emma's eyes through the kitchen window, and could imagine her indignation and Danilo's amused gleam.

'When shall I see you again, Shirley?'

'Can't tell you just now, Paul. Some time next week.'

'What nights are you working next week, Shirley?'

'*Mother!* Are you coming in?' Emma could contain herself no longer, and I had to say a firm and final good night, closing the side door behind him.

'For God's sake, Mother, what are you thinking of, letting a weirdo like that into the house?' Emma demanded angrily. 'And Danilo says you do *washing* for him!'

Treacherous Danilo had listened to every word we said.

'I'm sorry, Emma. But there's no harm in showing a little common humanity, surely.'

'Humanity be damned, he *stinks*, Mother, or have you lost your sense of smell? Look, this just isn't on, and I shall speak to Peter Crow or whatever his name is, and tell him exactly what I think of him, taking advantage of a soft-hearted widow living alone – sending a great creature like that round here to stuff his face and have his pants washed!'

'*Emma!* It isn't like that at all, it was nothing to do with Mr Crowne, I befriended Paul voluntarily,' I protested, hardly able to tell her that Crowne was broadly in agreement with her, though with far more compassion. 'You really have no need to worry, dear, Paul is brain-damaged, but I understand him and know exactly how to deal with him. It's a tragic situation.'

But Emma wasn't having it. 'Rubbish! You're running the most appalling risk, you silly woman!'

Danilo smiled and gently rebuked her. 'Your mother is very kind to the unfortunate young man, Emma.'

'Oh, be quiet,' she said impatiently. 'He could strangle her with those great paws of his. Or she could be raped! She'd have no chance at all against a brute that size, more than six feet tall and hands you could park a car on. Now, look here, Mother,' she went on, turning to me. 'You're to promise me that you'll never have him round here when you're alone, do you hear me? I absolutely forbid it!'

My daughter's beautiful blazing eyes demanded a response, and Danilo watched with unconcealed interest. The last thing I wanted was a row, but Emma was genuinely upset, and her anger rose directly from her anxiety for me.

My baby, my little girl. She had given me plenty to worry about since her discovery of boys, somewhere between twelve and fourteen, though I was slow to realise how far ahead of Ruth she always was in that area. Her first romance, if you can call it that, was a tearaway with a motorcycle,

118

and I don't think I slept for a week. He was mercifully soon eclipsed by a would-be rock star called Sonny Dark, though actually his name was Cyril, born late in life to Peggy Prickett who used to run the newsagents at the corner of Railway Road. He headed a local group, Double Vision, and drove them and their second-hand guitars around in a clapped-out transit van; Emma went with them on some of their engagements, and that was how she met drummer Sid Probus, who's since gone on to the northern club circuit and cocaine. More sleepless nights...

But then came University and a whole new world in which she had her pick of eligible males; I remember one upper-class twit whose constant phone calls during one Easter vacation irritated me beyond endurance. 'I want to speak to Emma Pierce,' he'd say, and I'd tell him she'd gone into Manchester with an old boyfriend, or was washing her hair – or sitting on the toilet.

Emma came to me, outraged. 'Mother!' It was always a bad sign when she called me Mother. 'What on earth have you been telling Giles? He says that the woman who answers his calls gives him the most extraordinary answers!'

'Oh, does he mean our half-witted daily help?'

'It's not funny, Mother, and I have no idea why you show yourself up like this when my friends call. In future will you please just say that Emma is not available at present, take the caller's name and number and say I'll get back to them. Is that quite clear?'

'It is, my darling daughter, quite clear. And let me tell you something else. If that stupid prat

Giles patronises me one more time on the phone, I'll tell him that Emma Pierce has had to go to the clap clinic. Is *that* quite clear?'

We didn't speak for the rest of the day, but of course we laughed about it later.

And now here she was, a smart, self-assured young woman on her way to the top, and fretting about her silly mother.

'I shall worry myself to death about you, Mum. You *must* promise me,' she repeated.

It wasn't worth spoiling our precious time together, though I could have slapped Danilo for the way he had subtly added fuel to the flames of Emma's disquiet while pretending to be sympathetic.

'I've taken note of how you feel, Emma, and I promise to be very, very careful,' I told her, and with that she had to be content, though I learned later that she had gone over to the Newhouses at some time during the weekend, and told Brian of her fears; she'd got his assurance that he'd keep an eye on the comings and goings at Number 50.

That evening Danilo presented me with a brilliant silk scarf with its own gold pin, and Emma had bought me a blouse in pale green crepe-de-chine to wear with the tailored slacks she'd given me on my birthday. They produced a box of Belgian chocolates, and we chatted until I went to bed at eleven, leaving them sprawled on the sofa watching an Italian film. It finished at some time after midnight, and I heard Danilo go into the little spare room where I'd made up the bed and put a hospitality tray on the dressing-table.

The next sounds I heard were splashes and

stifled whispers as they took a bath together.

What would my parents say if they knew about Emma's lifestyle, I wondered, and I thought about my mother who was thirty when she had me. She had grown up between the wars, one of a generation of girls who conformed at least outwardly to their parents' standards in general behaviour, morals and fashions; they went to church, learned house-wifely arts, didn't smoke or swear; their effective contraceptive was a deep fear of pregnancy. An illegitimate baby was a disaster, abortion was illegal, and the baby was usually adopted, though the girl seldom lived down her disgrace. 'Having to get married' was a lesser evil, and rather more common than was generally admitted, though such weddings were often hurried affairs with no white gown, averted eyes and shaming whispers. And a number of girls – and married women – died from septicaemia following septic abortions. Emma has the Pill, and can have sex when she wants it, with none of these dangers.

I had *not* had the Pill, and my thoughts went back to my meeting with Tom when I was twenty-two, a year younger than Emma, and I'd just become a State Registered Nurse, as we were still called then, and gone with two girl-friends on a week's walking holiday in the Lake District. Tom was staying at the same centre with a male colleague who'd suggested that it would do him good. He'd been widowed less than two years, and had a daughter of eighteen – she had not come with him, and how differently things might have turned out if she had!

He was forty-two, and resembled a married

121

surgeon I'd worshipped from afar. Our attraction was instant and mutual, and by mid-week had become a wild infatuation, sweeping us up into a new dimension, or so it seemed, away from the restraints of everyday life and routine. In such a heavenly setting, with those majestic peaks all around us, we climbed up and up, drinking in the pure air, completely lost in each other. On the Friday night we crept out of the house after our companions had retired, and climbed Helvellyn by moonlight; and there on the soft, cropped grass where we'd talked endlessly by day, we made ecstatic love beneath the night sky.

Tom was both elated and horror-stricken at what he had done, and I was dismayed by his almost immediate reaction.

'Oh, my God – my love! You'll have to let me know if you're all right, Shirley darling.'

And I wasn't all right. I was pregnant. We were married three months later at a hole-in-corner wedding, and I was catapulted into a Manchester suburb in November, living in a strange house among neighbours I didn't know, an unfamiliar foetus swelling up inside me and, worst of all, Tom's daughter Joy. It was not a happy pregnancy, and looking back on it now, I can see that I never made proper allowance for the fact that Joy's life had also been turned upside-down at an age when she couldn't cope with it, and much too soon after the loss of her mother. We were two self-centred young women, unable to see beyond our own interests.

It was in the third month of the marriage, and the sixth of my pregnancy, that my rage and frustration boiled over.

'Your daughter is the sulkiest, stupidest, most self-pitying *lump* that I've ever had the misfortune to meet, and either she gets out of this house or I do!' I shouted, tipping a tray of crockery into the sink after a particularly trying meal, and breaking at least half of the set that had been his first wife's pride.

'Oh, Shirley my dear, come on, come *on*, just calm down, you're overwrought,' poor Tom remonstrated, but I was like a cornered rat, and as savage.

'It's no good, I can't stand having her dripping around for another day! She can damned well park her fat backside somewhere else, anywhere but here. Or *I* shall go, and if I do, I won't be back. It's her or me, you'll have to choose, and choose *now!*'

This was when a decent flat or bed-sitter was affordable for a young person wanting a place of their own, and such a place had to be quickly found for Joy, who then put it all around Marston that she'd been turned out of her home by the woman Daddy had had to marry because she was pregnant. Which was no less humiliating because it was true.

I've sometimes wondered which one of us Tom would have chosen if I had not been carrying our child. He had no choice, because the new baby had to come before the officially adult daughter he dearly loved but who had become an inconvenience. By the time my first baby, Ruth, was born – a dear little round-faced thing with my brown eyes – Joy was pregnant by our GP's son, Andrew Bockett, and another hasty wedding followed, much to the fury of his parents. Her baby was also a girl, Jade, and the Bocketts had to make the best of becoming grandparents sooner than they had planned. Tom was deeply upset and blamed himself – or rather both of us – for what he saw as a disaster for all concerned. We never spoke about it because it was too dangerous a subject, but I resented the invisible, unmentioned barrier between us.

After I'd had our second daughter, Emma, I announced that I was going to enrol for midwifery training at Marston General Hospital, and engaged a middle-aged widow to come in and take care of Ruth and Emma at different times of the day, according to my shifts. I paid her out of my meagre students' allowance, and Tom got used to my absences; he consoled himself with the children, and often took them round to Joy's home to play with her children, for she had a boy at about the same time that I had Emma. I was sure that he discussed me with her, which did nothing to ease my bitterness against her, and the enmity between us was never healed.

I became a midwife rather than a housewife, and Tom withdrew into himself and an inner loneliness that he endured without complaint. And so ended the Lake District idyll, and if you're surprised and shocked by the Shirley Pierce of that time, remember that it was no picnic for me either, knowing that my husband saw his second marriage as a mistake. After his death the young Bocketts moved down south, and that was that. We never kept in touch.

It's only in recent years that I've understood the

extent of the damage resulting from my unforgiving spirit, but remorse always comes too late. I saw that my career had been a poor exchange for the happy marriage we could have had if I'd been reconciled to my husband's daughter. And I thought that perhaps my bitter regret has made me into the woman I had now become – nicer? Softer? More mature, or as silly as Emma said I was? I didn't know.

I found myself crying into my pillow while the Italian made love to Emma in her single bed on the other side of the wall.

'I wondered, Shirley, after all your kindness to Dora–' Martin Hayes's voice came hesitantly over the line. He'd been back in his own home in Wilmot Avenue for two weeks, and I could picture his tall figure in well-pressed trousers and summer-weight jacket, standing in the hall at the foot of the stairs and looking anxious as he held the receiver. 'Of course I know you lead a very busy life, and you must know so many people – I hope you don't mind me getting in touch, but I never really thanked you–'

But he *had*, over and over again, when I'd called with a cake and a couple of cottage pies to put in the freezer.

'It seems a shame to waste this nice weather, Shirley, and I wondered if you'd like a little drive out into the country,' he went on. 'Dora and I used to take picnics with us sometimes. Are you there, Shirley?'

Yes, I was receiving him loud and clear. Poor old love, he was obviously lonely, and it was scarcely a month.

'Actually I've got my younger daughter at home this weekend, Martin, with her boyfriend.'

'Oh, I'm sorry, my dear, you'll want to spend your time with them–'

'No, Martin, not at all,' I said, my mind working quickly as I considered his ultra-respectable image, a gentleman if ever there was one. If Emma needed reassurance about my friends and relationships, who better than Martin to provide it?

'Emma and Danilo are in Manchester this morning, and they've got some kind of outing lined up for me tonight, but tomorrow–' I paused significantly. 'Sunday afternoon would be an opportunity for them to spend some time here on their own – so if you *did* feel like a little drive, Martin–'

He cottoned on at once. 'Oh, that would be very nice, Shirley, and I'd be delighted.'

I could picture his beaming smile at the other end of the line. Good old Martin, I thought, here's something that will give pleasure all round, *and* make a good impression on Emma, for I hated any kind of friction or disagreement with my lovely, talented girl. We arranged that he would call for me at two-thirty on Sunday.

The young lovers returned carrying parcels and ready for drinks in the garden. The evening treat was revealed: seats in the circle at the Opera House – for *Phantom of the Opera*.

'So we'll expect you to dress yourself up to the nines, Mumsie. Wear your new blouse with that slim black skirt and Danilo's scarf – you'll wow them all.'

Of course I was thrilled and touched by their generosity. We had a taxi each way, and Emma sat between her mother and her lover in the theatre. We enthused over the music, the singing and the brilliant stage effects, and Danilo insisted on buying drinks in the interval, and another box of chocolates; he really did seem to want to make a good impression, and I tried to like him for Emma's sake.

When I returned from the 9a.m. Mass on Sunday, Emma helped me with the lunch, and I told her that I was going out for a drive in the afternoon 'with a friend'.

'Oh, no, Mumsie, there's no need for you to go out! We've got to go back this evening, and we want to enjoy every moment of your company while we're here!' Dear Emma's protest was predictable, and Danilo obediently echoed her, so things turned out exactly as I'd planned, and when Martin's Toyota appeared it was put to good use: I sat beside him in the front, with the young couple in the back. He'd already decided to go to Styal Country Park, a good choice, not too far away but within reach of some of Cheshire's loveliest countryside. Leaving the car, we followed Martin through woodland and beside the River Bollin; he knew all the best paths to take, having walked them many times with Dora over the years.

'There's the old mill, you see, Danilo – and those workers' cottages are two hundred years old, built by a cotton manufacturer for his workers. Nice, aren't they?'

Danilo showed his appreciation by asking

questions about the history of the place, while Emma and I chatted happily as we were led up into open country above the Bollin valley. Somewhere along our way we changed partners, and Emma walked with Martin while Danilo helped me over a stile to follow a footpath that gradually descended again to woodland and back to the car park. It was a perfect summer afternoon, and Emma was much impressed.

'Mumsie, what an absolute old *sweetie!*' she enthused. 'Oh, I feel so much happier about you now – and he admires you, even Danilo noticed. He'll be sixty-two this year, so he was telling me, so that makes him about fifteen years older than you – and he's got that house in Wilmot Avenue, and the car–'

'Ssh, Emma, the poor man's only just lost his wife. She was my colleague and friend,' I said rather confusedly, though I was pleased by her approval.

'But this will help him to get over his loss, Mum, and he's just the sort of man I like to think you're seeing, especially after – ah, well, 'nuff said. It's been a lovely weekend, and I'll ring Ruth when I get back tonight.'

And tell her about both Paul and Martin, I surmised. Emma could be very transparent at times, and I loved her all the more for it. Danilo's visit had turned out to be a success for more reasons than one.

Except that memories of Tom's other daughter had been reawakened. Tom was dead, but Joy was still around somewhere, and her children, my step-grandchildren, were the same ages as my daughters. Try as I would to forget the woman, her accusing image continued to stare from Tom's reproachful photograph: she had his eyes and jaw.

Philip Crowne was right: an unforgiven sin is an unhealed wound.

Chapter Seven

A Failed Attempt

The night staff soon got wind of my meetings with Martin Hayes, our drives out into the country, the shared meals at Wilmot Avenue and Chatsworth Road; he was my partner at the St Antony's Summer Parish Dance, where I introduced him to Father O'Flynn; they chatted over a beer, and Father casually mentioned that a new course of instruction in the Catholic faith would commence in September.

I found that I quite liked having an attentive gentleman friend, but it was early days; I didn't want to rush into a serious attachment, nor did I want him to become dependent on me, which looked all too likely. He was one of those men who need to be married, who find no compensations at all in a single life where freedom simply means loneliness. He constantly thanked me for my kindness, praised my cooking to the skies, and said I was his greatest comfort; but I knew perfectly well that if he had not got me he'd find somebody else, which wouldn't be difficult. There are plenty of lonely middle-aged women around, single, widowed and divorced, who'd be glad to be noticed by a courteous, generous widower with a nice home and a car – and a definite prospect of marriage on the horizon. One or two colleagues were frankly envious, and there were the odd whispers that Dora was hardly cold.

'Don't worry about what anybody says, Shirley, you just go for it and be happy,' said Linda, with the same defiant gleam she'd had in her eyes when she decided to leave Howard. She was looking a little strained during the school summer holidays, and was clearly not getting enough sleep. With his wife Miriam confined in a long-stay psychiatric unit, Charles wanted Linda to move in with her children, but her solicitor strongly advised against this while Grierson was contesting her petition for divorce.

'I don't intend to live in Charles's house until both our divorces are through,' she told me. 'In other words, not until we're married. It's going to be a long road, Shirley, but there's no turning back for either of us now. No way.'

She smiled, but there were dark smudges under her eyes from sheer fatigue. Her sister Jane and brother-in-law Frank both went to work, and the Grierson children could not be left unsupervised all day while Linda rested after night duty; and Howard was threatening vengeance for what he saw as a betrayal of their marriage and his rights as a father.

'He says he'll sue for custody, but my solicitor says he hasn't a hope,' Linda told us over coffee in the office, but I saw the anxiety in her eyes, and so did Bernie.

'How's little Cathy copin' with all this to-in' and fro-in'?' she asked. 'She's very close to her Daddy, isn't she?'

Linda frowned. 'Cathy's always been Howard's pet, being the youngest and a girl. He's bullied Simon and Andrew for under-achievement, as he sees it – never gives them a word of praise for their efforts, poor kids.'

'But how's little Cathy feelin' *now?*' persisted Bernie.

'We've had the usual tears and sulks, and of course all three of them feel restricted in somebody else's home,' Linda admitted. 'They miss their own rooms with their own belongings around them. We're a bit cramped for space at Jane's, and Frank likes to watch his own favourite TV programmes. I do what I can to divert them – took them to the ice rink this afternoon, that's why I'm feeling so whacked out tonight.' She yawned and poured out another cup of black coffee. 'But we'll get through it, and they'll have a much better life in the long run.'

'Can't the boys take Cathy to Dunham Park while you're resting, Linda?' I asked. 'They could take care of her, surely?'

'She's a bit of a handful for two thirteen-year-old boys to drag around with them, and I don't want to saddle them with too much responsibility,' she sighed. 'Don't worry about me, love. Things aren't easy, it's true, but I can look ahead to better times, which is more than I could before. I'd rather endure this difficult period, no matter how long it takes, than go back to Howard. Anything but that.'

A call-bell from the Delivery Unit cut us short, and for the next hour I was assisting with two epidurals – well, one really, because Mrs Marjorie Maybury was so huge that the anaesthetist had to concede defeat after two attempts to locate the intervertebral space beneath the rolls of fat. Lance Penrose wrote her up for a hundred and fifty milligrams of intramuscular pethidine, which I plunged deeply into her vast left buttock.

'How much longer will it be, Sister?' asked Ken Maybury, a worried-looking man of smallish build. ('Mind ye don't tread on him when ye turn round,' Bernie had whispered.) 'Can you give us any idea of when the baby will be born?'

The eternal question. I sighed helplessly, thinking that the true answer would have been that his wife was so grossly overweight that it was difficult to do a vaginal examination and impossible to palpate abdominally. The last scan had shown a vertex presentation and a foetal skull compatible with the outlet – but if she laboured for longer than eight hours she would probably be for a Caesarean section, in which case God help her and us. And I couldn't say that, could I?

Bernie answered for me. 'Ah well, now that's a question I wish we could answer for ye, Mr Maybury, and all the others who ask it,' she said, smiling. 'The fact is, y'see, we can't foretell the length o' labour at this stage, and if I could, I'd charge ten pounds a time, and then I'd soon save enough to retire to Donegal and keep chickens. Babies take their own time, y'see. Oh, yes, I've had four meself.'

Ken Maybury gave her a grateful look, and sat down beside poor Marjorie, who continued to thrash around like a harpooned whale for a further fifteen minutes until the extra large dose of pethidine took effect and she dozed fitfully.

In the D.U. office we studied the holiday list. I was off the third week in August.

'Going anywhere nice with a certain gentleman, Shirley?' asked auxiliary Sandra, nudge-nudge, wink-wink.

'No, we're not that close.'

'Not yet, you mean.'

'I'm going over to Shrewsbury to see my parents for a couple of days,' I said, 'and then I'm off to visit my daughter Ruth and her family for the rest of the time. No doubt I'll be doing a fair bit of baby-sitting, but I'll enjoy that, I don't see enough of Helen and Timothy. It'll be a welcome break from work and – everything.'

It would, too. I needed some time away from Marston and Martin, time to take stock of my life and what I really wanted from it. And what I didn't want.

Bernie broke in on these musings. 'Had any more love-letters from Mr Hawke?'

I wrinkled my nose. 'I think he's given up at last. I had a memo through Mrs Gresham's office, then two notes through the post, and finally I had this phone call from him at home, which I felt was an intrusion of my privacy.'

'Go on! What did he say?'

'Very smarmy at first – "William Hawke here, Shirley, sorry to ring you at your home, but I didn't receive an answer to my other communications, so I thought perhaps we could have a useful little chat on the phone." So I said, "If it's about that Blair man, don't waste your time, because I'd resign sooner than apologise when I've done nothing wrong."'

'Did ye really say that to him, Shirley?' gasped Bernie while Linda giggled and Sandra stared.

'Worse to come,' I told them grimly. 'He started wittering on about "I know what a wonderful job you midwives do," so I said in that case it was a pity he didn't stand up for us against the likes of Blair.'

'Good for you!' said Linda, awed but impressed.

'And I told him to stop patronising me. "What do you know about midwifery, Hawke?" I said. "It's non-nursing managers like you who are ruining the health service."'

'Jesus, Mary and Joseph! What did he say to that?'

'Dunno, I put the phone down. It rang again, but I didn't pick it up.'

'Oh, that's wonderful! You've made my night,' chuckled Linda, but Bernie shook her head ominously. 'Won't do ye any good, Shirley, gettin' on the wrong side o' Hawke.'

After the normal delivery of the patient who'd had the successful epidural, I went to find Dilly Fisher. She was on Postnatal, taking her rest hour. I found her in the day room, sitting with her feet up on a plastic chair, her eyes closed and her mouth open.

'Dilly.'

She jumped, and immediately began to gabble in the way that she does. 'Oh, sorry, I wondered who it was creeping up on me! Did you want me for something, Shirley love?'

'Sorry to disturb you, but I just wanted a word. It's about your son Mark, and this business with Paul Meadows.'

She sat bolt upright, and put her feet down on the floor in a defensive gesture. 'Now just a minute, Shirley, I don't want to hear anything about my son and that Paul Meadows. I'm sorry for him, of course, but–'

'Dilly, will you listen. Please? I only want to let you know that Paul had another bad experience the week the schools broke up, and by what he said, I'm pretty sure that Mark was involved. Paul was in an awful state and, if the trouble starts again in September, if Paul gets tormented one more time by *any* child, boy or girl, from Marston Comprehensive, I shall go straight to the headmaster and demand that he sorts it out and disciplines whoever's responsible.'

'It's got nothing to do with my Mark, so I don't know why you're telling me this,' said poor, silly Dilly.

'My dear, I'm telling you so that you can warn Mark and he can warn his friends that if there's any further persecution of Paul, there'll be trouble.'

'And I'm telling *you*, Shirley, that my Mark has been menaced by that – er – man for no reason at all, and if it happens again *I'll* go to the headmaster,' replied Dilly with uncharacteristic spirit, a mother defending her young. 'I just can't understand why you're picking on a perfectly innocent lad. It's really upset me, Shirley, and that's a fact.'

She looked so distressed that I relented a little. 'All right, Dilly, we'll leave it there, then. If I've been wrong about Mark, I apologise. But just remember, will you?'

And I left the poor soul smarting with indignation at such unjust accusation of her blameless son, by somebody she'd looked upon as a friend.

That night was a long one for the Mayburys. At half past four she was rolling from side to side again, and when I tried a cervical examination, thrusting my arm between the pillars of her thighs, my average-sized hand disappeared into the vagina and my fingers were too short to make an accurate assessment of the cervix. I thought I could feel a rim all round the foetal head, and told husband and wife that I hoped for delivery within a couple of hours.

It was when the cardiotocograph showed an alarming dip in the foetal heart rate to below ninety that I rang for Lance Penrose, who did not take long to decide on immediate Caesarean section. Anaesthetist and paediatrician were summoned, preparation of the theatre went ahead, and the all-important consent form was waved in front of the couple; Ken Maybury's hand shook as he signed his name beneath Marjorie's indecipherable scrawl. A porter was asked to come over from the main theatres to assist in transferring Marjorie from Room Three of the Delivery Unit to the Maternity Theatre, where the anaesthetist stood beside his trolley with its rows of syringes and intubation equipment.

'Blimey!' gasped the porter, clutching at his groin. 'I'll end up on industrial injury benefit at this rate.'

'Ssh!' cautioned Sandra, nodding towards Ken Maybury.

'Why, is he the – oh, my Gawd, how the hell did he–' Silenced by Sandra's glare, he disappeared down the corridor to share his ribald comments in the porters' lodge.

Penrose and the house officer began to scrub up and I, as theatre sister, did likewise, while Sandra stood by to help us on with our sterile gowns. Marjorie continued to moan and writhe on the operating table, and the anaesthetist looked thoughtful as he drew up an injection of intravenous pentothal into a ten-millilitre syringe.

'Just a little prick on the back of your hand, my dear, and then you won't feel another thing,' he said pleasantly, and Marjorie responded with a long, convulsive grunt. He put down the syringe and beckoned to Sandra to lift the operating gown that barely covered Marjorie's enormous abdominal dome. We stood open-mouthed as with another grunt and heave, a baby boy shot out from between her legs, unaided by doctor or midwife. Sandra lunged to catch him as he squirmed and yelled, flailing his little arms and legs as if in protest against his precipitate entry into the world. I have never seen a newborn child in better shape. The apparent deceleration of the foetal heart had been due to the monitor picking

137

up the maternal pulse through the intervening layers of fat.

In no time at all the happy mother was sitting up on the narrow table, cuddling her baby and beaming at his daddy, who was tearfully telling us all how wonderful we were. There was not a hint of reproach for our less than exemplary obstetric practice, not to mention the seven or eight hundred pounds of taxpayers' money thrown away on unused special services and equipment, including the failed epidural.

It's well known that obesity in maternity patients leads to mis-diagnosis, and Mrs Maybury was a classic example. Never mind! All's well that ends well in this game, and we ended up with a satisfied mother and a healthy baby – plus a proud father who thought us a brilliant team. Isn't that always the way?

'But of course I'll drive you over to Shrewsbury, Shirley,' insisted Martin when I told him I'd go by train. We'd just returned from a ramble over Alderley Edge, ending with a leisurely walk along a meadow path. Going through a kissing-gate, Martin had turned and pulled me gently towards him, pressing his cool lips against mine.

'You're a wonderful person, Shirley,' he whispered. 'I'd never have come through without your kindness.'

Poor old Martin's uncritical admiration of everything I did made me uncomfortable and ever so slightly irritated by praise I knew I didn't deserve. I wondered what Dr Goodson thought about our friendship, if she knew about it; on the few occasions I ran into her she was professionally polite as usual, but surely she must have known *something* about her father's new friendship, so soon after her mother's death. Unwelcome memories of Joy reared up from the past and, although I told myself that there was no comparison between a sulky girl of eighteen and a respected general practitioner with a family, the dreaded word *step* loomed like a cloud over my innocent relationship with Martin Hayes.

But how long would it remain innocent? Martin's gentle kisses and hand-holdings were clearly heading for a closer intimacy, and we had not far to look for an opportunity. We both lived alone and slept in the matrimonial beds we'd shared with our lawful wedded spouses, and sooner or later we would get into one or other of them together; but I wasn't yet sure how far I wanted to go.

I accepted his offer to drive me to Shrewsbury, and when I phoned my mother to tell her, she said he must stay to lunch before returning to Marston, where he'd agreed to look in daily on Pussage and Peppercorn; it was an ideal arrangement.

On the afternoon before we were due to go we were sitting on the patio having tea and scones and laughing over one of Bernie McCann's sayings when Paul Meadows appeared round the corner of the house. Martin's face fell. They'd met a couple of times, and distrusted each other. I got up to fetch another cup and to butter a scone for Paul.

'So, what have you been up to, young man?' asked Martin.

Paul glowered at him, and looked pointedly at me. 'I've been to Norma Daley's house-group this afternoon, and I didn't agree with a lot of the claptrap they talked there, Shirley. I mean, there's no need for people to be offensive, is there?'

'Well, no, and certainly not at that sort of meeting,' I replied, glancing at Martin who remained unsmiling. Paul needed no encouragement to continue: it seemed that he'd got into an argument about Jesus' attitude towards the rich and the poor.

'After all, Jesus was a socialist, wasn't he, Shirley?'

My heart sank. 'I don't think you can assume that, Paul.'

'Oh, come off it, Shirley, if He was walking around in this Tory-dominated country today, He'd have something to say about our so-called Government, that's for sure!' His voice rose, and Martin shifted uneasily on his seat.

'Now let's keep party politics out of it, Paul,' I ordered sharply. 'You've obviously never studied the Sermon on the Mount.'

'Oh, yes, I have, Shirley, and it was a socialist manifesto!'

'Rubbish,' I answered, keeping my voice level. 'Jesus kept *out* of politics, and even though He lived in an enemy-occupied country, He refused to join any military movement against the Romans. He even told the people to go on paying their taxes to the Roman emperor–'

'But He stood for justice, and said that the poor were more blessed than the rich! You can't get round *that*, Shirley!'

Martin intervened at this point. 'That's enough from you, young man. If you come here and eat at Mrs Pierce's table, you behave yourself, or I'll see you off. Now, then!'

Paul stared at him, his eyes dark with dislike, and then turned to me. 'Are *you* going to ask me to leave, Shirley?'

'If you argue with me and annoy my friends, I may have to, Paul. If you can't control that temper of yours, you won't have any friends left.'

He knew from my tone that I meant it. Heaving a long, melodramatic sigh, he picked up another scone and bit into it. Martin looked at me and then at his watch.

'If we're to be there by six, Shirley, we'd better be going.'

We hadn't planned to go anywhere, and I realised that this was a ruse to get rid of Paul. I glanced at my own watch. 'Mm, yes, it's later than I thought. If you'll excuse us, Paul, I'll ask you to finish your tea now, OK?'

A downcast Paul took his leave of us with the usual 'Shalom, Shirley, Shalom,' and as soon as he'd gone, Martin spoke with unusual firmness.

'I don't like him coming round here, Shirley, especially when you're alone. I shall have to insist that you stop him.'

Yet another warning to be careful. I had never heard Martin so stern before. I laid a placating hand on his arm. 'Sorry, love, he was in a particularly defiant mood today. Poor Norma, can't you just picture her little house-group!'

'It's no laughing matter, dear.'

How sweet he was, so concerned for my safety.

141

An idea suddenly occurred to me.

'Look, Martin, we told him we were going out somewhere, so why don't we make that the truth and go to your place? You're going to lend me your luggage-carrier, aren't you, so let's go and pick it up!'

I smiled up at him, and an unspoken signal was given. There is a chemistry between a man and a woman that has no need of words – or it gives spoken words a deeper meaning. He heard the invitation, *let's go to bed*. And the sudden startled widening of his eyes said *yes*.

He carried the tea tray indoors, I locked up and we left in his car for Wilmot Avenue. Why didn't we stay at 50 Chatsworth Road? Because I hadn't wanted it to be in my bed, mine and Tom's, so we were going to Martin and Dora's for our experiment. I was nervous, having acted on impulse, and told myself that this was a good moment to go further with our relationship, to see how we got on in that area, so to speak. If we were compatible, then we'd be nearer to making a decision about the future. And if not – well, then it would be a different decision, or a deferred one.

He parked the car in the driveway, and we went in by the back door, which he locked behind us.

'Would you like a drink, Shirley? Tea or–'

'No thanks, Martin, we've just had one.' I took hold of his hand and looked up into his face. 'Is this all right with you, love?'

'Ah, yes, it is, Shirley – dear little Shirley!'

He kissed my lips and led me up the stairs to the room he had shared with Dora.

'Which side do you–?' I asked awkwardly.

142

'Er – I'm usually on this side, dear.'

'Right, then I'll take that side.'

We took off our clothes and got in under the light summer-weight duvet. I put my arms around him. He was trembling like a leaf. 'I – I don't know if I can – er – it's been so long since I–'

'Martin dear, don't worry. Just give yourself time to relax.' I might have been talking to a frightened girl about to have a prostin pessary inserted. *Just let yourself go nice and loose, dear. Hold my hand.* I realised that this was going to take time and patience, and was not sure how best to help him, to encourage and arouse us both. We kissed slowly, my hands stroking his back and gradually exploring further: our feet touched at the bottom of the bed. His were as cold as a stone.

'Hold me close, Martin.' I nestled up to his chest, pressing my reasonably slim but middle-aged body against his lean, sinewy frame, well preserved by exercise and the healthy lifestyle Dora had dictated. Dora. Did I by any mischance whisper her name as I guided his left hand towards my now unsupported right breast? I heard him draw in a long breath, and as he exhaled he turned towards me, burying his face against my neck. That's when he cried out in anguish, *'Dora!'*

And again, 'Oh, my Dora – Dora, Dora, Dora!' And then the sobs began, a desolate storm of weeping as he clung to me in the bed they'd shared so recently.

This was not what I'd planned, and it required an abrupt change of tactics. So much for our experiment, but I had to forget my sense of anti-climax and do what I could for him. I sat up, covering my breasts with the sheet, and pushed a pillow behind my back. I soothed him, stroking the bald patch on the top of his head.

'Ssh-ssh. It's all right. Martin, don't worry. Ssh-ssh. All right, then. All right, Martin.'

While I tried to think of some wise word, some comforting quotation, a distant click caught my ear. I stiffened suddenly, alert and alarmed.

'Sssh, Martin! Did I hear something?'

He raised a tear-stained face. 'Eh? What did you say, dear?'

'Something downstairs – ssh, listen!'

We froze as we both heard the unmistakable sound of a key scraping in the front door lock.

'Oh, my God, Martin, somebody's coming into the house!' I whispered frantically. 'What shall we do?'

There was a soft thud of a step in the hall below, and then a voice called out, 'Dad! Are you in? Dad?'

It was Dr Goodson who had let herself in. Shit and double shit. I had to think very quickly.

'Martin, for God's sake, she mustn't find me here. Quick, get out and go into the bathroom and turn the shower on!' I hissed, pushing him off the bed. 'Hurry, get in the shower and then get out of it and call down to her – oh, be quick, do!'

The poor man stumbled into the bathroom, and I heard the shower start. I leapt out of bed and pulled on my knickers, throwing my dress over my head. *Oh, God, please don't let her come in here.*

'Dad, are you all right?'

Was she coming upstairs? I got down on all fours, ready to crawl under the bed. Then I heard

144

his voice, shaky but clear.

'Hallo, Laura! I was just having a shower.' His bare feet padded on the landing. 'Half a tick, I'll get my dressing-gown.'

'Oh, sorry, Dad, I didn't realise – have you finished?'

He dashed back into the bedroom to grab his dressing-gown and slippers, and I heard him going downstairs, followed by the murmuring of their voices in the hall, moving away to the kitchen. She'd called to pick up some rhubarb he'd saved her from the garden.

I tidied the bed and sat down on a hard little cane-bottomed chair to wait. My heart was pounding as if I'd just run up a flight of stairs. The sound of their voices went on and on, endlessly it seemed, though she probably only stayed a quarter of an hour. I heard them return to the front hall.

'Are you sure you're all right, Dad? You don't look so well today. Come over and have supper with us.'

'No, no, Laura, I'm all right, don't worry about me. There's a wildlife programme I want to watch tonight on BBC2. These nature programmes are very good – better than most of the rubbish they show these days.'

I had to admire his presence of mind, the way he'd pulled himself together so quickly after that torrent of grief.

At last his daughter took her leave.

'I'll be off, then, Dad. Let me know if you need anything.' There was a brief pause for what I supposed was a quick embrace. 'Take care, now.

See you soon. Bye! And thanks again for the rhubarb!'

'You're welcome, Laura. Love to the children – goodbye!'

And she was gone. I crept down the stairs, holding the banister and feeling shaken.

Martin was all apologies and concern. 'My dear, of all the unfortunate coincidences to happen – I'm so sorry.'

'Don't worry, Martin, it was my fault. I shouldn't have suggested it. Never mind about the car, I'll walk home.'

'It's no trouble, Shirley. I'll get dressed and run you back.'

'No, honestly, I'll walk. Need a breath of air.'

He stood there, looking at me helplessly. 'There'll be another time, Shirley dear.'

No, there won't, I thought. Not here, anyway. Too close to Dora.

'I'll be on my way, then, Martin.' I could hardly wait to get out of the house.

'Yes, all right, dear. And I'll be round tomorrow at about eleven.'

'Don't bother, Martin. Let's leave it for a bit, shall we?'

'But I'm driving you to Shrewsbury to visit your parents!'

'Oh, God, yes, of course, I'd completely forgotten. Right, then, see you at eleven. Thanks, Martin.'

And I got myself out through the back door without a farewell kiss.

Chapter Eight

Family Ties

My parents lived in a solid between-the-wars property that had been their home for most of their married life; another three years would see their golden wedding. My mother at seventy-nine was the elder by five years, an upright old lady who still did all her own baking and walked to church in her Sunday best, complete with hat and gloves. Dad was on sublingual tablets for attacks of anginal pain, and an hour's gardening left him short of breath; for this reason they seldom travelled far, so saw little of my brother Edward who lived in Kent, his family of three scattered here and there, like Ruth and Emma. If we wanted to see our parents we had to go to them, rather than expect them to come to us, and we only stayed long enough to assure ourselves that they were still coping satisfactorily, so as not to put them to undue inconvenience.

I've made it sound rather a cool relationship, but it was natural that in these latter years their first concern was for each other rather than for their grown-up son and daughter and the five grandchildren. They had drawn together like an old pair of swans whose cygnets had swum away, and they had that settled closeness which results from a lifetime of shared habits, as natural to them as breathing.

'Mum, this is Martin Hayes who has kindly driven me over.'

'Very good of you, Mr Hayes. Do come in.' My mother offered him her hand but not his Christian name on a first meeting.

'I'm only too pleased to be of service to Shirley, Mrs–'

'Wright,' I prompted.

'Mrs Wright. Shirley's been so kind to me–'

'Is Dad around?' I asked.

'Yes, he's in the kitchen washing his hands. He's been tying up the raspberry canes.'

'Martin's a keen gardener, too,' I said. 'Dad must show him around – let them compare notes!'

'Later on, Shirley, your father needs a break after working all the morning,' she said. 'I've got the kettle on, as I'm sure Mr Hayes would like a cup of tea. Can you carry your case upstairs? Fred mustn't lift anything heavy.'

'Please allow me,' said Martin at once, and I led the way up to my room, where he placed the suitcase just inside the door and retreated; after yesterday's fiasco all bedrooms were out of bounds, at least for the time being. I showed him the bathroom where my mother had put out a guest towel and a new bar of toilet soap.

Martin took to Dad straight away, pleased to find a mutual interest in fruit and vegetable growing. In due course Dad took him to see the abundance of cabbage, carrots, parsnips and onions, weed-free and neatly spaced in well-manured soil. Runner beans hung in bunches from poles that screened the compost-maker from view, and

148

Martin was profuse in his admiration as they sat on the bench seat beside the back door while I helped my mother in the kitchen.

'I didn't know what time you'd be here, so I've made a ham salad, and I'll put the rhubarb crumble in now,' she said, adjusting the oven. 'I'll make the custard when we're ready.'

'That's lovely, Mum, and thanks very much.' Once again I admired the energy of a woman in her eightieth year. 'We didn't want to put you to a lot of trouble.'

'It's no trouble, Shirley, we don't see you that often.'

Well, no, they didn't, which meant that we lived our separate lives without conflict of outlook or attitudes. There would come a time when they'd need me more, and I wondered how much longer Dad would be able to cope with the garden. I recollected that the house in Wilmot Avenue had a second lounge that could easily be converted into a bed-sitting-room for an old lady – or an old gentleman, or both. I hastily brushed such thoughts aside: no sense in looking ahead to a future that nobody could guess at.

Over the meal we spoke of Ruth and how much I was looking forward to seeing Helen and Timothy again.

'We sent Helen two little dresses for her birthday,' said my mother. 'Ruth wrote such a nice letter back.'

I told them about Emma's visit, and mentioned that Danilo had stayed at Chatsworth Road.

'Yes, she sent us some photographs of herself with the Italian boy,' said my mother. 'Let's hope she'll find herself a nice English lad when she's ready to settle down – though I suppose the Italian's a Catholic.'

'That's not to say as he practises it,' added Dad.

'I've been to Shirley's church and met her priest, Father Flynn,' said Martin, forgetting the O. 'Very nice chap, I thought.'

'Oh, are you Catholic, Martin?' asked my mother.

'Er – no, Dora and I used to go to – a different church,' he said hesitantly. 'But I think St Antony's is very nice. I might even–'

'I see you've got a big new supermarket going up – that'll be handy for you, Mum,' I cut in, not wanting to get into the minefield of religion just yet, and the talk turned to local news and changes.

'What a very nice gentleman!' exclaimed my mother after he had left amidst much cordial hand-shaking. 'And so much in common with you, Fred.'

I wondered what they would have made of yesterday's ignominious escape.

On the Saturday morning my mother and I left Dad to potter around while we went into Shrewsbury by bus to do some shopping, after which we had a wander round St Julian's Craft Centre, which always has such lovely things on display. I bought her a velvet beret of multi-coloured segments hand-stitched together, and of course she protested at what she called the extravagance, though her obvious pleasure more than compensated for the price. I suggested we stopped for coffee, and found a café with pavement tables; as soon as we were served she began to question me about Martin.

'Do you think this friendship could develop into something more, Shirley?' she asked, smiling over the top of her upraised cup.

I shook my head. 'It's less than two months since he lost Dora.' However many times had I said that, both to myself and to colleagues at work.

'Yes, dear, but time goes by, and you can be a comfort to him, being a widow yourself. He seems to me like the kind of man who needs a wife – a woman in his life,' she said, unconsciously echoing my own impression of Martin. 'So if I were you, Shirley, I'd start thinking ahead. I know it's not my business, dear, but–' Our eyes met across the table. 'What I'm saying is that if you wanted him, you could have him. I could see that straight away, and so could your dad!'

We both chuckled a little awkwardly. 'Oh, Mum! All in good time. The poor man'll need at least a year, and meanwhile we can just be friends, surely?'

'Mm-mm.' She shrugged, and I felt pretty sure that she was wondering how long it would be before we embarked on a more intimate relationship. My mother knew the ways of the world.

On Sunday morning the three of us went to Mass, leaving a joint roasting in the oven. After dinner I could see that Mum was tired, and I told her to go and rest on her bed while I cleared away and washed up. Afterwards I made a pot of tea and sat outside on the bench with Dad in the August sunshine.

'So he's coming back here to fetch you

tomorrow, then?'

'That's right, Dad, after dinner.' My parents had dinner at midday and high tea or supper in the evening.

'Shirley–' he began, and then hesitated.

'Go on, Dad,' I smiled, anticipating a similar conversation to the one I'd had with my mother in the café.

'I reckon you'd best think very carefully before you decide anything,' my father said slowly. 'You could have him tomorrow if you wanted, but you're a girl who's all right on your own, aren't you?'

'I'm hardly a girl, Dad!' I protested lightly, though I was a little taken aback at his attempt to give me – not exactly advice, but his honest opinion.

'It wouldn't be the same as with Tom, but you'd still be second fiddle, Shirley – and he's got a daughter as well, hasn't he?'

Such uncharacteristic candour deserved a carefully considered reply.

'Yes, but she wouldn't be like – Joy. Dr Laura Goodson's a mature woman with a family of her own.'

'Oh-ah, but she's still his daughter, like you're mine – and she won't take too kindly to seeing somebody in her mother's place, 'specially if it's too soon.'

In her mother's bed was what he meant. I hadn't expected this, and my father's reversion to the broad dialect of his childhood reflected the effort it cost him to speak so plainly. I felt my colour rising in sudden embarrassment.

152

'It's true that I had problems with Tom's daughter, Dad, but that was a long time ago when I was young and – well, very self-centred,' I said, changing my position on the seat.

'Yeah, but you never made it up with her, did you, Shirley?'

In went the knife, finding its mark. I knew that he would not hurt me without a good reason, but I still protested. 'I'm not in touch with her,' I said irrelevantly. 'I'm not even sure where she lives now. And I don't see what she has to do with Martin!'

He turned round and looked me straight in the face. 'Think about it, girl. I'd think it over very carefully if I was you.' There was a pause, and then he continued with a certain reluctance. 'It was hard on Tom when you and his girl took against each other, and your mother and I were sorry about it. Only–' An expression came into his eyes that I hadn't seen before. 'Only I thought it served him damned well right for what he'd done to you.'

'*Dad!* Whatever do you mean?'

'Well, what d'you think, a man of his age and a youngster like you, just got your nursing exams, a bright little kid with everything ahead o' you – and then *that*. Your mother was that upset, I didn't know what to do with her. I could've throttled him bare-handed. Worst day o' my life that was, when you told us you was – like that.'

The garden was very quiet; not a bird sang in the still air. And I had nothing to say. At the time of our engagement Tom and I had been so deliriously in love that I hadn't given much thought to 'having to get married'. It was what we wanted, there was no pressure on either of us, and I'd scarcely considered the impact on my parents. Now, after all these years, I faced the fact of their shock and disappointment.

Dad reached out for my hand. 'Sorry to rake up the past like that, Shirley. Only I always knew that things were never really right. You wouldn't've gone and worked all them hours at the hospital else. Your mother couldn't understand it, but I kept me own thoughts to meself. We never interfered, 'cause that wouldn't've done any good.' Again he looked into my face, his eyes probing. 'But you're all right on your own, aren't you, Shirley? You can please yourself what you do, go to this Shalom thing and have odd characters in the house if you feel like it. You couldn't do all that if you was married, could you? Eh?'

'Dad – oh, Dad, I didn't realise how much you–' I turned away, unable to say more. He still held my hand.

'I'm your father, Shirley, and I'm only saying it for your own good. You've got a nice little home and your work and Ruth and Emma. You don't have to tie yourself down again. He can always find somebody else.'

I couldn't speak. I needed to blow my nose, and besides, there was no answer. I got up and went indoors to brew fresh tea for us both, and to splash my face with cold water.

When Martin arrived to collect me, my mother presented him with two jars of her home-made raspberry jam and a sponge-cake. He made the predictable remark about a mother passing on her skills to her daughter.

'And granddaughter,' I added. 'Ruth's sponges are just like her grandma's, lighter than mine.'

Dad told me to help myself to ripe tomatoes from the greenhouse.

'Thanks, Dad, but Martin's got a good crop coming along.' I glanced at Martin, who nodded.

'And Shirley can have her pick of them,' he said. 'And anything else in the garden.'

'Oh-ah, reckon she can,' replied Dad cryptically.

My mother told Martin to call any time that he was in the area, and we took our leave with smiles, handshakes and kisses as appropriate.

'Have you enjoyed your weekend, dear?' he enquired as we headed towards the A49.

'Oh, yes, it was lovely – and reassuring to see them still managing so well on their own.'

'Such a delightful couple – they must be very proud of you, Shirley.'

What for? I wondered.

I spent Tuesday at home, washing, ironing and repacking for the visit to the Butlers. Paul appeared on the doorstep in the afternoon with a Gospel CD.

'I've been trying to persuade Philip to use this sort of music at Shalom, Shirley. I think it would bring in more young people – I mean the sort of young people who occasionally think seriously about God, and want to change their way of life, as it were.'

'I'm a bit busy today, Paul.' He followed me as

I went to take the washing in off the line.

'He wasn't even willing to give it a run-through, which I thought was mistaken on his part, and I told him so.'

'Perhaps he feels that we make our own music at Shalom,' I suggested, folding up the sheets and duvet cover. 'Our singing is part of the worship, isn't it? Gospel is more like entertainment, really.'

'I beg your pardon, Shirley, but I'll take issue with you on that, if you don't mind! Gospel is a lot more than just entertainment, in fact it's a great deal more. Haven't you ever studied its African and American roots in the negro slavery culture?'

When Paul got a bee in his bonnet like that, I found it best to let his words flow over me without argument. I started ironing the clothes I was taking with me the following day, while he sat at the kitchen table lecturing me on Gospel and Soul between chunks of cake and mouthfuls of coke.

Martin's mouth tightened when he came in through the back door.

'I want a private word with you, Shirley.'

I looked at Paul. 'If you wouldn't mind finishing your cake, love, I've got some arrangements to make with Martin.'

Paul looked rebellious. 'Quite frankly, Shirley, I'm getting a bit tired of being turfed out whenever somebody comes round here wanting a quiet word. I suppose I shan't see you again until you come back from Birmingham. You're always gallivanting off somewhere, and you'll miss Shalom on Friday.'

'But *you* needn't miss it, Paul. Rod Daley will be there, and his friend Gareth – be nice for you

156

to have some young company for a change.'

We exchanged the peace in the Shalom way, and he put his arms tightly round me, lowering his head to kiss my forehead and cheek. When I extricated myself I told him I'd listen to the CD some time the following week.

As soon as he'd gone, Martin spoke with uncharacteristic heat. 'It's got to stop, Shirley. Just suppose I hadn't turned up, there you were alone with that surly fellow, completely defenceless if he'd attacked you, as he might well have done. I cannot and will not allow you to put yourself in danger.'

'It's not as bad as it looks to you, Martin. I *know* Paul, and I can cope with his various moods,' I assured him, but he wasn't buying it.

'But there's no *need* for you to do so, my dear, no good reason at all why you should.'

It was useless to argue, to try to explain my sense of commitment to Paul Meadows, let alone my very real affection for him.

Richard Butler met my train at Birmingham New Street Station, wearing a dark tailored suit and the air of a confident young businessman. Not yet thirty he was now a senior sales manager, and told me that he was being sent to Milan and later to Tokyo as a representative of his firm, which made car accessories.

'So I'm having to swot up a bit on languages, Shirley. The company's paying for a crash course in Italian, so I should be able to get around in Milan, but Japanese is going to be something else.'

'Rather you than me,' I said, looking at his firm

157

hands on the wheel as he manoeuvred the car through the heavy, fast-moving city traffic. Ruth had chosen well: in Richard she had security and stability, a man who would make his way in the world and be able to provide her and the children with every comfort.

The Butlers lived in an attractive three-bed-roomed house at Steephill, a suburb well out of the city. It was twice the size of 50 Chatsworth Road, but apparently not large enough for the upwardly mobile Butlers, who had their sights on a big old property in Solihull.

'We need more space for the children, Mummy, and a bigger garden,' Ruth explained, settling little Timothy into his high chair. The children were being allowed to share the evening dinner as a special treat in honour of my visit, and Helen sat beside me on a dining chair with a thick cushion under her little bottom; Timothy was next to his mother at the table, a plastic sheet spread under his chair to catch the flying morsels from his Beatrix Potter bowl. Ruth smiled at him, her big brown eyes softening; she had put on a little weight and looked every inch the contented young matron that she was.

'My dolly's name is Bertha, Nana,' said Helen.

'Bertha? That's a name I haven't heard for a long time, dear. Why did you choose it?'

'After Richard's grandmother,' said Ruth. 'We had to think of names for the three new dolls she had for her birthday.'

'My word, aren't you a lucky girl, Helen? And Grandma Wright was so pleased with your letter, Ruth.'

'Oh, yes, poor Grandma Wright, she sent Helen two little dresses, but of course it's all jeans and leggings these days, with lots of different tops. Helen sets the fashion at her play-group, don't you, darling?'

'I get all my clothes from Marks 'n' Spencer's,' said the young model with a satisfied air.

'Oy-oy-oy-oy-oy!' warbled Timothy, banging his spoon on the white plastic tray of his high-chair.

'Now, now, Timmy, that's enough. You don't like being left out of things, do you?' murmured Ruth fondly, pushing a spoonful of mince and mashed potato into the rosy gap he presented to her.

It was a joy to see two such happy, well-loved and well-cared-for children. Ruth made a big point of staying at home and devoting her time and talents to the all-important demands of motherhood and home-making. Was it a reproach to me for my division of time during my daughters' growing years?

'Richard won't let me even think of going out to work, Mummy and, besides, there's simply no need. Of course when both the children are at school there might be some time to spare, but I don't quite see myself in an office again,' she said, wiping her son's chin.

'But my dear Ruth, there's any amount of voluntary work to be done,' I pointed out. 'The WRVS always needs new members for all sorts of things – meals on wheels, hospital cafés and mobile libraries, cars to take old people to their appointments and day centres–'

'Oh, Mummy, Richard would hit the roof if I used the car for anything like that! Just imagine if some old person leaked on the upholstery, and then the children had to sit on it!'

She shuddered, and began to recount stories she'd heard from her private daily help.

'My Mrs Hughes has a friend who's a home help, and has to go to the most appalling houses. She takes her own vacuum cleaner in the car because it's so much easier to use than some of the awful old models they've got – isn't she a *saint?* And they don't get paid all that much, Mrs Hughes says.'

The good Mrs Hughes was paid between thirty and forty pounds a week to clean for Ruth and tackle such extra duties as washing and re-hanging curtains, changing bedlinen and getting through mountains of ironing. An automatic washing machine and dishwasher took care of the jobs that had taken up hours of my mother's time in her early married life. Although she disliked housework, Ruth was an excellent cook and enjoyed entertaining, with all the planning and preparation it involved.

'I have to give the odd dinner party now and again for Richard's business associates,' she told me with modest pride.

'Yes, Ruth puts on a better three-course meal than most restaurants, and for a quarter of the price,' added her husband with an appreciative smile which clearly delighted her.

'Richard sees to the wine, of course, I'm not too well up in that side of it,' she said as they exchanged well-satisfied glances; after a while the talk turned to Emma and her life in London.

'What did you make of the Italian Romeo, Mummy? She seems to think that it's the real thing at last.'

'Oh, he seemed pleasant enough, though I'm not sure that he's as much – er – involved as she is,' I replied, not wanting to discuss one sister with the other in any depth.

'And what's all this she's saying about a certain charming old gentleman who's apparently besotted with *you*, Mummy? Richard and I are most intrigued, so tell us more!'

'Oh, poor Martin Hayes, he's newly widowed and very much at a loss without Dora,' I replied, trying to sound casual. 'She was a retired colleague of mine, and their daughter's Dr Goodson the GP. As a matter of fact he very kindly drove me over to Shrewsbury to visit your Grandma and Granddad, and came to–'

'Whoops! *No*, Timothy, you mustn't try to wriggle out of your chair, darling,' cried Ruth, jumping up to rescue the red-faced infant who had tangled himself up in the protective straps that belted him to the chair seat. 'Look, his leg's curled under his bottom, and he can't get it free, poor pet.'

Timothy began to bawl loudly, and Helen took advantage of the diversion.

'Can I have some ice cream now, Nana?'

'Not until you've eaten all that nice mince, dear, and the vegetables,' I answered. We grown-ups had steak-and-kidney pie from which the children's mince had been made, with their carrots and greens suitably mashed: a delicious meal, though punctuated by these frequent interruptions.

I found that I enjoyed my grandchildren more when I had them to myself, and so was perfectly happy to babysit for Ruth and Richard during my stay – in fact those were my favourite times. The little sister and brother were as demanding as all young children are, and Helen had learned to say 'I want' as soon as she could string two words together; but they were happy and affectionate, and alone with them at their bedtime I read aloud a few stories from the book I'd brought for them, *A Child's Life of Jesus*. Watching their eager little faces as they pored over the coloured illustrations, I remembered hearing Richard say that he was opposed to any form of religious indoctrination, though he was tolerant towards his mother-in-law's misguided piety, for Ruth's sake.

But wouldn't he have been surprised by the scene at Wilmot Avenue?

As well as the evenings I spent with the children, there was also Sunday morning. Ruth asked me somewhat coyly if I could mind them while she and Richard had a lie-in.

'Is that what you call it?' I asked with a grin, and she coloured.

'Oh, Mummy, we never get a chance these days! You'll be Richard's friend for life if you'd keep them out of our room for a couple of hours,' she pleaded, and of course I was only too happy to oblige. Not only did Helen and Timothy come to my room for an early morning romp and have a picnic breakfast out of doors, but I told them that they could come to church with Nana as a very special treat. The nearest Catholic church had a Mass at ten-thirty, so with a certain air of secrecy we set off, Helen trotting along beside Timothy's trolley.

It was all new and strange to them. I pointed out the altar, lectern and font, and held Timothy up to see the votive candles flickering in front of the statue of Our Lady. There were several families there with young children, some of whom fidgeted and wailed throughout the service, so Helen's chirpy questions and Timothy's shouts went unremarked by a congregation used to these diversions. On our way out I introduced myself to the parish priest and asked him to give my grandchildren a blessing.

'The man put his hand on my head and went like this,' Helen told her parents at the dinner table, making a sign of the Cross with her little hand in the air. Ruth smiled discreetly, and I glanced at their father to see if he showed disapproval.

Evidently not, for having taken full advantage of their absence, Richard had that sleepily contented look of a man who had had his fill of sexual gratification.

On the train back to Manchester I found my thoughts straying uneasily back to that revealing talk I'd had with my father, and once again I was troubled by memories of my stepdaughter. Was she going to haunt me for the rest of my life? In vain did I tell myself that it was futile to dwell on the mistakes of the past; I must forget about a woman who no longer had any relevance to my present life, and who probably never gave me so

163

much as a passing thought these days. But my conscience, or whatever it was, refused to be persuaded, and by the time I reached 50 Chatsworth Road I had decided to try to make contact with her.

A search through old letters and address-books failed to yield any information; I knew that the Bocketts had moved somewhere south, but had no idea where; how determined I had been to forget her!

Then I remembered a friend she'd had from schooldays, a girl called Jo Parsons who'd visited her at Wellington Avenue. Her parents still lived in Marston, and it was through them that I eventually tracked her down; she was now married and lived at Marple. Her response to my telephone call was wary.

'I'm afraid I can't give you Mrs Bockett's address without her permission, but I suppose I could contact her and say you want to get in touch,' she said without enthusiasm. In the end she agreed to forward a letter from me.

After half a dozen unsuccessful attempts, I bought one of those *Thinking of You* cards with a picture of a table set for tea beside an open window with a garden beyond, and, after some careful thought, this is what I wrote:

You'll be surprised to hear from me, Joy, but I have been thinking about you for some time and wondering how you are. I'd like to get in touch again if you are willing. There are many things I now regret about the past. Jade and the boys are more or less the same ages as Ruth and Emma,

164

and I'd like to have news of them, too. I know it's been a long time, Joy, but I hope it's not too late.

With good wishes, and hoping to hear from you,

Shirley

I enclosed a stamped, self-addressed envelope, and put it in a larger envelope addressed to Jo Parsons, to be forwarded, checking by telephone that she had done so.

There was no reply.

Chapter Nine

Angry Words and As You Like It

'Oh, *no!* It *can't* be!'

But it was. The back tyre of my trusty bike was flat, and I was due on duty in twenty minutes. I'd have to ring for a taxi, or – what about Martin? He'd drive me in to work if I asked him. I rushed back indoors and picked up the phone. No reply. He was probably at Laura's, and I wasn't going to phone there. Damn and blast. By the time I'd ordered a taxi and waited for it to arrive – they were usually busy at this time, especially on a Friday – I'd be late. Better ring Maternity and let them know.

As I picked up the phone there was a tapping at the window, and I pulled back the curtains I'd drawn against the September dusk.

165

Brian Newhouse was outside, raising his black eyebrows at me. I went to the front door.

'You all right, Mrs Pierce? Saw your shed door open, and the bike still in it – you off to work, then?'

I grimaced. 'I should be, but I've got a puncture.'

'Want a lift?'

'Well – yes, if it wouldn't be too much trouble, Brian.'

What a relief! I picked up my bag and closed the front door behind me. 'Thanks a million, Brian,' I said, getting into the passenger seat and fastening the safety-belt. 'Have you just got in from work?'

'Not long. Saw you come out and go to the shed, then dash back indoors. I thought something was up, so I came round.'

'I'm very glad you did. I hate being late.'

'Specially in your job, eh? Babies won't wait!' He laughed. 'My mum says she wishes you could be around when my sister has hers next month.'

'Really? Is your sister booked for Marston General?'

'No, they live up in Bury. She didn't like it much in hospital with her first one – said she never got any rest. You'd think they'd take the babies out of the ward at night, wouldn't you?'

I groaned, and turned down the corners of my mouth. 'Oh dear me, no, that's right out of fashion now. The idea is that babies should be with their mothers all the time so that they get bonded together from the start. In actual fact it means it's absolute pandemonium on the Postnatal ward at

166

night.' I could have held forth at length on the vexed question of 'rooming-in,' but we were at the hospital and he drove up to the entrance of the separate Maternity Unit.

'Here you are, then – and there's a lady who'll soon be needing your services, by the looks of her!'

A very heavily pregnant woman was just going in. A man carrying a suitcase supported her vast bulk with his free arm. Heavens above, they were our neighbours the Tippetts!

'You're here just in time for her!' said Brian as I got out of the car. 'What time do you finish?'

'Oh, don't bother, I'll get a lift off somebody going home in the morning,' I said quickly. 'Cheers, Brian – bye!'

What a good sort he was, I thought; pity his marriage had broken up. I suspected that Lilian didn't give him much opportunity to meet suitable girls.

The bicycle puncture was only the first set-back in a night fraught with tension. I was on Delivery Unit with Staff Nurse Sue Weldon and we shared Dilly Fisher with Linda on Antenatal. Sister Amos, a handsome Barbadian woman in her thirties, was on Postnatal with another auxiliary. There were no student midwives on, but we had two medical students from Manchester University, sent to get practical experience, which included ten normal deliveries each. One was nice Jim Digweed, who didn't mind what we asked him to do, like shoving a bottle-feed down a hungry baby as he held it on his knee in the office; he chatted easily with the mothers and staff, and

167

had clocked up five deliveries to date. The other boy was Adam Rapley-Blade who was now sitting at the desk in the D.U. office, reading *The Unbearable Lightness of Being*. He'd already got on our nerves with his lofty attitude towards staff and patients. As one of the midwives said, you'd have thought he'd fallen among a tribe of savages who spoke a different language from his own upper-class drawl.

June Tippett was in advanced labour with her third child, while the only other patient in D.U., a Mrs Endicott, was getting weak, irregular contractions as yet; I settled her down with a couple of paracetamol tablets, and concentrated on June. It can be tricky, dealing with people you know.

'Who's next for a delivery?' I asked in the office. 'Mrs Tippett won't be long, so you'd better decide which one of you's on for her.'

'I suppose that dubious privilege falls to me, then,' sighed Rapley-Blade, closing his book.

'Right, well, here are her case-notes, so go and sit with her in Room Three and show a bit of interest.' My voice was sharp.

'But there's already a man sitting beside her.'

'Yes, her husband, Don Tippett – so *you* go and sit on the other side of her and make yourself known to *both* of them,' I snapped. 'Make an effort, check her pulse and blood pressure.'

'But she's got the cardiotocograph to do all that.'

'Yes, and a fat lot of use it is if you don't look to see what it's telling you! And a machine is no substitute for personal contact – so would you mind doing what I've already asked you to do, and go and *sit* with Mrs Tippett? Her name's June, by the way.'

'Do I have to call her June? Won't the man mind?'

I rolled my eyes heavenwards in exasperation. 'Look, do you want this delivery or shall I ask Mr Digweed to come for it? For God's sake use a bit of initiative, and go and tell that couple that your name's Adam and that you're a medical student from St Mary's, and would they mind if you delivered their baby under a midwife's supervision!'

'It's chumps like him who give us a reputation for being bossy and bitchy,' I grumbled to Linda as we grabbed a quick coffee in the kitchen. 'Just when I want to give a good impression to June Tippett, too. At this rate I'll be ready for Carrowbridge by morning!'

Damn, I could have bitten my tongue off for mentioning the Psychiatric Unit where Charles King's wife was confined. Linda tactfully didn't hear.

'Adam's probably scared stiff, and trying to hide the fact,' she said reasonably. 'Don't let him irritate you, Shirley, just take a deep breath and count to ten. Anyway, I must dash, I've got a couple of diabetics in for blood sugar profiles, and one of them's got the most inaccessible veins – and the prem labour you sent over last night is still niggling, even though she's on maximum ritodrine and it's giving her the shakes. Her pulse is racing like hell, poor girl.'

She hurried back to the ward. At least it kept her mind occupied, I thought. With the children back at school she was getting a little more rest during the day, though the search for affordable rented accommodation was proving more difficult than she and King had anticipated.

As I went to check on June's progress, I heard the front doorbell. We weren't expecting an admission, and I thought it might be Mrs Endicott's husband. Dilly went into the office to speak on the intercom, and I heard the click of the door as she pressed the control button.

Trust Dilly to let Grierson in.

The upraised angry voices of a man and a woman echoed down the main corridor, his full of menacing threats, hers of defiance.

'I'm not going to let you stop my little girl from seeing her father!'

'How dare you come here, throwing your weight about! I've got nothing to say to you.'

'So you're not content with committing adultery with that bastard and destroying our marriage – you break my child's heart as well, just to spite me!'

'That's rich, you talking of hearts – you haven't got one! But you won't bully us again, we're free of you now – you and your foul temper!'

'Now just you look here, Linda–' Was there a hint of pleading in his bluster? If so, it had no effect on Linda.

'Oh, just shut up and get out of here!' Her voice was dangerously shrill, and I could hear mutterings from the Antenatal ward. No doubt some of the women from Cockshott would think it was home from home, but others would be frightened. I had to intervene. I left Room Three and hurried to the scene in the corridor.

'What on earth's going on? Have you no consideration at all for the patients in this place and at this time of night? Stop it at once!'

The words were addressed to both of them, but my glare was directed at the man. He glared back.

'You've no right to be here,' I told him. 'Sister Grierson is on duty and responsible for the patients in her care. Leave her alone!'

I turned to my colleague and, summoning up all the authority I could muster, I spoke quietly and clearly. 'Get back to your ward at once, Sister, and attend to the patient with the ritodrine drip. And don't forget that you have two blood sugars due to be taken.'

She and I looked at each other meaningfully. We both knew that I was not in a position to give her orders, being senior only in age. We also knew that the blood sugars were not due again until two o'clock. What I was actually signalling to her was, *disappear, Linda, and let me deal with him.* She hesitated.

'At once, Sister, do you hear? I'll speak with you later in Mrs Gresham's office.'

She saw that I was trying to save her worse trouble. 'I'm terribly sorry, Sister Pierce,' she muttered, lowering her head and walking back towards the Antenatal ward. Grierson lunged after her, but the door closed in his face, and I stood myself between him and it.

'Right, Mr Grierson, you'd better go now.' I nodded towards the exit. 'I'm not your wife, so don't try to bully me.'

For a moment he was defiant, and pushed his

171

face close to mine. I smelt the drink on his breath. Sister Amos had come out of Postnatal with an auxiliary, and Sue Weldon appeared behind me, drawn by the angry exchanges. A frightened-looking Dilly Fisher hovered in the background.

'I'm warning you, if you lay a finger on me, you'll regret it, Grierson,' I said levelly, and caught Sister Amos's eye. 'Sister Amos, will you telephone the porters' lodge and ask them to send up two men to escort this gentleman from the building?'

It worked. Grierson was sober enough to realise that he was at the mercy of petticoats and threatened with worse humiliation. He clenched his fists.

'All right, but you haven't heard the last of me, Madam Pierce. I shan't forget how you've connived with my wife to break up a marriage. Home wrecker!'

'Go on, get out before you're thrown out.' I simply couldn't resist that parting shot as he stomped through the exit door. My heart was thumping, and I just wanted to sit down with a cup of tea, but the call-bell was ringing loud and long from Room Three. Hurrying back to June Tippett, I found her pushing, and Rapley-Blade trying to pull on a sterile gown; he had it inside-out.

'Gloves on first, then gown,' I told him. 'Not much longer to go now, June, love.'

'Thank God you're here, Mrs Pierce, we thought we were gonna be left with just *him*,' muttered Don Tippett in relief.

I switched on the heater above the resuscitation

cot, and began to undo the delivery pack on the trolley. I poured warm sterile water into the two bowls, and tied the tapes of the student's gown, then drew up the routine injection of syntometrine, ready to give to the mother as soon as the baby was born, to aid early expulsion of the placenta. The head was advancing well with each contraction, and June moaned as she clung to her husband's arm.

'Take a deep breath in and hold it, June,' I told her. 'Now push right down into your bottom – push – push – *push* down hard – good girl!'

It would have been plain sailing if I hadn't had Rapley-Blade dithering about, and I was still feeling shaky after the slanging-match with Grierson. 'Come on, get your swabs ready,' I said to the student; 'cord-clamps, scissors – no, not that dish, that's for the placenta. Spread the green towel out on the bed – keep your knees drawn up, June love – now, just wash her down on each side of the labia – no, use the cotton-wool swabs, not the pad, that's for holding over the anus when the baby's head is emerging.'

'What about an episiotomy?' he asked.

Give me strength, I prayed silently. 'This is Mrs Tippett's third baby, and she doesn't need an episiotomy. Just try to prevent a tear along the scar of the previous one. Put those scissors down, and have the pad ready – quick, the head's coming now. All right, June, don't pay any attention to all this, everything's fine.'

With the next push, the widest diameter of the baby's head filled the outlet: we still say 'crowning of the head,' like the midwives of the

173

past, and like them we try to prevent a too rapid delivery of the head and consequent tearing of the perineum. 'Stop pushing now, June, and pant quickly in and out like a puppy-dog, in and out, in and out, that's the way – well done!'

While she panted in and out for all she was worth, I hissed to the student. 'Look, hold the pad over the anus, *guard* the perineum as the head's born – gently! – there you are, the head's out. Now feel to see if there's a cord round the neck – just insert your forefinger–'

'I'm not really sure what I'm supposed to be feeling for, actually – this is only my third delivery, after all.'

'Oh, for heaven's sake, let *me* feel – God, *yes*, the cord's there, right round the neck, and tight – too tight to pull over the head. We'll have to cut it now, quickly. No, not before you've clamped it! Get the clamps on, and have the cord scissors ready – the *clamps*, man!'

The baby's face was turning blue and congested with the pressure on the neck. I took the two plastic clamps from the trolley, pushed the student's hand away and applied them myself; picking up the scissors, I severed the cord between them: it was not easy, with it being so tight against the baby's tender neck. The two ends fell apart, and with a gush of blood and amniotic fluid, the body slithered out immediately.

'Is it born?' gasped June, and Don leaned over to look.

'Yeah!' he told her, 'And hey, it's a girl! We got another little girl – hooray! How much does she weigh, Mrs Pierce?'

The weight of the silent, blue-tinged baby was the last thing on my mind as I gathered her up in the towel, and took her to the warmed cot, switching on the oxygen supply. I applied the mucus extractor to her mouth and nostrils and, muttering a prayer, I placed the tiny plastic face-mask over her nose and mouth.

'Is she all right, Shirley? Shouldn't she be crying?' asked June anxiously, and at that very moment the child gave a gasp, providing an air-way for the life-giving stream.

Don came over to see what was happening. 'She's all right, i'n't she?' he asked, demanding assent. I nodded as the baby's skin turned from blue to pink. She took another breath, and her arms flexed; then another, and she drew up her little legs. And then she gave a weak cry.

'Hey, d'ye hear that, June? She's making a noise!' Don said with a shaky laugh.

And so she was. Less than two minutes after her birth her cries filled the room, her colour was good and her muscle tone normal. She was all right. I carried her back to the bed and put her into her mother's arms. Words cannot express the thankfulness I felt, though I did not show my emotion in front of the parents.

The injection had not been given, but the placenta was easily expelled within the next min-ute, as June held her daughter to her breast. She had a small superficial tear that would heal with-out stitching, and baby Gemma weighed 3.460 kilograms, or seven pounds, ten ounces. Dilly was summoned to brew up tea for the parents, and that was that – except for the examination of the placenta in the sluice, where I could hardly bring myself to speak to Adam Rapley-Blade. I blinked back tears of vexation at such a badly conducted delivery, and my own lack of self-control.

'Bit of a cliff-hanger there with that cord round its neck,' he commented without much interest. 'Oh, well, that's three notched up, and seven to go.'

'You can't count that as a delivery,' I said.

'Why not?'

'Well, for a start, *you* didn't deliver the baby, *I* did. You were just in the way, taking up space.' I knew I shouldn't be so vitriolic, but I had been concealing my own emotions for too long, and had reached the end of my tether.

'I say, I don't think that's fair,' he protested. 'You midwives won't let us get near the women! God knows how we're supposed to learn when you keep panicking and interfering. I've heard other chaps and girls say the same about the midwives at Marston Gen–'

That was enough for me. I rounded on him in fury.

'And suppose you'd been on your own in there, without me *interfering*, as you call it, what would have happened? That baby would be dead from cord strangulation. Look here, I've had all I can take from you,' I rushed on, unable to stop myself. 'You showed not the slightest interest in Mrs Tippett, who happens to be my next door neighbour, you didn't speak a word to her or her husband, you had no idea what you were doing – you're just plain *useless!*'

I choked on a sob, and he stood stock-still,

staring incredulously.

'I – I – I shall see Mr Horsfield in the morning – I mean after the weekend,' he managed to say. 'And I'll let him know what you–'

'Oh, just bugger off and leave me to clear up the mess – and to apologise to Mr and Mrs Tippett for this fiasco!'

I know I shouldn't have said it. It was rude and unprofessional and let down the whole of the Maternity Unit. I lowered my head over the sluice sink to spread out the reddish-purple placenta, and then realised that Adam Rapley-Blade was still standing at my elbow, and speaking with a tremor in his well-bred tones.

'Only too glad to oblige, Sister, because quite honestly I find the whole process unspeakably repugnant, and God knows why any normal person wants to do obstetrics. I can't think of anything more – more *unsightly* than the external female genitalia thrashing about under my nose. It's – it's–' He gave a sort of *ugh!* sound. 'You've done me a favour, really, because I'm getting out of it, and going for a law degree. So thank you and good night!'

And he strode away, leaving me miserably aware of my own failure as a clinical instructor. If we could have sat down and talked in a civilised manner – as Bernie might have done in similar circumstances – I might have helped him to realise that he was not alone in his feelings about midwifery, that others had also found it very different from the books, but that with experience and increased understanding, it got better as time went on.

It had been an opportunity lost.

Mrs Endicott progressed quite quickly once she got going; it was her third baby, too, and I told Sue to supervise Jim Digweed with the delivery, while I hovered in the background, ready to give assistance if required. Polly Endicott was a nice, thirtyish woman with tinted spectacles and a giggle.

'Hope John gets here in time,' she said, when Sue had telephoned her husband. 'My mum's come over to look after the other two, even though she's had to cancel her hospital bed. Been waiting for months to have her hammer toes done, and as soon as they send for her, I go into labour, don't I? I told her John could manage, but she wouldn't hear of – ooh, aaah, here we go again!'

On Jim's instructions she took a deep breath, closed her lips and, gripping her hands behind her knees, she pushed down with all her strength.

'That's just great, Polly, you're doing champion!' cried Jim Digweed. 'Put your right foot up against my side if it helps you to push – go on! – that's the ticket! Pain gone now? All right, breathe away, make the most of the intervals.'

'We'll have to make a tape-recording of you, Jim, and play it when we need a bit of extra encouragement,' smiled Sue, while I thought glumly about Rapley-Blade. Had the boy really walked out, never to return? What would he tell Mr Horsfield? I kept quiet while the three of them chatted away like old friends – four of them when Endicott hurtled into the room to the accompaniment of a cheer from Jim, and took his place beside Polly, who started asking him about the children and her mother.

'Don't let them play her up, John – and see that she puts her feet up whenever she – ooh, here comes another one!'

'Here we go, here we go, here we go,' chanted Jim. 'I'm a Manchester United supporter myself – come on, Polly, time to score a goal!'

'Don't make me laugh, I'll lose what breath I've got,' she gasped, her teeth clenched in a grimace as she pushed again.

'This is your big moment, Polly,' he told her as Sue tied the tapes of his gown. 'Now, with your next contraction, I'll tell you exactly what I want you to do.'

And he did, too. It was all so well managed, the timing was just right, the teamwork smooth and friendly; and yet it was exciting, too, as baby Michael emerged into Jim's hands, thrilling his hearers with his lusty howls. John Endicott kissed his wife for joy, Jim got kissed by Polly – and I didn't miss the sly kiss that Jim gave Sue Weldon as she straightened up from giving the syntometrine injection. And how pretty she looked as she blushed and smiled. If only all births could be as happy, I thought; no matter what rules and guidelines are laid down for the conduct of a normal delivery, it is the human element that makes each one different from the rest.

At last, just before five o'clock, there was time for a word with Linda. A rather subdued Dilly brought a tray of tea and toast into the Antenatal ward office, and then left us alone.

'If only that daft Dilly had called one of us before pressing the door button,' she sighed. 'But you were marvellous with Howard, Shirley, though I'm terribly sorry it happened – what with him and that awful student, you've had a right old night of it.'

I shrugged. 'Howard's not going to go quietly, is he, love?'

'He'll have to in the end, when we're divorced and I'm married to Charles. I cling to the thought of that, but meanwhile it's pretty grim, as you can see.'

'What about your sister Jane?' I asked tentatively. 'Is she OK about you and the children still sharing with her and Frank?'

'They're putting up with us pretty well, really, and of course it's Cathy that's the main problem. The boys have got each other, that's how they've always coped in the past when Howard used to go for them – but Cathy's playing up, saying she misses her home and her Daddy, all that stuff. It's difficult to be patient with her when she refuses her food and complains of a variety of ailments, from headaches to a tight feeling in her chest. You don't know how much is real and how much is just put on.'

Linda rubbed her hands across her eyes and went on to describe the chaos in the mornings when the boys had to get their sister up and breakfasted before taking her on the bus from Altrincham to Marston, depositing her at her junior school before going on to their own.

'I fetch them home in the afternoons, but I can't get home in time to take them in the mornings. We'll simply have to move nearer to Marston before the winter sets in. Those dark, cold mornings don't bear thinking about.'

'Have you thought of letting Cathy visit her Daddy, if that's what she says she wants, Linda?' I ventured. 'If she spent a Saturday or Sunday with him, it might settle her a bit, and give you a break, too.'

Linda's face hardened. 'I'm not letting him have time with her until the legal side's sorted out and he's been granted official access to the children,' she declared. 'Personally I think it would disturb her even more, and besides–' She stopped speaking, and again I saw that fear in her eyes, and guessed what she could not bring herself to say: that the unhappy, uncooperative little girl might not return from such a visit, but choose to stay with her father who would then use her preference in his application for custody.

'And how's Charles bearing up?' I asked.

It was good to see her smile. 'Don't know what I'd do without him. We manage to see each other every day, but of course there's not much opportunity to – to be on our own.'

I could imagine. Poor Linda.

Eight o'clock, and time to hand over to the day staff. I decided not to say anything to Mrs Gresham about Howard Grierson's visit or the clash with Rapley-Blade. If the student had really walked out and given up his medical training, there would be questions from Mr Horsfield about what had taken place at the Tippett delivery, but if the wretched boy changed his mind and turned up again as if nothing had happened, then the less said the better. Even so, I wasn't happy; not even the prospect of four nights off compensated for my general sense of dissatisfaction with myself. Damn Grierson and damn Adam Rapley-Blade, I muttered as I went to say goodbye to a rather sleepy June Tippett in the Postnatal ward. Oh, the dangers attendant upon birth that mothers know nothing about!

Then I remembered the puncture. Damn again, I'd either have to walk or wait for a bus. I couldn't delay Linda by asking for a lift, and Sue had already left.

And there was Brian Newhouse, sitting in his car outside Maternity, reading the morning paper. He looked up with a grin.

'*There* you are! Thought you might've gone,' he said.

I got in, dumping my bag on the back seat. 'You shouldn't have bothered, but thanks all the same.'

'Well, seeing that you hadn't got your bike – I had a look at it last night, and found a piece of glass right through the tyre, so I took it round to Charlie Babcock and asked him to put a new inner tube in.'

'But surely he was shut by that time!'

'Yeah, but I went round the back. Known old Charlie for years.'

'It's really very good of you, Brian.'

'It's no trouble for a lady, Shirley.'

On arrival home I was greeted by Don Tippett with a huge box of milk chocolate assortment and a card from him and June. Of course it was gratifying, though I knew I didn't deserve a thank-you present for that badly managed delivery. Damn Rapley-Blade, damn Grierson – and damn the silence from my stepdaughter Joy.

It was over three weeks since I'd sent that card, and her total lack of response seemed to indicate that there was nothing I could do for her now except to stay out of her life. But would I ever get her out of mine? Is it possible to forgive without being forgiven? My rest that Saturday was troubled by many unwelcome thoughts.

At three o'clock I went downstairs and made some tea; picking up the new *Radio Times* I saw that there was a production of *As You Like It* on BBC2 that evening. Martin didn't care for Shakespeare, and in any case I was no fit company for anybody, so I planned to watch it on my own if I could stay awake.

I got dressed and wondered whether to do a little tidying-up in the garden. It was a dull, over-cast day with a warning chill in the air, a reminder that summer was over. In another month the clocks would go back and the evenings would quickly draw in.

When the front gate clanged shut and footsteps sounded in the passage beside the house, I knew at once who it was.

'Paul! How good to see you,' I said, holding out my hands.

'You too, Shirley.' He enfolded me in one of those Shalom bear-hugs.

'How're you doing, love? Everything all right?'

'Yes, I suppose I can say so, Shirley. I do what you said, and try to keep quiet when the little bastards hurl verbal abuse at me in Boreham Road – not that it's easy, I can tell you!'

'Come on, let's go and sit down and you can tell me all about it,' I said, replugging in the kettle and leading him to the living room where he sat on the sofa. He wore jeans with an assortment of tops, one layer on another. I lit the gas-fire.

'What about the Weasel?' I asked. 'Is he behaving himself these days?'

'He hasn't actually said anything since the new term started, though he's usually there in the background, egging the others on to make snide remarks.'

'Can you be really certain of that, Paul?'

'Yes, I can. I'm not as daft as some people seem to think, Shirley.'

'And did you find out if his name is definitely Fisher?'

'Yes, he definitely is. Mark Fisher.'

I went out to the kitchen to make tea and get out the cake-tin. 'I'll make a nice, tasty supper for us a bit later, Paul,' I told him, and was rewarded by a brilliant smile. He was as easy to please as Martin Hayes, and my heart warmed: what were my silly scrapes at work when compared to this tragically damaged life?

'There's a Shakespeare play on tonight, Paul, *As You Like It*. Would *you* like it? To watch it, I mean?'

'Oh, yes, Shirley, that'd be marvellous! What exactly is it about?'

I took down the hefty tome of the *Complete Works* from the bookcase, and we pored over it together while I gave him an outline of the romping pastoral comedy written four hundred years ago and, at eight o'clock, seated together on the sofa with plates of scrambled eggs and bacon on potato cakes, we drank in a lively new production of the play. For three hours we were transported to the Forest of Arden, far away from the Weasel, Grierson and Rapley-Blade; all the plagues and disappointments of everyday were forgotten. When we put our plates aside, I leaned my head comfortably upon his shoulder; we were enfolded in a little world of our own, safe and warm. I realised too that I was weary of Martin's grief for his dead wife and his desperate attempt to make me a replacement for her.

'Mm-mm,' Paul sighed happily. 'Rosalind makes me think of you, Shirley.'

I smiled. Only Paul could have imagined the slightest resemblance between middle-aged me and the vivacious actress who so delightfully teased her lovelorn Orlando whilst reflecting on the fragile nature of love. She was well-matched by the young Scot who played opposite her with understanding and wit, expressing as much with his eyes as with his words.

'He must *know* that it's Rosalind dressed as a man, Shirley.'

I agreed. To judge by the adoring looks bestowed on the breeched and booted 'Ganymede,' it was clear that Orlando was only pretending to be deceived.

'Yes, I think he's humouring her, and not letting on he knows,' I replied, not inclined to go into the stage traditions of Shakespeare's day, and the acceptance of improbable disguises.

It was magical from the first scene to the last, and when Rosalind delivered her saucy epilogue, she did it sitting on the greensward, propped up against her lover's chest. From time to time he slyly stroked her neck and played idly with her cascading hair, now released from Ganymede's cap. As she uttered her final words she turned and buried her face in his neck; the camera drew back to show fields and woodland behind them, and the frame froze on a pretty rural scene over which the credits rolled.

It was eleven o'clock. I got up and stretched. 'I'll make some coffee – or would you prefer hot chocolate?' I asked.

'Shirley – could *you* say Rosalind's last speech? I mean in the way she just said it. You could read it from your book, and I'd pretend to be Orlando. He doesn't have to say anything.'

'I suppose I could try,' I said, smiling, for I too was in no hurry to leave the Forest of Arden. I picked up the book, found the place and began to read.

'"It is not the fashion to see the lady the Epilogue; but it is no more unhandsome–"'

'No, no, let's be as we were before, Shirley. Sit here and lean back against me like you did when we were watching the play, the way Rosalind was leaning against Orlando. Like this.'

And so we resumed our former positions on the sofa, my head on his chest and his arm encircling me. With the big book propped unsteadily on my updrawn knees, I had to twist my head slightly to see the lines but, even with such disadvantages, my reading delighted Paul, and he chuckled at intervals as I continued through to the end.

'"If I were a woman, I would kiss as many of you as had beards that pleased me, complexions that liked me, and breaths that I defied not: and

I am sure, as many as have good beards or good faces or sweet breaths will for my kind offer, when I make curtsy, bid me farewell.'''

And Rosalind found herself gathered to Orlando's heart, his lips upon her forehead, then her cheek, and then sweetly upon her mouth, not probing as a man would have done, but lingering softly. This was the Forest of Arden which had nothing to do with life's ugly realities. My hand guided his to the swell of my breasts beneath the dress material – Paul's big, well-shaped hands that should have played a piano keyboard, plucked strings, wielded a bow, held a pen, a paintbrush, a tennis racquet – hands that should have caressed a pretty girl and stroked her hair.

Touch me here – and here.

Go on and call me a silly woman, call me whatever you like, it makes no difference now. Even after all that's happened since, I don't regret it. I gave that boy those few minutes, those few short minutes: just for once I let him experience a passing glimpse, a faint echo of the fulfilment he had been denied by an evil chance. I was willing to be the woman who offered him this miserable pittance, this apology for what should have been his true rights.

By midnight he was gone. We parted in the usual way, exchanging the peace.

'Shalom, Shirley, Shalom.'

Chapter Ten

Date Rape – or One Night Stand?

The news of Adam Rapley-Blade's abrupt departure from Marston General that weekend had the hospital grapevine buzzing, and I waited in some apprehension for a memo from Mr Horsfield. None came, however, and by the end of a week I breathed freely again. Whatever reasons the young man had given for abandoning his medical training at such a late stage, it seemed that the Tippett delivery, and my part in it, had not been cited as a factor in his decision. I suspected that he'd left my name out for fear that I'd retaliate by repeating his crudely expressed repugnance for obstetrics. So I got away with it, though my conscience was far from easy, and I've often wondered whether he went in for law and did better at it.

The matter of Grierson's visit was not so easily dismissed, and I got rapped over the knuckles for not reporting it; so did Linda. The patients in both Ante- and Postnatal wards were full of what they had overheard, and somebody's husband complained that his wife had been upset. I can withstand a ticking-off from Mrs Gresham, but it was with dismay that I heard that Linda and I were both summoned to Mr Hawke's office for further ear-ache.

'You do realise that this could have very serious

consequences, Mrs Grierson – Mrs Pierce,' he said, full of his own importance as usual. 'How am I expected to uphold the standards of the department if I'm not even informed of an incident like this? How can I defend the staff against the inevitable complaints? And more to the point, how can I guarantee the safety and well-being of the patients when such incidents occur? You should have telephoned the switchboard and put a call through to me at my home to inform me of this intruder.'

Linda stared straight ahead, and I looked out of the window.

'I take it from your silence that neither of you have anything to say.'

'Only that I got rid of Grierson in less time than it would have taken to phone anybody,' I said coldly.

'It was an auxiliary who mistakenly let my husband in, and I'm sorry that the Unit was put to inconvenience over my domestic problems,' added Linda. 'Sister Pierce was wonderful, and deserves to be thanked, not blamed.'

'I'm afraid we differ on that, Mrs Grierson. It's most unfortunate that you have this marital problem, and it's to be hoped that it can be sorted out before too long.' He cleared his throat. 'Right, well, that's all I have to say to you, so I'll wish you good morning – no, not you, Mrs Pierce, I'd like you to stay a little longer. Good morning, Mrs Grierson.'

When the door closed on Linda, Hawke and I stared across the desk in mutual dislike.

'I just want to say this, Mrs Pierce, for your

own good. You seem to think that you are a law unto yourself but, if you don't change your attitude, you could find yourself in a tight corner one of these days, with nobody to bail you out.'

'Is that all?'

'Believe me, it's meant as a friendly warning, Mrs Pierce.'

'Good, so I can go home now and get some rest after a busy night, OK?'

I got up and walked out without another word being spoken. Linda was waiting for me in the Maternity entrance hall. Her eyes were haggard.

'I can't tell you how sorry I am, Shirley. I should have stood up for you in there.'

'You *did*, only there's no love lost between Hawke and me, so whatever you said wouldn't've made any difference. Forget it, love, and let's go home to our beds. You look knackered. Will you be able to get a decent sleep today?'

'Charles is calling this afternoon before the children are due out of school, to arrange about us moving into his house.'

'What? But I thought his solicitor said–'

'Charles is moving out. He's found this little flat in Beckenham Road, so I'm moving into his house with the children, and he'll be able to visit us – discreetly, of course.'

'Thank God for that,' I said with feeling.

'Yes, the children will be back in Marston and close to their schools, for one thing. And they'll have some space of their own.'

'And you'll be living in the house that'll be your home anyway when – er–'

'Yes. I've told Charles all along that I wouldn't

move into his house until we're married, though he's been on at me for some time to change my mind, and up to now I've stood firm. But now – oh, Shirley–'

She swayed against me, and I quickly put an arm around her. 'Linda dear, sit down, sit down here – there, now.'

There were a few chairs in the entrance, and she sank down wearily on to the nearest one.

'It's the children, Shirley,' she almost groaned. 'I'd share a bed-sitter with Charles and think it heaven, but the children need a proper home with space and – and security. We can't afford to rent anywhere that's half adequate – so I've agreed.'

'And the sooner the better,' I told her. 'You'll be no good to Charles or the kids if you go under. Oh, Linda dear, you *must* take better care of yourself!'

My heart ached for her, for her problems were by no means over. Her love for Charles and her faith in the future had kept her going so far, but she was now defeated by sheer exhaustion. It occurred to me that King was taking on an enormous commitment with the three Grierson children. Did he truly realise what he was in for? Declarations of love beside the lake at Tatton were one thing, but the presence of a whining little girl forever saying how much she missed her Daddy could put a strain on the most romantic relationship. What kind of stepdaughter would Cathy be? Time would tell, and meanwhile I tried to give my friend what support I could. Which wasn't much.

By the end of September the move had been

made, and the effect on Linda was immediate and wonderful to see. Overnight it seemed as if she'd regained her bloom and optimism.

'I hate to think of Charles being turned out of his home like this, but he says he'd much rather see the four of *us* in it!' she told us gaily in the D.U. office. 'And the children are so happy with everything, even Cathy's decided to stop playing up – she's like a different child. Of course it's been a pretty horrendous time for them, I know that.'

By which she meant that she felt guilty about them. 'But Charles is so *good* with them,' she went on, her eyes shining. 'Just think about it, girls, how many men would be willing to put up with another man's children? Not to mention the lack of privacy – though we manage to get an hour or two while they're at school.' She paused, colouring self-consciously.

'How're the lawyers goin' on, apart from linin' their own pockets?' enquired Bernie.

Linda shrugged. 'Grinding along, and Howard's going to end up with one hell of a bill. And would you believe it, the only one eligible for legal aid is Charles's wife, though there's no contest there. It's all to do with protecting her interests.'

Bernie's face was expressionless, and Linda felt her lack of sympathy.

'Remember that Charles has had twenty years of worry and anxiety with Miriam, Bernie, no marriage at all since Jonathan was born, not to mention life-threatening experiences, like when she set fire to the bed with him asleep in it. He's had to be father and mother to the boy, and I think he's earned the right to some happiness at last.' She sighed. 'Now it seems they've taken Miriam off the anti-depressant she's been on for years, and put her on another with a lot of dietary restrictions. I'm sorry for her, of course I am, but it's been no picnic for Charles either.'

'How's *your* divorce going ahead, Linda?' I asked, to get away from the Kings' problems.

She turned down the corners of her mouth. 'You'd never believe what Howard's coming out with now. Says that his prospects for putting up as Parliamentary candidate have been damaged by my desertion and his mental suffering at being deprived of his children!'

'Really? Did he ever say anything about running for Parliament, Linda?'

'No, never, it's all talk, he'd stop at nothing to gain sympathy. Well, it won't wash with me, I know him too well after sixteen years. Look, girls, you must come and visit me now that I've got a place I can call my own, more or less. What about lunch on Thursday? We're all off then, aren't we?'

I duly went to lunch with her, and Pearl Amos came too. Bernie said she couldn't because she had relatives coming over from Donegal.

'And wouldn't I be lookin' over me left shoulder all the while, Shirley, in case the real lady o' the house walked in and asked me what I was doin', sittin' at her table?'

The Irish can be very superstitious.

September passed into October, and the leaves whirled down, driven by strong north-easterly gales; it was that dismal time when the year starts sliding down towards Christmas, and I was another year older. Changes were in the air, for instance at Shalom. Philip Crowne had begun to move in a new direction, with a shift of emphasis away from inward self-examination and towards an outgoing spirit of public service to the community. When a wealthy old lady died and left her solid Edwardian mansion to Shalom, Crowne saw it as confirmation of his call to provide a refuge for runaway teenagers, a haven where they would be safe from drug-pushers, pimps and pornographers. Crowne was an early voice in the campaign against paedophilia and, never one to shun the limelight, he importuned companies and supermarket chains to make well-publicised donations, and got a sizeable grant out of Manchester City Council. He was interviewed on local radio stations and in the press, and actually appeared on a national breakfast TV show. His denunciation of what he called a spiritually impoverished society earned him plenty of sneers, but we were all delighted when Celia was interviewed and photographed at his side, a beautiful woman who didn't fit at all with Crowne's image in some quarters as a sexually repressed Holy Joe.

The downside to this was that it took him away from Marston, leaving local Shalom meetings in the hands of lesser preachers who lacked Crowne's remarkable power to stir the hearts of his hearers. Bible readings and carefully prepared expositions were no substitute for ecstatic utterances, and Norma Daley had to speak quite firmly to a woman who noisily fell to the floor, passing out in the spirit just as a visiting preacher was getting into his stride. Gradually but inevitably attendances began to decline.

Changes were on the way for me, too, though as yet I couldn't see my way forward. Paul Meadows continued to visit, though I insisted on restricting him to once a week, and preferably in the afternoons, to avoid the dark evenings and drawn curtains; Martin Hayes had repeated that he simply would not stand for it, and I had no wish for a confrontation, though Martin himself was another problem. I was no nearer to making a decision about the future of our relationship, and our meetings continued; he was as attentive as ever, and I privately set myself a deadline for the end of the year to decide. Meanwhile, as with Paul, I avoided any occasions of too-close intimacy, and stuck to public appearances like the dances at the Winter Gardens, the Police Silver Band concert at the school, and the Marston Operatic Society's production of *Oklahoma!* in the gymnasium of the leisure centre. You name it, and we were there, an item, as they say.

Even so, I longed for some sign, some signpost to point my way: I wanted something to happen that would make up my mind for me.

I had not long to wait.

As the school half-term approached Martin came to me and said that the Goodsons were taking a late holiday in Spain and had asked him to join them.

'I'd much rather go on holiday with you, Shirley dear, and I hate leaving you. Perhaps at Christmas or New Year we could take one of those winter breaks together if you could get the time off?'

I told him to go and enjoy himself. 'It'll do you good to get a bit of sunshine before the winter sets in, Martin.'

'It's very kind of Laura and Vic to ask me,' he said hesitantly, willing to be persuaded.

'Most thoughtful,' I replied, thinking he'd probably be put to the same use as I'd been put by Ruth and Richard. 'Off you go, and have a good time with your grandchildren! Send me a postcard!'

'And will you promise not to have that Meadows fellow round here after dark, Shirley?'

I told him I'd remember his wishes.

Arriving home at the end of four nights on duty, I noticed the Newhouses' front door open and Brian coming out carrying a large suitcase.

'Heavens, you're not leaving home, are you?' I called to him.

'No, just taking my mum to our Jean's. She's been rushed into hospital, and it doesn't sound too good.' For once he was without his customary grin, and Lilian was in floods of tears.

'Woke up and found she was pouring blood, Shirley,' she sobbed. 'All over the sheet it was, Bob said. The doctor called an ambulance straight away, and they had to take little Billy and Diana in with them, they couldn't leave them, could they? Bob's asked me to go over to look after them, and I was going to anyway when Jean had the baby, but I haven't done my shopping or anything, and there's nothing for Brian's tea–'

'Come on, Mum, stop moaning and get in,' called Brian from the driver's seat.

'And you'll be late for work, son, taking me all the way up to Bury.'

'It's all right, I've phoned 'em and swapped my shift. Be on from eleven to seven. Come on, Mum, the kids won't want to see tears, will they?'

I didn't know what to say, not knowing enough about the severity of this antepartum haemorrhage. The baby was due in another two weeks, and I could only assure Lilian that her daughter was in the best place, and that every effort would be made to save the baby.

'Don't worry about anything this end, Lilian – I'm off for a few nights, and I'll keep an eye on your Brian,' I said, trying to sound jocular. 'Tell you what, Brian, come and have some supper with me when you get in from work this evening.'

The offer was more for Lilian's benefit than her son's, as she made a point of always having a cooked meal ready for him. He was a grown man, and there was surely a staff canteen at the airport, but this was no time to tell her that she treated him like a child.

'That's very kind of you, Shirley – see you!' said Brian as he let in the clutch and I waved them off with a shout of 'Good luck!'

I needed to do a little shopping, so cycled off to the local shops straight away. I bought a pound and a half of steak and kidney, enough for a good-sized pie, and got some fresh greens. I had some frozen blackberries from the garden, and got some cream to serve with them; I also bought a packet of paper serviettes, so as to do the thing in style.

I prepared the meat before I went to bed, cutting it up and rolling it in seasoned flour before browning it quickly in a little fat, and then transferring it to a covered casserole dish with just enough water and a large chopped onion; it would cook very slowly in a low oven while I slept.

It was nearly five when I got up and made the pastry, prepared the vegetables and defrosted the blackberries. If Paul Meadows called there would be enough for three, and he'd be able to stay longer because of Brian being there.

When the telephone rang it was an emotional Lilian Newhouse with the good news that Jean was safely delivered of a little boy weighing seven pounds, eleven ounces. The delivery had been normal, and the bleeding nothing more than a heavy 'show' when the cervix had begun to dilate. Of course I congratulated her, and joked that I was getting Brian's tea ready.

When the pie was in the oven and the table laid I went upstairs to change into a comfortable house-dress in two shades of violet. It buttoned down the front, with a longish skirt, and I twirled in front of the mirror with satisfaction: it looked really nice, and so did I – not bad for forty-eight.

When the doorbell rang at a quarter to eight, Brian stood on the step holding a couple of packages. 'Good evening! Am I too early?'

He wore a beige cashmere sweater over a shirt with a grey tie that matched his corduroy trousers. 'A little something for the hostess,' he said, producing a bottle of good French wine and a pound box of Belgian chocolates, a real luxury. I was quite taken aback.

'Thank you, but you had no need to be so extravagant, Brian.'

'Ah, I don't often get a date like this, Shirley!' His dark eyes sparkled, and I wondered about that word *date*. Is that what he thought this was? If so, he had another think coming.

'I've heard the wonderful news about your new nephew,' I said. 'So the bleeding can't have been as bad as it sounded.'

'No, Bob's a bit inclined to panic, and it worried my mum half to death, getting that call first thing this morning.'

'Let's have a sherry to celebrate, anyway,' I said. 'Perhaps you'd like to watch the television while I see to a few things in the kitchen.'

But he followed me through to the kitchen where saucepans bubbled and the pie was nicely browned. I put my apron on.

'Aha, something smells good in here!' he said, sniffing appreciatively and lifting lids. 'These spuds are ready – I'll drain and mash 'em, shall I?'

'Thanks – er, you'll find the butter dish over there, and the milk's in the fridge.' My face was flushed with the heat from the gas cooker and the complexities of dishing-up, though I needn't have worried; the meal was a huge success, and Newhouse passed up his plate for a third helping of pie. He opened the bottle of wine and poured out two generous glasses.

'This is really living!' he declared, and I felt absurdly pleased. I was used to cooking for Paul, who simply ate his way through the food while he talked, and Martin would have praised my culinary skill if I'd opened a tin of baked beans.

This man showed true appreciation by doing justice to a good meal.

It was time for a little post-prandial conversation, I thought.

'What exactly do you do at the airport, Brian?'

'Ground staff mechanic. We work in shifts around the clock, like you do.'

'It must be a very responsible job, making sure that those great passenger jets are in top condition when they go off on those long flights.'

'Yeah.' His eyes gleamed with amusement beneath jet-black brows. 'Oh, yes, Shirley, any aircraft needs to be well screwed together before take-off.'

Had I said something silly? Was he teasing me? I took another sip of wine.

'What happened about your marriage, Brian? It seems such a shame, and of course it's none of my business, but – well, there must be plenty of nice young girls around who'd like to settle down and have–'

'Babies? Yeah, I dare say, but I'm not in any hurry.'

He didn't seem to mind me asking, so I went on, 'Have you any children, Brian? From your marriage, I mean?'

'Or apart from it? None that I know of,' he answered cheerfully. '*She* had one, but it wasn't mine. That was the trouble.'

'Oh, your wife, you mean?'

'My ex-wife, I mean. Have some more wine, Shirley.'

It was time to change the subject, and we talked about his sister's family and the new arrival who was to be called Gary. Coffee with cream rounded off the meal, and I couldn't resist opening the chocolates.

'I'll help you with the washing-up,' he said, carrying a tray of used crockery and cutlery through to the kitchen. I'd intended to leave it till later, but he was well organised, and as I washed the dishes he wiped them dry. The job was done within fifteen minutes, and as I reached up to put away plates, cups and saucers in their cupboards, I felt my apron-strings being untied at the back.

'Come on. Shirley, let's get back to the fireside on a chilly evening like this!'

And back we went. I picked up the *Radio Times*, and flicked through the pages. 'There's a programme about gorillas in the Rwandan jungle,' I said. 'Or an Inspector Wexford mystery over on ITV if you'd prefer that. It's up to you, Brian.'

He grinned. 'I can watch the goggle-box when I'm on my own. I see you've got a cassette player. Any nice tapes to put on?'

I ran my forefinger doubtfully along the rack. It was rather a limited assortment, from composers like Vivaldi and Monteverdi which Paul enjoyed, to the 'Songs of Faith and Fellowship' recorded at Shalom. What about 'The Best of Luciano Pavarotti'? Ah, here was one, Simon and Garfunkel's 'Hits of the Sixties' that Emma had given me.

'Let's have something *you* like, Shirley,' he said, settling himself on the sofa and patting the space beside him. Soon the room was filled with 'The Sound of Silence'.

I sat beside Brian Newhouse as I'd sat beside Paul Meadows and Martin Hayes on that same sofa, its patterned cover now somewhat shabby and clawed by the cats. And he put his left arm lightly round my waist.

Heavens! I stiffened and sat bolt upright, but before I could marshal my thoughts together and find suitably discouraging words, he kissed me on the cheek: an experimental kiss, a try-out, a little kiss that seemed to say, there now, how's that for starters?

I gasped and turned my head away; his arm tightened around me just a little. This was ridiculous. *Brian Newhouse?* He'd made a mistake, and I'd have to let him know – at once.

He kissed me again, aiming for my cheek but landing on my right ear because of my turned-away head.

'Brian–' I began, amazed and foolish and all sorts of things at once.

'Yes, Shirley?' He smiled with apparently the same pleasure that he'd shown for the pie. 'That was a very nice meal you cooked for me – for us. As good as anything my mum makes, and what man can say more than that, eh?'

'Er – yes, Brian, your mother. I think of her as being in my own age group, you see,' I babbled, my heart fluttering away like a captive bird. 'What I mean is, well – I must be old enough to be your mother – so this is not really – er–'

His low chuckle made gentle fun of my embarrassment.

'I doubt that, Shirley. I mustn't ask a lady her age, but how old d'you think *I* am?'

I turned and stared at him. 'Thirty? Thirty-one?'

'Thirty-seven.'

'G-good heavens, I didn't think – you don't look it.' With his mischievous dark eyes and black curly hair, he really wasn't a bad-looking man, in a swarthy sort of way.

'Aha, remember I haven't got a wife and kids to put years on me. A jolly bachelor's life for me!'

'But don't you want to marry again and have children?'

'Not right now, no. Let's talk about you instead of me, Shirley! When I first saw you I thought you were probably divorced, but mum says you're a widow.'

'That's right. For nearly four years.' It was like being in a dream, and I'd done nothing to put a stop to this impossible scene in which I was taking part. His arm still held my waist.

'Four years, eh?' he repeated. 'But you've got a few men friends, haven't you? There's young Paul.'

'*Paul?* He's just an unfortunate young man I've befriended. You can see for yourself that he's not like other – men.'

He nodded. 'Yeah, I can see that you've got to be careful with him. But there's that nice old chap you're always going around with. Nothing wrong with *him*, is there?'

'Well, no, but – he only lost his wife three months ago, and we're not in that kind of relationship, not exactly – not yet. I mean we've never – we haven't–' I floundered into silence, feeling an idiot. Why on earth was I telling him this? It had nothing to do with him.

And he seized on my hesitation, drawing me quickly into his arms and pressing his lips against mine.

203

'So is *this* what you've been missing, Shirley?' And he kissed me again, a kiss that took my breath away, literally. It should have filled me with panic, but it didn't. I suppose he was right, and that it *was* what I'd been missing, because neither Paul or Martin had kissed me like that, and it had been many, many years since Tom had. This was something else, this was a vigorous body and hard male flesh, this was uncharted territory for me in my middle-age. With Martin I'd had to be gentle and kind, with Paul I'd had to be on my guard, but this Newhouse, this *Casanova* needed no guidance, nor, obviously, did he expect any resistance.

So why didn't I struggle and break free, get up from the sofa and order him to leave at once? Suppose I'd banged on the wall and summoned Don Tippett to my assistance? Suppose I'd dialled 999 and asked the police to come at once? A picture came into my head of a sympathetic woman police constable taking details of a date rape, a crime usually committed by a man known to the victim. I pictured the report in the *Manchester Evening News*:

Weeping and distraught, Mrs Shirley Pierce, 48, a widow and practising midwife, of Chatsworth Road, Marston, said she had only tried to be a good neighbour. Father Gerard O'Flynn, parish priest of St Antony's Church, Marston, told our reporter of his 'deep shock' at this attack on a valued parishioner.

Newhouse would stand in the dock at Manchester Crown Court, his mother weeping in the public gallery while witnesses would be called to testify to the good character of his victim. He could be convicted of rape and given a prison sentence: he would be completely ruined, and it would be the talk of the neighbourhood, with no doubt a few voices muttering that I'd asked for it.

But it wasn't rape, date or any other sort, because I responded to him in an uprush of physical passion, kissing him again and again in return. He began to undo the buttons of the dress, and in no time his hands were on my naked breasts, a heady sensation that brought back memories of Ruth and Emma sucking nourishment from me.

'You're a beautiful woman, Shirley,' he whispered, then changed it to 'a beautiful lady'.

Simon and Garfunkel had got as far as 'Feelin' Groovy', and their la-da-da, dah-da, dah-da provided a backing to our kisses. The smell of his after-shave mingled with the floral perfume I'd sprayed behind my ears. My arms went round his neck, and my fingers clenched convulsively among his black curls. He was a gypsy, a bold gypsy boy who took me by the hand and led me upstairs, where all rational thought was swept aside, all caution thrown to the winds.

It was as if Mr Newhouse and Mrs Pierce had been taken over by two strangers whose bodies communicated independently of them; a man and a woman were naked and impatient for each other, for the man's forceful entry, the woman's eager cry as she received him. Oh, moment of truth! My world held nothing but Newhouse, his thrusting movements, his quickening breath, his groans of release.

'Christ! Ah – sexy woman – oh!' Incoherent words and sounds to express the inexpressible. Why do unbelievers use Christ's name at such times? Real Christians don't – or at least, I don't think they do.

But how quickly it is all over. As he lay sprawled and spent, with one arm flung across me, I gazed up into the semi-darkness and thought that I had just committed fornication in the bed that I'd shared with my husband. The old cynical saying came to my mind, that all cats are grey in the dark, meaning that all men (and women too, I suppose) are essentially the same in bed. A faint light filtered through the curtains as I pondered on what had happened, and what it had revealed to me. That was certainly no rape, but had I in fact planned it from the start?

Tell you what, Brian, come and have supper with me when you get in from work this evening.

To this day I can't be sure, though Newhouse had clearly seen it as a straight come-on, and had prepared accordingly, bringing wine and chocolates. He might even have dropped off at the airport chemist's, just to be on the safe side, for although there was no fear of putting a woman of my age in the club, there might still be a risk of AIDS and other STDs. I recalled his mention of Paul and Martin: had he been checking up on my recent activities? In the end he hadn't taken precautions, and if anybody was at risk, *I* was.

What in God's name would my daughters think? Or my parents? Not to mention poor old

Martin. What shamelessness! And what hypocrisy! Father O'Flynn was in for a surprise next time I went to Reconciliation – we older ones still call it Confession – but priests hear all sorts of things that nobody else suspects, and are pretty well unshockable. This is going back ten years, before all the scandal broke about paedophiles in the priesthood.

So was I ashamed? No. This one random collision with a man I hardly knew had given me the sign I'd wanted. The earth had moved for me, and moved on: I now knew, or thought I knew, where my future lay.

Newhouse stirred and murmured, 'Shirley'.

I stroked his tousled hair and whispered, 'Casanova'.

He opened his eyes. 'Eh? What did you say?'

'Your name, New House – it's Casa Nova in Italian.'

'Go on, is it?' He raised himself on one elbow. 'You all right, Shirley? No regrets or anything?'

'No, Brian, no regrets. In fact I've come to a decision about something.'

'Oh, ah?'

'Yes. I shall marry Martin next year. The nice old gentleman.'

'Yeah? Just made up your mind, then?'

'Yes, Brian. I'd like to be a married lady again. You've helped me to see that. This has been wonderful, but it's a one-off, isn't it? And I can make Martin happy, I'm sure of that.'

He looked a bit bewildered. 'I shan't ever forget this, Shirley. Lucky old Martin, eh? But if that's what you want, if he can make *you* happy – well–'

He never finished the sentence, and I wondered what he felt as he dressed and returned to No 52. Relief, probably, that I didn't expect it to go any further than just that once. A man like Newhouse couldn't afford to do anything stupid.

Like falling in love with an unsuitable older woman.

Chapter Eleven

Tragedy

Martin Hayes telephoned me twice from Nerja on the Costa del Sol, saying that they were having a nice holiday, that the weather was quite warm and that he wished I was there to share it with him.

'I'm on duty up to the weekend, Martin, but call me on Friday when you get back,' I told him. 'Yes, fine, thanks – been busy at work as usual – yes – and so pleased to hear that you're having a chance to relax – and Laura, too. Sorry, what was that? Oh, yes, we should be all right for Saturday and the Hospital Ball!'

There was no mistaking the dear man's concern, and the fact that he was missing me. I found myself looking forward to his return, and the annual ball given by the Hospital League of Friends.

Meanwhile, Brian Newhouse went to work and came home again, nodding to me as he got into and out of his car. He told me that 'our Jean' and baby Gary had been discharged from hospital on the third day following delivery, and Lilian was staying for another week to take care of them all. I did some shopping for him, making sure that he had sausages, chops, baked beans and oven chips enough to satisfy hunger; even if somewhat low on vitamin content, it would see him through until his mother's return.

'I really appreciate it, Shirley, and if ever I can do you a favour in return some time, you've only got to–'

'Thanks, Brian, I'll let you know. Bye!'

Paul called on the Monday, and how could I shut the door on him? He shared my evening break-fast before I cycled off to work the first of four nights.

'D'you think we could watch another play some time, Shirley?' he asked wistfully. 'I heard that there's been a film made of a Jane Austen novel, so a lady said at the Seagull's Nest the other night. She said it was about a girl called Emma, and I remembered that, because it's your daughter's name.'

'You can always watch plays on your own TV, can't you, Paul?' Some dear old soul at Shalom had given him her television set because her sight was failing, and she preferred the radio anyway.

He looked me straight in the eyes. 'That's not the same, and you know it, Shirley. We're not the same as we used to be, are we? Not since you started being friends with Martin.'

'Oh, Paul, it's nothing to do with Martin,' I lied unhappily. 'I'm such a lot older than you, aren't I?'

'And *he's* a lot older than *you*, Shirley, and he doesn't even like Shakespeare, not in the way we do,' he retorted, which made me feel even worse because I knew what he meant. Our special relationship would eventually have to end if I married Martin, but I still shied away from telling my poor young friend.

When I saw Martin again, it was all so simple. There was hardly need for words.

'Shirley, darling, I've missed you more than I can say.'

'Me, too, Martin.'

He held me close, and our lips met in a tremulous kiss. 'I'll be fine for the dance tomorrow, Martin.'

'I've been looking forward to it ever since I was away from you in Nerja,' he said, and made it sound like a place of exile.

The Christmas Ball at the Marston Winter Gardens was quite a prestigious affair, well supported by medical, nursing and administrative staff. I saw William Hawke with a woman I presumed was his wife, and Lance Penrose with a lady I knew was not. Sue Weldon was there with Jim Digweed, now returned to the University but drawn back regularly to see Sue. I introduced Martin to them, and we chatted over the buffet supper; they were clearly surprised to see us taking to the floor for a Latin-American medley, and I was delighted to see Hawke's expression as he stared at us kicking up our heels and tossing our heads like experts. I'd bought a new dress in clinging red jersey that flared out around my calves and showed more than a glimpse of lacy underskirt; it really was the most tremendous fun.

We danced the last waltz in semi-darkness, and my arms went up around Martin's neck. I felt his lips upon my forehead, and we both sighed contentedly; I suppose that was the moment when we became unofficially engaged, though after the experience at Wilmot Avenue I wanted to wait for the right time and place before embarking on a closer intimacy. Or making an official announcement.

'Let's keep this between ourselves for the time being, Martin – we won't say anything to Laura or to my daughters,' I whispered. 'Our secret, Martin, until next year – next spring will be early enough, don't you agree?'

'Just as you think best, Shirley darling.' He kissed my cheek as we swayed to the music. 'I'll go along with whatever you say.'

But did he? The very next day he told me that the Goodsons had invited us both to dinner at their home. I was a little taken aback, especially when it turned out that we were to be the only guests, and I was her father's partner. The children were sent to bed early, and we were invited at eight-thirty for dinner at nine. My offers of help in the kitchen were firmly declined, and Martin and I sat perched on the settee in the lounge while Victor Goodson served drinks from a well-stocked cabinet. I allowed myself one sweet Martini, and then steered away from alcohol. Laura complimented me on my dress, long-sleeved and paisley-patterned, which contrasted nicely with her own sleeveless green gown over which she tied a frilly apron for serving the excellent three-course meal. Victor was both butler and waiter, hovering at her side, easing her way – 'Do you want these taken out now, darling?' – and I got the impression that he was in overall charge. Had this dinner been his idea, I wondered, a move that he had suggested in order to show their guarded approval of the liaison? Or was it simply to indicate that they knew perfectly well what was going on?

Our dinner conversation gave no clues. We talked hospital shop over the mushroom soup with melba toast, and Laura spoke of the rising insurance costs to GPs as litigation cast its widening shadow. Over the roast shoulder of gammon that Victor expertly carved at table, placing the pink, clove-studded slices on each plate, they talked of their children, and I felt able to mention Helen and Timothy as we passed round the new potatoes, parsnips, carrots and parsley sauce. By the time we got to the lemon sorbet topped with maraschino cherries, Victor was waxing lyrical over the charms of Nerja, ideal for a family holiday away from the more obvious tourist attractions of Torremolinos.

'We felt that we were sharing the life of the people who actually lived there, didn't we, darling? Those little whitewashed houses, and of course the caves–'

I put my hand over my glass when Victor approached with the wine bottle, and refused brandy with the coffee. All in all I think I acquitted myself pretty well, but by eleven I was worn out by being on my best behaviour for so long, and was thankful when Martin said it was time for him to drive me home.

I pleaded tiredness as a reason for not asking him in, and he rang me the next morning to say how charming I'd looked and how proud he was of me; I sent Laura a spray of flowers with a polite note of thanks.

Needless to say, the Maternity Unit was by now positively buzzing with the news of our engagement, however unofficial, so I smiled graciously and accepted my colleagues' congratulations, though I told them firmly that the wedding would not take place until some time next summer, a full year after Dora's passing. Even so, Dilly Fisher sent me a card, and so did Pearl Amos, expressing their good wishes to the happy couple.

This meant that I had to let Ruth and Emma know, and their response was touchingly generous. The Butlers sent a congratulations-on-your-engagement card, and Emma a cheeky letter, kindly offering to give Martin a try-out and report back to me with her findings. 'But seriously, Mumsie, I couldn't be more pleased to think of you and that sweet old darling getting together. You'll be so good for each other!'

Lilian Newhouse said how pleased she was for me, though I avoided her son's eye. After all, it was thanks to him, in a way, that I had reached a decision about my future, but I had not quite recovered from our neighbourly encounter.

And then came the terrible day that changed everything, for ever.

It was the last day of October, All Hallows' Eve,

when local children came knocking at doors and demanding, 'Trick or Treat?' I was on duty that night, and had no intention of getting out of bed and going downstairs every time the doorbell rang: yet when it rang loud and long shortly after four o'clock on that dank, chill afternoon, the sound was like an alarm-bell, penetrating down through my mogadon-induced sleep, rousing me to consciousness.

'Eh? Who is it? What?' I stirred as the continuing noise reverberated through the gloom of the unlit house. I sat up, blinking away the cobwebs of sleep. Still it went on and on.

'All right – wait, I'm coming, keep your hair on,' I muttered, slithering out of bed, stepping into my slippers and throwing my dressing-gown around me as I padded downstairs and opened the front door. A dark figure stood before me, his face a pale mask.

'Paul–!'

He rushed in, flinging his arms around me so violently that I staggered backwards and would have been knocked over if I hadn't grasped the shelf below the hall window.

'Shirley, help me, don't send me away, please – I've done something wrong, Shirley – I couldn't bear it any longer!'

'Ssh, ssh, Paul, calm down now, quiet, quiet,' I ordered, though my heart was pounding. 'Come into the kitchen, and I'll put the kettle on. Come on, Paul, come on now, tell me all about it. What have you done?'

Taking him by the hand I led him through to the familiar table and sat him down in his usual chair. There was something in his eyes when he looked up at me that filled me with both pity and terror. I plugged in the electric kettle and lit the grill to make toast.

'You'll be angry with me, Shirley, when I tell you – and – oh, Shirley, you wouldn't hate me, would you?'

'Never, Paul. Sometimes I get cross with you, but that's all. Now, tell me – is this about the Weasel – Mark Fisher?'

Even as I said the name, I shivered. *Please, God, don't let it be Dilly's son – please!*

But it was. Between incoherent gasps, sobs and bursts of speech, he told me that a gang of children had surrounded him outside the gates of Marston Comprehensive School at four o'clock. The usual puerile insults had been shouted, and they'd dared each other to run up to Paul, touch him and shout, 'Wanker!' – then rush off before he could make a grab at them. It sounded like a monstrous game of tag, and Mark Fisher had stood watching from what Paul called 'a safe distance,' and that he had 'smirked' at the sight of the big, bewildered boy trying to keep calm in the face of his tormentors. It made me think of bear-baiting.

'You've always told me to ignore them, Shirley, but you don't know what it's like,' he sobbed. 'I couldn't *stand* it, Shirley, I couldn't bear it any longer, so I called out to him, "Hey, you, Fisher, you've put these little bastards up to this, haven't you?" – and he said, "You talking to *me*, Mr Meadows? I haven't said a word, have I?" And that's what did it, Shirley, that's what drove me to it – all I could see was his horrible face, all blurred and red – and there was this noise inside my head, and I rushed up to him and got hold of him – I held on to him and shook him and shook him – I can't remember what I said, but all the kids were yelling and I threw him down on the pavement and hit him in the face with my fists – I punched him and punched him, Shirley, until the smirk was gone.'

'Oh, my God, Paul. Oh, *no.*' I covered my face with my hands to shut out the picture, only it wouldn't go away.

'I heard a sort of crack, Shirley, so I may have broken one of his front teeth. But that can be put right by a dentist, can't it?'

'For God's sake, Paul, did he – did Mark get up again after – after you'd done this to him?' My voice sounded weak as I forced out the question. 'Did he get up? Did he speak?'

'I don't think so, but I can't be sure. All the other kids were screaming and hollering and running away in all directions – and so I ran away too, and came straight here. You'll look after me, won't you, Shirley? You'll explain why I had to do it?'

The kettle had boiled and the toast had burned. I made tea and put more bread under the grill with shaking hands.

'Look, Paul dear, I'm going to leave you in the kitchen with a nice, sweet cup of tea–'

'I'd rather have coffee if it's all the same to you, Shirley.'

'All right, coffee, and buttered toast. I'll go and ring up about the boy. I know his mother, you see. I work with her.'

'I know you do, Shirley, and will you tell her that I wouldn't have slammed into him like that if he hadn't set those kids on me? He asked for it, Shirley, he put them up to it!'

'All right, just sit there, Paul, and wait a few minutes, there's a good boy.'

I went to the telephone and dialled Bernie McCann's number. One of the children answered, and I tried to sound casual as I asked to speak to his mother.

'Bernadette McCann here – God's grief, Shirley, what're ye ringin' for at this time? Ye're on again tonight, aren't ye?'

'Bernie, listen carefully. I want you to ring Dilly Fisher for me *now*. No, listen, you mustn't let her know I asked you to. Make up some reason for phoning her, like asking when she's on next week.'

'Ye've lost me, Shirley. Why should I call up Dilly when the poor soul's gettin' tea ready for those thankless kids, with no proper reason for botherin' her?'

'Believe me, Bernie, this could be very serious, and you must help me. I've got good reason to think that her son Mark may be injured, perhaps badly.'

'Jesus, Mary and Joseph! Ye mean run over or somethin'?'

'No, Bernie, he's been attacked. Listen, will you please trust me as a friend, and ring Dilly to ask – oh, anything – I know, ask her if she's attended a fire lecture this year, say you're checking up that all the night staff have been to one.'

'And how will askin' about a fire lecture tell me if her son's injured?'

'Well, if he *has* been badly hurt, she'll tell you, won't she? Maybe the daughter will answer the phone, and say her mother's gone to hospital with the boy. I mean, if there's any serious news, you'll be told about it, just as you'd tell anybody if they rang up and one of *your* children was – oh, for God's sake, Bernie, just ring Dilly's home, and whatever you hear, ring me back to tell me – please, Bernie!'

She must have heard the rising note of panic, because she replied quickly, 'Sure I will, I will so, if ye can't ring her yeself.'

'It'd be better if I didn't, Bernie, because it's my friend Paul Meadows who – thanks, love, I'll wait for you to call me back.'

We rang off, and I waited. I went upstairs and hurriedly dressed, putting on my uniform. There was a resounding silence from the telephone. Surely Bernie must have got through and found out something by now? It was ten to five, and seemed like an eternity since Paul had held his finger on the doorbell. I went back to the kitchen where he had finished a mug of coffee and eaten two slices of toast.

'Have you found out anything, Shirley? What did Mrs Fisher say?'

'Er – I'm just waiting for my friend Mrs McCann to ring back, Paul. She's getting some details for me,' I said with an effort at re-assurance, though my smile faltered a little.

Five o'clock, and no return call. At five minutes past there was a loud ring, and I leapt up with an involuntary 'Ah!' before I realised that it was not the telephone but the doorbell. Would it be a couple of kids on an early round of 'Trick or Treat'?

On the doorstep stood two uniformed police officers.

'Good evening, Mrs Pierce. You *are* Mrs Shirley Pierce, I take it?' the older one asked gravely.

I leaned against the door frame. 'Yes, I'm Mrs Pierce.' I knew what they had come about. I knew what they were going to say.

'I'm Detective Sergeant Cross, Mrs Pierce, and this is Police Constable Smith. We're looking for a Mr Paul Meadows, and we believe he may be here with you. Is he?'

A thin, faraway voice that didn't sound like mine answered. 'No, he isn't. You're wrong, there's nobody here.'

They glanced at each other. The sergeant smiled patiently. 'You do realise, Mrs Pierce, that it's an offence to harbour a person wanted for questioning by the police? I'll ask you again, is Paul Meadows here in this house?'

'I – I don't know where he is. Why do you want to see him?' asked the same disembodied voice.

There was a pause while again they exchanged questioning looks, and the sergeant adopted a firmer tone. 'I don't want to have to insist, Mrs Pierce, but we have good reason to believe that you are harbouring Meadows. If you are charged with–'

That was when my poor friend called out from the kitchen. 'Tell them I didn't mean to hurt him, Shirley, tell them what he did to *me*. You explain to them, Shirley!'

The officers at once entered the house and

went straight through to the kitchen. I followed them, and saw Paul cowering back against the wall as he and Cross recognised each other from previous encounters.

'All right, son, I know you're Paul Meadows of Flat 3, Brankton Court, Boreham Road, Marston.' Cross nodded to Smith, who produced a pair of handcuffs, while the sergeant made the formal arrest.

'Paul Meadows, I am arresting you on suspicion of the murder of Mark Fisher.'

The constable clicked on the handcuffs, and I heard myself give a low groan as I slumped down on a chair at the table. There was a dreadful inevitability about the whole scene, as if a nightmare was coming true. Paul's eyes seemed to widen and darken with fear.

'It's not true, Sergeant Cross! I didn't kill him, I just gave him a well-deserved thrashing!'

'Maybe you never meant to, son, but the fact is that he's dead. You don't have to say anything now, but anything you do say may be given in evidence later.' The man spoke kindly enough, but did not waste words; he turned and nodded to Smith.

'All right, Les, you look after him, and I'll radio for the van. Sorry about all this in your home, Mrs Pierce, but we do know young Paul, and we'll make allowances for – er–'

'Don't leave me, Shirley, don't leave me!' implored Paul, his voice rising as it always did at times of emotion, and Smith restrained his manacled hands. 'Keep 'em down, there's a good lad.'

'You can come with us in the van if you like,

Mrs Pierce,' said Cross, 'and stay with him when he sees the custody officer. Looks as if we could do with a responsible adult around when he's interviewed.'

I went to get my coat. I heard Cross mutter to his assistant while they waited for the van, which was only just round the corner. 'He's blown it this time, Les. I always said something like this'd happen sooner or later.'

As we left the house I heard the telephone ringing in the silence, and wondered if it was Bernie calling back at last with the terrible news she had heard.

On the short journey they let me sit beside Paul, his handcuffed hands in my lap as he continued to whimper and protest his innocence. I knew that I had to be brave for him, and my training now stood me in good stead; I composed myself, and kept my thoughts away from Dilly Fisher looking down upon her son, his face an unrecognisable bloody pulp.

At the police station Paul was taken straight into the custody office. Cross beckoned me to follow, and introduced me to Custody Officer Phillips, thick-set and unsmiling. Paul was searched and his wallet and watch taken from him, in spite of his protests. He was asked about his next of kin, and stammered out the address of his married sister in Fleetwood.

'Don't tell my Dad about this, will you?' he begged, but as his elderly father lived with his sister, I did not see how it could be kept secret.

'Do you want a solicitor present?' Phillips asked him, but seeing Paul's blank look, he turned to

221

me and repeated the question, 'Does he want a solicitor present?'

I asked if I might telephone my own solicitor, whom I hadn't seen since Tom's death, but he sounded distinctly reluctant to leave his fireside.

'We can call in Courtney, he's used to this kind of thing,' said Phillips briskly, and a Mr Courtney duly arrived, as did Paul's social worker, a youngish, cocksure man – 'Call me Bob' – who at once lit a cigarette and told me with a knowing grin that he knew all about me, whatever that meant.

'This is a very serious charge, and the CID are sending over a couple of officers to interview the accused,' said Phillips bleakly. 'The Home Office pathologist should have a post-mortem report within the hour, so–' he glanced up at the clock – 'the interview will take place at around nineteen hundred hours. Mr Courtney and Mr – er – Bob Simmons may be present, but the Inspectors won't want a crowd.' He looked meaningfully at me as he spoke, and Paul protested wildly.

'Let Shirley stay! Don't send her away, she's my very best friend!'

The sergeant frowned and told him to keep his voice down, at which Paul shouted all the louder. 'Don't go, Shirley! Don't let them send you away!'

'You've got Mr Courtney and your social worker, Meadows, and that's enough,' barked Phillips, at which Paul began to shout at the top of his voice.

'Damn Bob Simmons, he's never done a thing for me, he's never there when I want him, he's only visited me twice, and he's been bloody useless!' he roared, shaking his handcuffed fists. 'Let Shirley stay with me instead of him, she's got far more sense!'

If I hadn't been so racked with fear and foreboding I'd probably have been amused at Simmon's discomfiture, as PC Smith evidently was. By the time the CID interview took place in a soundproof room with a tape-recorder going, my presence was accepted as necessary if they were to get any sense out of Paul, much to the annoyance of Simmons, who spouted a lot of psycho-babble about Paul, but clearly knew nothing of his sensitivities, his artistic appreciation and capacity for friendship.

The grisly details of the post-mortem report made it clear that death had been due to severe head injuries, including a fractured base of skull and brain haemorrhage; these injuries were consistent with a violent assault on the deceased, and death had been virtually instantaneous. In reply to the charge of murder, Paul repeated again and again that he had never set out to kill Mark Fisher, but that the boy had tormented him beyond endurance over a long period, and he had wanted to teach him a lesson.

'You ask Shirley, she knows what I've had to put up with!' he shouted. 'She told me to ignore people who behave like that, but nobody knows what it's like, not even her! I couldn't bear it any longer, and it was about time he was punished for it!'

'That's as may be, Meadows, but the fact remains that this fourteen-year-old boy is dead.'

'Yes, well, I'm sorry he's dead, but I never

wanted to kill him.'

It needed a lot of probing to get the right answers, but eventually the essential evidence was recorded: that Paul had wanted to hurt Mark Fisher, though not seriously, and had never intended to kill him. And that he was very sorry that the boy was dead.

At length the two CID officers declared that there were sufficient grounds to support a charge, and Custody Officer Phillips intoned the fatal words:

'You, Paul Jeremy Meadows are charged that on the thirty-first day of October 199- you did murder Mark Fisher against the Queen's Peace and contrary to Common Law.' That said, he added briskly, 'You'll be kept in a police cell until the next sitting of the Magistrates' Court.'

'That'll be tomorrow morning, Mrs Pierce,' explained Sergeant Cross kindly, 'and it'll only be a formality, really. He'll be remanded in custody until his trial comes up at the Crown Court, and that could be some months. You can come along to the courtroom tomorrow, but you'll have to leave him now. You can't come into a police cell with him.'

There was an extraordinary sense of unreality about the whole scene, and Paul gazed at me with fearful, silent pleading as the constable rose to lead him away to the cell. It was nearly half past eight, and I had to go to work anyway; my courage almost deserted me when I thought of what lay ahead, but I stayed calm when we said goodbye.

'I'll pray for you, Paul,' I whispered, putting my arms around his neck in front of them all in the usual Shalom embrace, though he couldn't respond because of the handcuffs.

'Shalom, Shirley, Shalom.' His tears were wet on my face as we kissed.

Chapter Twelve

Night of Sorrow

Ill news travels fast, and the shock waves from Mark Fisher's death and the dire circumstances of it had reached the Maternity Department before I hurried into the Delivery Unit office to find Sister Amos talking in a low tone with the day sister. They assumed wary expressions when they saw me.

'Ah, hallo, Sister Pierce. Mrs Gresham wants to see you as soon as you've taken the report,' said the day sister. 'Would you like a cup of tea first? You look all in.'

'Has anybody heard how Dilly Fisher is?' I asked abruptly.

'Completely devastated, I believe – well, it's been the most fearful shock to us all, needless to say.' She sighed and picked up the case-notes on the desk. 'And I'm afraid there's more sad news to tell you, Shirley. We've got Mrs Kathleen Rogers in, she's the daughter of Madge the ward clerk–'

'Oh, my God, what's wrong with her?' I cut in. 'It's her first baby, and they're so looking forward to it – don't tell me it's – oh, *no!*'

'Intrauterine death at thirty-eight weeks,' came the sombre reply. 'She came up to Mr Horsfield's clinic this afternoon, and there was no foetal heart. She hadn't felt movements since yesterday, so she's in Room Four for induction and delivery.' The sister gave a helpless shrug and Pearl Amos clucked her tongue. 'Madge is with her, and her husband, Alex. She's had prostaglandin gel inserted, and seems to be getting a few niggles. Lance Penrose says if there's any delay he'll put up a syntocinon drip. It should be over by morning.'

My heart sank even further, if that were possible. This patient would need all the sympathy and support that I could offer, and my own troubles would have to be kept hidden.

'Does Mr Horsfield have any ideas as to why?' I asked.

'He thinks it might be a concealed antepartum haemorrhage associated with toxaemia, though she's had no signs of it up till now – slightly raised blood pressure, a trace of albuminuria and oedema of ankles, nothing dramatic. Or it could be something hormonal, or an infection, who's to say?'

We groaned in unison. 'Is she for the usual diamorphine?' I asked. The powerful sedative and pain-relieving effects of heroin have become notorious through misuse, and it is only used in obstetrics when there is no need to consider the baby.

'Yes, and I gave her an injection of five milligrams at seven-twenty to settle her after the prostaglandin. Oh, it's such a shame.'

The inadequacy of words in the face of tragedy...

'And in Room One you've got Anna Sands, likes to be called Nonnie – baby number three, forceps for the first, second was normal, and she wants a natural childbirth this time – no enema, no drugs, no drip, no interference of any kind. Her husband's with her, he's called Hill.'

'Shouldn't he be called Sands?'

'He is, Hill Sands. Hill and Nonnie. Actually they seem a very nice couple and, with it being her third, there shouldn't be any problems.'

'Better not be, because I'm in no mood for fooling about,' I said wearily. 'Would you like to take over Mrs Sands, Pearl, with student midwife Bhimjee to deliver? Poor Kathleen Rogers is going to need pretty constant attention, and what with everything else today–'

I left the sentence unfinished, and the sister gently reminded me that Mrs Gresham was waiting to see me.

'Don't worry, Shirley, I'll check the drugs and hold the fort till you're through,' said Pearl Amos. 'You go and get it over with Mrs Gresham.'

Which I did.

'Ah, hallo, Sister Pierce, what a frightful business this is about Auxiliary Nurse Fisher's son,' she said. 'Take a seat.' She poured out two cups of coffee and handed me one, though I'd just drunk a cup of tea.

'Mrs Fisher will obviously be off work for the foreseeable future, and I've removed her name from the duty roster,' she said in her practical way. 'I've started a collection for her among the staff, but meanwhile I've ordered flowers to be sent tomorrow morning, with a card from the Unit. I'm afraid you'll have to manage with only one auxiliary tonight, so the two student midwives will have to help out with the ward work. What an additional blow about poor Mrs Rogers – but I'm glad that you're on duty for her, and for Madge. I believe she's starting to contract, so hopefully it should be over by morning.'

'Let's hope so, Mrs Gresham.' It was time to get to the point. 'Have you heard anything about – about Mrs Fisher?'

'Only that she's in a state of shock, which is to be expected. Sister McCann has been at her home, and her minister from Moor End Methodist Church. She seems to have plenty of support. And while we're on this subject, Sister Pierce – Shirley – there's something I have to say to you.' She cleared her throat and hesitated.

'Yes, Mrs Gresham?'

'Look, Shirley, I believe you know this – er – person, this man who's responsible for the boy's death. I've heard that you befriended him and that he has visited your home on several occasions.'

'That's right, Mrs Gresham. As a matter of fact he was arrested at my home this evening, and I went with him to the police station. I've come straight from there.'

She gasped involuntarily, her hand to her mouth in genuine horror. 'Oh, my dear, how awful for you – how simply *awful!* But I'm glad you've told me that, because – well, I have to advise you not to speak about this – er – association, not to anybody. There's a lot of sympathy for Nurse Fisher, naturally, and I strongly recommend that you play down any acquaintance you may have with this – er–'

'Paul Meadows,' I said.

'Yes, Meadows, that was the name. If anybody asks you about what happened, don't mention any connection you have with him, do you follow?'

'You mean I'm to say that I've never heard of Paul Meadows – is that it, Mrs Gresham?'

'Of course it's up to you what you actually say, Shirley, but think about it. This is going to be headline news, especially at the trial. It's bad enough having poor Mrs Fisher involved in the way that she is, and we don't want any further involvement, not here at the Maternity Department.'

I took a gulp of the coffee, and set down the cup. 'I hear what you're saying, Mrs Gresham.' I was pretty sure that I could also hear William Hawke's voice in this.

'Good, my dear, I thought you would. I think that's all we need say. I hope you don't have too busy a night. You'll deliver Mrs Rogers yourself, won't you?'

'Of course.'

'Good. Right, then. I'll be on my way. See you in the morning, Shirley, and good luck!'

At the door she stopped and turned round to face me. 'My dear Shirley, I'm just so terribly sorry about all this, I really am.'

'So am I, Mrs Gresham. Thank you.'

I went straight to Room Four where Kathleen Rogers lay in a diamorphine haze that many an addict on the streets of Manchester might have envied.

'Hallo, there,' I said softly. 'I'm Shirley, and I'll be around until eight o'clock in the morning. Hallo, Madge dear, and Kathleen. And Alex, how're you doing?'

'Oh, Sister Pierce, I'm so glad you're on tonight,' said Madge, getting up from her armchair. Her eyes were red-rimmed and strained from suppressing her own grief. 'It's difficult to tell whether she's getting pains or not. Do you think it will be long?'

Alex looked up and gave me a nod. ''Evening, Sister.'

'I'll just take her blood pressure,' I murmured, and noted a significant rise since the last recording, in spite of the heavy sedation. I laid a hand gently on the abdomen, which was tightening with a contraction; it felt quite strong. I looked at the husband and mother.

'Like a drink of something?' I whispered. 'Tea, coffee, hot chocolate? Toast? Or a sandwich?'

They shook their heads. 'We're just about swilling with tea, Sister Pierce,' replied Madge ruefully. 'Do you fancy anything to eat, Alex?'

'Couldn't touch it, Madge.'

'How long do you think it's likely to be, Sister Pierce?' asked Madge again.

'It doesn't usually take any longer than a–' I began. 'Once she's getting some good, strong contractions, the cervix will probably dilate up fairly quickly.' I crossed my fingers.

'Will she see the baby when it's born?' Madge's voice trembled.

'Oh, certainly. Alex may want to hold the baby and show it to her – and you, too.' I patted her shoulder. 'We'll take each step as it comes, love, and do whatever the parents want.'

I telephoned Lance Penrose to report her rise in blood pressure.

'Should settle once she delivers, Sis. Too bad we didn't have her in for induction before the weekend. Bloody shame. Anyway, keep an eye on the b.p. and don't stint on the dope. I'm here if you want me.'

As soon as I put down the phone there was an outside call. It was Martin, and he was very upset. 'I know you don't like being telephoned at work, Shirley, but I've been trying to call you at home and there was no answer. Laura's told me about this horrible murder, and it's been a terrible shock, dear. When I think of what might have happened to *you* – oh, thank God he'll be behind bars now!'

'Please don't get into a state about it, Martin. It's a terrible thing to have happened, I know, but–'

'But you had this deranged creature at your *home*, dear, eating at your table and *alone* with you. It just doesn't bear thinking about, Shirley! When did you last see him?'

'You'll have to excuse me, Martin, I've got a patient here who needs my attention. *Do* stop worrying, there's nothing to be gained by harping on about it now. Look, I have to go–'

'Laura says that this poor little boy's mother is

one of your nurses, Shirley. Did you know that?'

'Yes, of course I know. I'll have to ring off now, Martin. Speak to you tomorrow, OK?'

And I hung up. He clearly considered this calamity to be a complete vindication of all his warnings, and one could hardly argue over that; but tomorrow I was going to the Magistrates' Court to support Paul, whatever Martin thought. I'd promised.

Pearl Amos was with the Sands couple who were planning a jolly do-it-yourself delivery, and were currently sitting on the floor, playing Scrabble. Pearl rolled her big eyes at me and said that everything seemed normal – temperature, pulse, blood pressure and foetal heart.

'She doesn't want any vaginal examinations or pain relief – do you, Nonnie?'

Nonnie smiled and shook her head. Every time a contraction came on, she stopped the game, drew up her knees, Hill put his hands under her arms from behind, and she did the breathing exercise she'd learned at relaxation classes, a series of rapid pants, 'blowing the pain away,' though as the pains got stronger she made odd-sounding noises in her throat:

'Ooh-aah, ooh-aah, ooh-aah – wooh-whoo-whoo-whoo whoo!' She rocked backwards and forwards, so Hill had to do likewise, and had a job keeping his balance. As soon as the pain passed they were back at the Scrabble board, arguing good-naturedly about whether *orgasmically* was a dictionary word. They were doing all the things that the Blairs had hoped to do, using the force of gravity, relaxing between contractions and 'blowing the pain away'; only whereas Nonnie had had two babies before, Constance Blair had been a primigravida of thirty-seven with an occipito-posterior position, which made a big difference. Nonnie was flushed, her cropped hair stuck to her forehead with perspiration, and her 'Ooh-aahs' were getting louder; I reminded her that she could change her mind about pain relief at any time, and she and Hill smiled and nodded, then shook their heads in unison, like two mandarins.

'Nurse Bhimjee has gone to help out on Post-natal until things get cracking here,' Pearl Amos told me. 'She says she doesn't like to intrude!'

It was now ten-fifteen. 'Telephone for you, Shirley!' called Linda Grierson from the Antenatal office. 'Councillor Crowne,' she added significantly. I flew to the phone.

'Philip!'

'My dear Shirley, I do apologise for calling you on duty, but I thought you'd like to know that I've been to see our friend Paul at the police station.'

'Oh, Philip, thank God. I should have phoned you as soon as he came to me this afternoon after he'd – oh, Philip, isn't this just the worst – what we've dreaded–' My voice failed, and I choked back tears.

'Yes, my dear, there's going to be a lot of agonising over this, and we're all involved. I've been to see poor Mrs Fisher and her daughter, and she's in a bad way, of course, though she seems to have a fair bit of support, and most of all she's got her faith, which is so important to her. With Paul, on the other hand, we must just pray that he won't be destroyed by this. I've prayed with him, and I'll be at the Magistrates' Court tomorrow morning. He says you're coming too. Would you like me to call for you?'

'Oh, yes, please, Philip. Thank you. It's all so ghastly, isn't it?'

'Don't give way to despair, dear. Don't let the Other One get the better of you.' (He meant the devil, the evil one, Satan – we called him the Other One at Shalom.)

'I'm so thankful for your support and understanding,' I murmured with a sniff.

'Bless you. I'll call at about twenty to ten tomorrow, shall I?'

'That would be such a help. I'd better go now, Philip, there are two patients in labour – but thanks a million.'

'Take courage, Shirley, and never forget that Jesus is Lord. Just say that to yourself when you're feeling overwhelmed.'

'Thanks, Philip, I'll try. Good night.'

'Good night, Shirley. Peace be with you.'

Linda came in with a tray. 'Coffee's up, love. Have you time to grab a quick one?'

'Yes, only it'll have to be very quick.' She looked at me searchingly.

'I can't tell you how sorry I am, Shirley. And for poor Dilly. And now Madge's daughter's in with an IUD, it makes me so ashamed of the fuss I've made over my own ups and downs this year.'

We were alone in the office, so exchanged a brief hug. 'Oh, Shirley love, this is the pits. If only there was something I could do.'

Which was exactly how I'd felt about her for the past six months. When the telephone rang again, it was Bernie.

'I know ye're busy, Shirley, but I must speak to ye. Ye weren't there when I phoned back to ye at last – and didn't I imagine all sorts!'

'Bernie, I'm so sorry about asking you to phone Dilly's home. It must have been such a shock when you heard–'

'It was, because I got a policewoman on Dilly's phone, and she asked me to go round there as soon as she heard I was a colleague. That's where I've been this evenin', though Dilly's had lots o' visitors, the minister from Moor End and your Mr Crowne. And her ex-husband, who's shattered, o' course, because Mark's his son too. Dr Goodson's given her a sedative for the night, but God help her, Shirley – whatever would we do if it was one of ours?'

I swallowed, and could not answer.

'Listen, Shirley, I'm tellin' ye this as a friend. There's goin' to be a lot o' hard things said about Paul Meadows, so don't let on about him bein' a – a friend o' yours, like.'

'I know, Bernie, I know,' I said tiredly. 'Mrs Gresham's already warned me along those lines.'

'Has she? Good, then ye won't mind me tellin' ye again. Everybody's so sad for Dilly, but there'll be no tears for him who did it, Shirley. D'ye get me meanin'?'

'I do, Bernie. Keep my mouth shut, right?'

'Right. And Shirley me darlin', I'm just so sorry for – well, for *him*, even though I can't go round sayin' so. He'll be in me prayers, along with all

235

the others.'

Somehow or other I got through that night, as we always do. I made a conscious effort of will not to think about Paul in the police cell, wondering whether he was asleep or awake during the hours of darkness; still less did I dare to touch upon the young body in the mortuary further mutilated by the pathologist's cold dissections. My mind reeled away from Dilly Fisher as I gave my attention to Kathleen Rogers and her mother, and when a patient was admitted in labour with her second baby, I asked student midwife Bhimjee to admit her in the delivery room next to Nonnie Sands. But she had no sooner introduced herself than Pearl Amos rang the bell in Room One to say that Nonnie was in second stage, so I sent Nurse Bhimjee in there and took over the new admission myself. It was her second baby, and she was cracking on, as we say.

Twenty minutes later I looked in on the Sands, expecting to see Nonnie cuddling her baby, but there had been a tiresome delay in the second stage, due to a loaded rectum. The most appalling smell hit me as I opened the door, and Pearl was muttering crossly.

'As soon as she began pushing down, it started coming out, and it's just gone on and on.'

Poor Nonnie was groaning with pain and discomfiture as Nurse Bhimjee used up sheet after sheet of paper towelling to scoop up the seemingly endless discharge of – well, let's call it poo. Hard lumps at first, then softer and smellier. Hill had to let go of Nonnie while she knelt on all fours and Nurse Bhimjee wiped her bottom.

'Come on, Nonnie, let's get you on to the bed,' ordered Pearl, and Hill helped us to heave her up.

'I'm so sorry, Sister,' she wailed, almost weeping with embarrassment at this unforeseen nuisance, and of course we told her not to worry, it didn't matter; not a word about the enema that would have emptied the rectum and stimulated the contractions. Once on the bed, Nonnie stayed there and delivered lying on her back, as if to confirm the old midwives' saying that the best position for birth is the same as when it went in, nine months earlier.

Having had the obstacles cleared out of his way, baby Peregrine Sands followed easily. Nonnie bled quite briskly for a minute after delivery, and Pearl gave the injection of syntometrine that had not been part of the birth-plan; Nurse Bhimjee got the placenta out by controlled cord traction, and the blood loss was just short of the five hundred millilitres that would have made it a statistical postpartum haemorrhage.

'Phew!' gasped Hill, and excused himself to go to the en suite lavatory, where I suspect he sat and put his head down between his knees.

'All's well that ends well, Nonnie,' I smiled, and at that moment Linda appeared at the door to tell me that Kathleen's membranes had ruptured spontaneously and her contractions were getting stronger.

'She's coming on quite quickly, Shirley. I'll hang around if you need any help, love.'

But there was no need of help with the delivery of the dead baby girl. Not with the mechanics of it, anyway. By twenty minutes past two the child's body was out, and the placenta took another five minutes. Kathleen moaned softly with the expulsive contractions, but seemed barely aware of what was happening. Alex held her hand as her body parted with its burden, and when I'd wiped away the moisture and wrapped the little body in a cot blanket I put her in Madge's arms to let her show the parents. Alex and I propped Kathleen up on pillows, and Madge gave her the baby to hold for a minute, still supporting it from beneath. The new mother gazed blankly down at the still face: the skin was white with faint bluish shadows around the closed eyes and half-open mouth. The features, like the rest of the body, were perfectly formed – a beautiful baby, but without life.

Kathleen looked dazedly at her husband. 'J-Joanna?' she asked like a woman in a dream.

'Yes, my love,' he whispered. 'Our Joanna.'

Madge whispered to me, 'They'd decided on Joanna for a girl,' and covered her face with her hands.

There is no silence like that which accompanies a stillbirth: the whispers seem only to emphasise it. We have some taped music that can be put on, Handel's Largo and slow arrangements for piano and guitar, but I never think it's appropriate – it's too much like that canned music in a crematorium.

I left them alone while I wheeled the trolley out to the sluice to examine the placenta and give the family a few moments of privacy, a time to share their grief while the baby was still with them.

The placenta explained the reason for the

tragedy. There was a large blood-clot on the maternal surface, evidence of an antepartum haemorrhage that had separated the placenta from the uterine wall, cutting off the vital oxygen and food supply. It had happened only recently, associated with the onset of toxaemia. With the pregnancy now over, the condition would immediately subside.

I went back into the delivery room. Guided by her mother, Kathleen kissed the baby and Alex also said his farewell; then I took the little body to weigh, label and prepare for the mortuary. I also took the two routine polaroid photographs, one to give to the parents and one for the case-notes. When Madge and Alex had left, Sandra and I transferred Kathleen to a single room in the Antenatal ward, away from the sound of babies – and although I should then have telephoned for a porter to remove the baby's body, I did not do so, but placed her in a covered cot in the corner of the vacated delivery room, and left the IN USE sign on the door. Midwives get these strange impulses from time to time.

Pearl Amos supervised the other student midwife with the normal delivery of the mother I'd admitted, and by four o'clock we sat down to begin the paperwork, including the stillbirth certificate and the hefty register of births. I put my elbows on the desk and leaned my head on my hands. *Jesus is Lord.*

'Tea and toast for you, my girl, before you do another thing.'

Linda looked anxiously at me as she set down the tray. 'Will you be able to go straight to bed this morning, Shirley?'

I shook my head. 'Philip Crowne's taking me to the Magistrates' Court for ten. I promised Paul I'd be there.'

'Oh, honey-bun, d'you think that's wise? You're on again tonight, and you'll be like a zombie.'

'You've had your share of sleepless marathons this year, kid, and you've survived.' I sipped the tea gratefully. 'There have been times when I've worried about you, God knows. It's great to see you looking better these days – is everything going ahead all right?'

There was the briefest of hesitations. 'It's Charles who's beginning to show signs of strain lately, poor love. He's got an appointment with her consultant psychiatrist at Carrowbridge on Thursday. It's got to be put to her that this is the best way for everybody concerned, but of course it bothers him. He's been so good with her for so long, but now–' She shrugged and shook her head. 'It's got to be faced.'

I ventured a question I'd never been able to ask her before.

'Linda, if she – if Miriam King was ever stable enough to be discharged from Carrowbridge – I mean, she's had these better times at home in the past, hasn't she? What would happen then? Where would she go?'

'Miriam has a twin sister who has given Charles plenty of advice and criticism over the years, and *that's* where Miriam will go if she's ever discharged. The sister's never married and lives alone – she's a senior tutor at a teachers' training college, and a bit of a virago, by all accounts.

She'd get an attendance allowance, but Miriam's so unpredictable, a danger to herself and other people, so let's hope she stays where she is. Her solicitor will squeeze what he can out of Charles under the divorce settlement,' she added bitterly, and I could see she had little sympathy for Charles's wife or his sister-in-law. When I asked if Howard was still suing for custody of the children, she gave a grim little smile.

'I think he's beginning to see reason at last. When I finally let Cathy go to spend a weekend with him, it must have made him realise that he'd never cope with them on his own. It sounded pretty awful, actually – the weather was cold and wet, so they couldn't go out to the park, and although he took her to see that Robin Hood film with Alan Rickman, she didn't sound very thrilled with it, and said "Daddy was so sad". I think she was glad to be back with me and the boys, quite honestly, and serve him damned well right.' She sighed heavily. 'The cost of all this is going to be astronomical, and poor Charles is looking so tired and strained, though he tries to hide it from me. But listen to me, Shirley, when Dilly's lost her son, and that poor girl's lost her baby – oh, *God*, did you ever hear of such trouble?'

The misery of that night was not yet over. At half past five I went to check Kathleen's blood pressure, and she sat up in bed and looked straight at me, her eyes wide and clear.

'Sister, where's my baby? I know she was born, but I was so drugged, I can hardly remember it. I know it wasn't a dream.' She looked down at her abdomen, soft and flabby. 'I held her in my arms, didn't I? Alex held her, too, and my mother – we called her Joanna, and she was warm and – where is she now, Sister?'

How can one woman tell another such grievous news? I sat down on the bed and held her hand. 'Kathleen dear,' I began quietly, 'you remember when you came up to the clinic yesterday, and Mr Horsfield said that your baby's heart had stopped beating, and she was – was not alive any more. You hadn't felt her moving, had you?'

She grasped my hand in both of hers. 'But I *had* her, Sister, she was *born* and I *held* her – she was lying in my arms, and I kissed her – where is she? I want her, Sister, I want to hold her again – what have you done with her? Joanna! Joanna!'

Her voice rose as the memories returned with the realisation of her loss. My impulse had been right. I would not have to go over to the mortuary with a porter and keys to remove the baby's body from the refrigerated cabinet.

'All right, Kathleen dear – you can hold your baby again. Wait while I fetch her now.'

Joanna's body had cooled in three hours, and there was no need for me to say anything as I placed her in her mother's arms. Kathleen gave a low moan, and rocked to and fro, holding the child's body against her breasts as if to warm it; and then the heart-wrenching sobs began.

It has happened before and will happen time and time again, all over the world. A mother loses her baby, and no power on earth can bring the dead to life. The midwife can only stay beside her and share the agony, the lamentation of a woman weeping for the child of her womb, and refusing to be comforted.

It was in that desolate moment that I truly faced the fact of the other woman who mourned for her lost child: Dilly Fisher. My own tears flowed silently with my patient's in her darkest hour. These are the experiences that don't get recorded in case-notes or in letters to the official journal of the Royal College of Midwives, but they stay with us for life, and become part of what we are.

It was nearly half past eight before I was ready to leave the Unit and mount my trusty bike. Home! On went the gas-fire, the radio and the electric kettle, and I opened the fridge to get out the milk and cat-food for Pussage and Peppercorn. And then the kitchen floor suddenly tilted and rose up towards me; Radio 4 was replaced by a buzzing in my ears, and then there was nothing; I had simply passed out on the floor.

I opened my eyes to find myself lying on the cold tiles, a bruise on my forehead and the telephone ringing. Somehow I dragged myself into the living room and picked up the receiver with shaking hands. It was Philip Crowne.

'My dear Shirley, how are you this morning?'

'Ah, Philip, yes. Sorry I only just got in.'

'Heavens, you're late. Was it a very busy night?'

'Er, yes – look, Philip, I won't be able to come with you this morning. I – I'm sorry, but–'

He asked if I was ill, and did I want Celia to come over?

'No, no, I'll be all right when I've had a sleep. I'm just knackered, that's all – exhausted.'

I choked on weak, useless tears, and he was full of concern. 'I'll tell Paul you're not well, but that you're praying for him, my dear—'

'And give him my love,' I croaked. 'And please phone me this evening to tell me how it went – will you?'

As I crawled into bed I thought I heard the telephone ringing again, but sleep mercifully claimed me.

Martin appeared at the door that evening, and insisted on preparing a meal for me, a ham and cheese omelette with a crusty French stick which he put on a tray with a pot of tea for two. Of course he said I shouldn't go into work again that night, and of course I said I must.

'I shan't let you go on slogging at that hospital when we're married, darling.'

I smiled and sipped the tea gratefully. It was nice to be pampered, especially after the bleak experience of fainting alone and unattended. We were just finishing the meal when Crowne telephoned shortly after seven. Martin came with me to the phone and put his arm around me.

'What happened, Philip? How was he?' I asked.

'It was just a formality, Shirley, and he made only a very brief appearance in front of Miss Jarvis – I was glad she was the presiding magistrate this morning.' It took me a moment or two to make the connection: Miss Jarvis had been the headmistress of the Girls' Grammar School when Ruth and Emma were pupils. 'And what did she say?'

'He's been put on remand. He can't be allowed

bail because of the seriousness of the charge, and now the Crown Prosecution Service will have to prepare a file of evidence to use at the trial when it comes up at the Crown Court.'

'When will that be?'

'Not for a few months, probably well into the New Year, February or March, maybe.'

'Oh, *no!* Will he have to spend Christmas there – in prison?'

'No, my dear, not prison. Miss Jarvis recommended that he goes to St Botolph's Remand Centre out in Cheshire, the place that used to be an approved school. It's used for juveniles, and it's less formal, no uniforms – he should be all right there.'

'Will I be able to visit him?'

'Yes, of course you can, but I'd leave it for a day or two. And when his case comes up, you'll probably be given an opportunity to testify on his behalf – about his character and special problems – and so will I. Would you be willing to do that?'

'Yes, of course, if it will do any good. Was anybody else at the court today besides yourself and the police?'

'Yes, his sister and her husband. She was very tearful, and said she didn't know how she was going to break the news to their father who lives with them.'

'I can imagine. He hardly ever mentions her, and I thought it sounded as if she'd washed her hands of him some time ago.'

'Anyway, Shirley, I was able to have a word with him, and explained that you weren't able to come to the court after a very busy night.'

'Did he accept that?'

'Well, you know Paul. He can never understand that we all have other commitments and responsibilities in our lives.'

By which I gathered that Paul had been hurt or resentful, or both, because of my absence.

'Oh, the poor boy! I – I could visit him tomorrow afternoon after a few hours' sleep–'

'My dear Shirley, what absolute nonsense, you'll do nothing of the sort!' This indignant interruption came not from Crowne but from Martin who had been standing beside me and listening, his arm still firmly around my waist.

'Who's that?' asked Crowne in surprise.

'Sorry, Philip, I have a visitor here, a very good friend,' I began, but Martin was really extremely annoyed. He took the receiver from my hand.

'I'll have you know that I'm rather more than a friend, Crowne,' he said firmly. 'I'm the man who's going to marry Mrs Pierce and take proper care of her. Good evening to you.'

He hung up, and at that moment the doorbell rang. 'I'll answer it, Shirley,' he said, and strode off ready to do battle with whoever was about to make further demands on me. I heard Lilian Newhouse's voice, and went out into the hall to see her. She was holding a huge bunch of yellow and bronze chrysanthemums tied up in cellophane with a large bow and those curly little ribbons dangling all over the place.

'Here, Shirley love, I got these for you. I knew how upset you'd be, seeing that you've always been so good to him, like, and him not knowing any better. Brian gave me the money, and said to get the very best. They're from us both. Hey, I'm sorry, love, I didn't mean to make you cry.'

Martin looked on in utter bewilderment as I stood there holding the flowers and weeping.

Chapter Thirteen

End of an Affair

Looking back now upon that miserable winter, the weeks blur together, indistinguishable in greyness, with Christmas and New Year standing out as being especially fraught. I did not let a week go by without a visit to St Botolph's, an hour's journey each way by train and bus, dark by the time I got home. It was something I had to do, and I declined a lift from Brian Newhouse, preferring the relative privacy of public transport; I didn't want to talk about where I was going or whom I was visiting.

The first visit was awkward and strained. Paul and I faced each other across a table, alongside other inmates and their visitors, and under the watchful eyes of supervisors. I wasn't allowed to give him the home-made chocolate cake and other goodies I'd taken and had to bring them back. However, as time went by it began to improve. There were things that couldn't be mentioned, first and foremost the tragedy that had brought Paul there. We didn't talk much about Shalom, either – it didn't seem to have relevance at St

Botolph's, and I didn't attempt to pray with him as the Crownes did when they visited. And yet conversation was no problem: Paul had always been happy to meet new friends, as he put it, and he now had plenty of hair-raising stories to tell about boys like Billy whose mother was in prison for drug-dealing, and Ziggy who was black and had run away from every foster home he'd been sent to. There were enough sad stories to fill a book, and Paul thrived on them; the place had its bullies and baddies, of course, but Paul and his friends were fairly well protected by the strict discipline and segregation of the more vulnerable inmates, and gradually he began to be accepted by these other youngsters whose lives had also been blighted, though for different reasons. They were brothers in adversity.

Martin continued to be in daily touch, and I was warmed by his obvious devotion. We never spoke of St Botolph's because he disapproved of my visits, and I didn't want to upset the dear man, still less to have a row. We went on our usual drives into the wintry countryside, returning to an appetising casserole of beef or lamb that had been simmering slowly in a low oven, either at Wilmot Avenue or Chatsworth Road. I did not go to his bed again, nor invite him to mine; there was a tacit agreement not to repeat that particular experiment until we were into another year and could look ahead to a definite wedding date. We enjoyed our times of cosy domesticity, but I didn't have the same enthusiasm for social occasions like dancing; for me time was suspended while waiting for Paul's trial to come up, and I felt unable to make plans or look forward to better times until that ordeal was over and the outcome known. The weekly visits to the remand centre had a draining effect, and night duty didn't get any easier.

We heard that Dilly Fisher was not to return to work until the new year; Dr Goodson had put her on two months' sick leave. The inquest was held on Mark, and he was cremated at Altrincham after a moving funeral service at Moor End Methodist Church, which was packed to capacity. The headmaster, teachers and classmates were there to represent Marston Comprehensive School, which was closed for the day; similarly the Maternity Unit was headed by Mrs Gresham and a gloomy William Hawke, with as many of the night staff as wished to go. I didn't, because I thought the very sight of me would distress Dilly, and to be honest I shrank from facing her. She did not reply to my sympathy card and letter, though I heard she'd received hundreds, many from people she'd never met. Philip and Celia Crowne were there with Norma Daley and other friends from Shalom.

Outside the church afterwards Linda found herself face to face with Councillor Grierson, who tried to say something about making arrangements for Christmas and spending some time with his children.

'I told him I had nothing to say,' she reported the following night. 'And I said that a child's funeral was hardly the place to talk about matrimonial disputes.'

'Ouch!' I replied. 'You know, Linda, I can't help

noticing how times have changed.'

'How do you mean?'

'Well – Howard caused you a lot of aggro in the past, and we were often upset on your behalf. But now–'

I paused, and she waited for the follow-up. I knew what I wanted to say, and various mixed metaphors came to mind about who had now got the upper hand, and the boot being now on the other leg – but they didn't sound right, so I changed tack and simply asked her how Grierson had looked.

'Not too special, Shirley, in fact I got quite a shock,' she admitted. 'He's lost weight, and that hideous black suit hung on him – it used to be a good fit. And there was a sort of – I don't know, he seemed to have lost his arrogance, or he was hiding it very well. He was like a man who's had the stuffing knocked out of him, somehow.'

I said nothing, because she had said it. So much for Grierson's hopes of a Parliamentary career, plus any ideas he may have had about turning the clock back.

And so to Christmas and the usual wranglings over the duty roster – who was entitled to what time off over the festive season. I was everybody's favourite when I offered to work the nights of December 24th and 25th; I was then off for Boxing night and the following two nights, on for the 29th and 30th, and off for New Year. It was no great sacrifice, really; Linda, Bernie and Pearl had children, and I lived alone with my cats. As always, Ruth and Richard had asked me to go and stay with them, and Emma had parties and all sorts of goings-on in London, so it was decided that I should go to the Butlers' for New Year, and that Emma would join us on New Year's Day for a family get-together. It meant that Martin would be free to go to Laura's for Christmas Day, which seemed only right on this first Christmas after Dora's death. Next year he and I would be married, and I wouldn't even be on the duty roster, because he'd made it quite clear that there would be no need for his wife to work.

'Dora and I both retired at the same time, and we only had two years to enjoy it, Shirley. I want you at home with me, not spending half your nights away!'

Linda hugged me gratefully as she contemplated Christmas at Charles's home.

'He's got the time off, too, Shirley, so we'll all be together, and that includes Jonathan who'll be home on university vacation for Christmas!'

'Have you met him yet?' I enquired.

'No, he spent his summer vacation abroad, but he'll be home for Christmas, and if he wants to bring his girlfriend to share his room, fair enough!' She laughed indulgently. 'I'm determined to show him that his father's life is better – or will be, when everything's sorted. And being off duty means I'll be able to give all my time to making it a real family Christmas for everybody!'

Her happiness, and my own prospect of spending the following Christmas as Mrs Hayes at home with Mr Hayes, made up for being on duty this year, going home to Pussage and Peppercorn

251

to sleep through the jollity going on all around, then getting up and going on duty again.

On Boxing Day I got the offer of a lift from Celia Crowne, who said she was going to St Botolph's with the mother and grandmother of a lad who'd cracked the skull of another boy with a club.

'We can both see Paul,' she said, and so I got up at half past two and was ready when she called with the two women in the back seat. If they thought she was a soft touch, they realised their mistake when she told them she didn't allow smoking in her car, and put on the tape of Songs of Faith and Fellowship for the journey. Philip was spending the day painting and decorating Shalom House, soon to be opened as a refuge for homeless youngsters. Oh, for such faith and certainty, such willing obedience to the teachings of Christ! Let me say it now, in case I forget later on, that the Crownes and others like them are lights shining out in a dark world, and I'm thankful to have known them, even though I'm not and never can be truly one of their number.

Paul had been visited by his sister and her husband on the 23rd, and they'd brought his frail elderly father to see him. There was no visiting on Christmas Day, but there had been a carol service in the chapel and a specially written pantomime put on by a group of students from Liverpool University, apparently well received by the captive audience. Paul, Billy and Ziggy eagerly told us about their part in audience participation, and the roars of laughter that had greeted the carefully censored jokes. In a place where a few extra goodies is a feast and some relaxation of the routine makes for a holiday atmosphere, there is less chance of disappointment, and Celia and I agreed that there were worse ways of spending Christmas for these lads.

I spent that evening with Martin and the Goodsons, who'd invited me to join them. I didn't mention the visit to St Botolph's, and Martin thought I'd been resting all day, though by nine o'clock I felt unutterably tired. Laura had been called out a few times, and got involved in a blazing row with a pharmacist on call who'd refused to dispense some drug or other. It had quite upset her, and Victor had sounded off on the phone to the man, who in turn had accused him of being drunk.

'Damned cheek!' snorted Victor. 'I shall certainly take the matter further, darling, I'm not standing for that.'

Weary and bored out of my mind, I fell asleep on their settee while they rabbited on interminably. Another Christmas was over.

Curious to know how Linda's Christmas with the family had gone, I rang her at work on the night of the 27th. By the tone of her voice I knew at once that there had been problems. And of course it was Jonathan.

'The children enjoyed themselves, Shirley, but that boy was a real pain in the backside. So downright *rude*, you've no idea.'

(Ah, but I had.)

'What about the girlfriend?' I asked. 'Didn't she help at all by being there?'

253

'She didn't turn up, and now he's gone to stay with her and her parents. Good riddance! But of course it's upset Charles, and I feel so sorry for him, poor love.'

'Of course, Jonathan is his son,' I said carefully. 'And I should imagine they've been fairly close, considering all the trouble with Miriam.'

'Oh, and don't I know it! The boy talked about her all the time and, the minute Christmas dinner was over, he whisked Charles off to Carrow-bridge, leaving me for the whole afternoon.'

'But you had the children—'

'Yes, and I suppose I should have been thankful when Charles returned alone. Jonathan had suddenly decided to go straight to the girlfriend's people, without saying goodbye to me or thank you for anything. I thought it was too bad of him – after all, he's not a child, and knows when he's causing trouble.'

I was silent.

'Well, don't you agree, Shirley? You went through the same sort of thing with that step-daughter of yours, didn't you?'

I winced. 'Yes, love, I did, and I wish I'd managed things differently. Anyway, did you have a better time after Jonathan had taken himself off?'

'Yes, I guess so, but Charles is finding it a strain, and I can't help worrying about him. He looks quite dreadful. Anyway, love, I must go – speak to you again soon.'

She rang off, leaving me troubled by the memories that had been stirred yet again, the regrets I could now do nothing about. I'd have to speak very seriously to Linda, I thought, and warn her of the dangers ahead if she did not conquer – or at least conceal – her negative feelings towards Jonathan. As a friend I owed it to her, painful though it would probably be.

But fate stepped in and gave me a different role to play in Linda's domestic drama.

I was walking home from the 9a.m. Mass on the 28th, enjoying the bright, clear morning after a frosty night, when Charles King's car drew up to the pavement and the passenger door opened for me, I smiled and was about to decline his offer of a lift.

But one look at his face told me that something was very wrong. He leaned across and spoke in a low, urgent tone. 'Mrs Pierce – Shirley – have you got a minute or two to spare?'

What could I do? I got in and closed the door, clicking on the seat-belt.

'Better not stop here,' he said. 'I'll drive you home, and we can talk in the car outside.'

Off we went. He asked me where I'd been, and when I said church, he gave a laugh – well, more of a mirthless grunt, really.

'My wife used to go, but I lost any faith I might have had years ago. A born-again atheist, that's me, I'm afraid.'

'Fair enough,' I said, there being no point in arguing, and I'm no Celia Crowne, always seizing opportunities for evangelisation. When we stopped outside 50 Chatsworth Road I turned to him and smiled. 'Come on then, Charles, if there's something you want to say.'

He began to speak, staring straight ahead. 'You've been a good friend to Linda, and I'm

255

glad about that, because you're going to have to stick even closer to her.'

I think I knew then more or less what was coming, and all I could say was, 'Oh, dear'.

'I'm in a terrible situation, Shirley, like a rat in a trap trying to find a way out – but there's only one way that's acceptable, and that's the hardest way.'

I laid a gloved hand lightly on the sleeve of his duffel coat. 'All right, Charles, go on. I've got a feeling you're not going to surprise me. Is it about Miriam?'

'Yes – yes, it's my wife, Miriam. How much do you know about her?'

'Only what Linda has told me. She's been in Carrowbridge for a long time, hasn't she?'

'Yes, the poor girl's had twenty years of mental misery through no fault of her own – so much for her religion – and now at last she's responding to these new anti-depressants they've put her on. For years she was on dothiepin, with chlorpromazine for the manic phases. She's had electroconvulsive therapy and all the psychotherapy going, with varying degrees of temporary effect, but no real basic change. Then in September they started her on these MAOI inhibitors – they've got a hell of a long name, and basically they cancel this enzyme that causes the chemical imbalance. Bloody tricky, too, there's any number of dietary restrictions, and her blood pressure has to be monitored all the time – but her consultant says that these MAOIs have done the trick on quite a few long-stay patients who've been successfully resettled in the community.' He paused, as if searching for the right words.

'And does he think Miriam could be another?' I prompted quietly. 'Well enough to be discharged from Carrowbridge?'

He turned and faced me, his features heavy, his eyes behind the horn-rims staring at mine.

'Yes, that's it. Only he didn't have to tell me, I've seen for myself the change in Miriam. She hasn't been like this for years. It's a miracle.'

What could I say about this ill-timed miracle that should have been a cause for rejoicing? I was silent, and he went on talking as if to himself.

'The shrinks say that she should be able to live a normal life – and Miriam herself says that she's only too happy to cooperate with the medication and diet. Anything to be well again. Poor girl, all those lost years when she couldn't enjoy Jonathan and his growing-up. But he always knew she loved him – oh, *Christ*.'

It's always unbelievers who use Christ's name like that, but when King buried his face in his hands over the steering-wheel, I felt he had some cause to blaspheme. I asked him if he'd like to come into the house for coffee, but he shook his head.

'Thanks, but I should be at the lab by now'

'Charles, what about this twin sister of Miriam's? Linda told me that Miriam would go to her if – if something like this happened.'

'Yeah, that's what I told Linda, but I never thought it would work out if push came to shove. Her sister's all talk, always has been,' he answered without raising his head. 'Besides, Miriam wants to come *home*. She says so. She looked at me and

257

Jonathan on Christmas Day and she said – she said–'

I never did hear what Miriam said to her husband, probably because it was too intimate to repeat: something about how much she loved him and wanted to be his wife again. Poor Miriam. Poor Charles.

And poor Linda, who would now have to get out of his house with her children. A horrid suspicion came to my mind. 'Are you asking me to tell Linda?'

'No, that's my job, and I've had to keep it to myself over Christmas. Linda was entitled to that much after all she's been through, though there were tensions, with Jonathan resenting her in Miriam's place. And I've had to find somewhere for them all to live – it's been the one bit of luck I've had, thanks to a chap at the lab who's going abroad for six months and letting his house in Marston. Linda and the children will be able to go there. And you'll have to be ready to stand by her, Shirley.'

I was amazed to think how he'd kept his secret hidden over Christmas for Linda's sake. No wonder she'd said he looked dreadful.

'Let me know when you're going to tell her, Charles, and I'll be standing by, I promise.'

It cost me dear to keep my word, for Charles telephoned the following day to say that he was off for the New Year, and Linda had three nights off after working New Year's Eve. He said he was going to tell her in the evening of New Year's Day, and could he count on me being available for her?

Of course I said yes, and telephoned Ruth to cancel the New Year visit. I'd been looking forward to this meeting with my daughters, because I so seldom saw both of them together these days. Ruth was quite put out, and said so.

'Helen has talked for days about her Nana Pierce coming to see us, and they've both got presents for you. It really is too bad, Mother, and I find it hard to understand how this midwife's marital troubles can be more important to you than your own family. You've said yourself that you don't see enough of your grandchildren.'

I pleaded to her that I felt just as badly about it, and said I'd visit as soon as possible. She replied that it wouldn't be the same, and she was sorry, but quite frankly she felt let down.

From Emma came another wail when I telephoned her.

'Oh, for God's sake, Mumsie, I was relying on you being there to ease the atmosphere a bit. All that bloody domestic bliss, Ruth going on about the wonder-kids and those God-awful business associates Richard brings home to dinner, and how marvelously she copes – I honestly don't think I can bear it on my own.'

'Oh, Emma, you *must* go – I can't tell you how sorry I am, but it's going to be a much worse New Year for my poor friend Linda, and I've promised that I'll be around for her when – when–'

'Is that the one who left her husband for a mortuary attendant?'

'Pathologist. Yes, Linda Grierson.'

'And her lover's called Mr Rochester?'

'No, Charles King. His wife is–' And I saw the

connection. Trust Emma to joke about it.

'Listen, love, I'll come down to London one Saturday, and treat you to a nice restaurant and a tour of the January sales. How does that sound?'

'Exhausting. And there'll be nothing decent left, anyway.'

It was a big disappointment, but I'd promised to be there for Linda and, as it turned out, I was certainly needed. So was Bernie, who had to come in on it and take the Grierson children to the pantomime matinée at the Palace Theatre with her own on New Year's Day. The extra three seats were in a different part of the theatre, so her husband had to sit with the Grierson twins and Cathy occupied his place with the McCanns, which upset Bernie's children. After the show she returned Simon, Andrew and Cathy to me at Chatsworth Road for tea, while she went home and tried to get a couple of hours' rest before going on duty.

'D'ye think he'll have told her by now?' she asked as we grabbed a quick cup of tea in the kitchen. 'I'm glad he's doin' the right thing by his wife, but God help them all. Are ye goin' to say anythin' to these poor children now, while they're havin' their tea?'

'I'm going to try to prepare them a little, Bernie – let them know that their mum will be feeling sad,' I said glumly.

'God love them, haven't they been shunted from pillar to post this year! If Linda had never given way to the temptation o'–'

'Thanks for all you've done this afternoon, Bernie,' I said quickly as Cathy appeared at the kitchen door. 'Hope you're not too busy tonight. Bye!'

The children tucked into sausages with beans, chips and grilled tomatoes, followed by ice cream and a choice of cakes. I broke the news to them about their coming house move, emphasising that their mum would still be with them, but that Charles would be living with his wife again. The boys heard the news in silence.

'And will Daddy come to live with us?' asked Cathy at once.

'No, dear, but I'm sure you'll be able to visit him.'

Simon muttered to his brother and then asked me, 'Are our parents still going to be divorced?'

'I really don't know about that, Simon. It's something your mum will tell you about.'

'Isn't she going to marry Mr King, then?' asked Cathy.

'No, silly, she's just said that he's going back to his wife,' cut in Andrew, and turning to me, he asked, 'Is she better, then?'

'Yes, Andrew, she's better.'

'Not mad any more?' asked Cathy, her mouth full of chocolate cake.

'That's right, dear, she's going to be happy again.'

But of course Linda wasn't, and I ended up keeping the children with me overnight after a frantic phone call from Charles. Linda had reacted badly to his news, first with sheer disbelief and then with uncontrollable fury, attacking him with hammering fists and screaming that he had

261

betrayed her. He'd restrained her as gently as he could, and waited for the first phase of the storm to pass. Then she had collapsed in a flood of tears and reproaches.

'She's in a terrible state, Shirley, and I'll have to stay with her tonight and hear it all out. If you could manage to keep the kids until tomorrow, I'll be in your debt for ever.'

Poor old Charles. I told the children that mummy was not very well but would be better in the morning. The boys slept in Emma's room, but I hadn't the heart to put Cathy in the other small room on her own; I took her into my bed, where the poor little thing was violently sick. Definitely not the New Year I'd planned.

Two days later I got a letter from Mr Courtney informing me of the date of Paul's trial: it was the first Monday in February, and I would be called upon to give evidence for the defence. I was due for another week's annual leave before the end of March, so asked Mrs Gresham if I could have it that week. Some holiday.

Linda returned to duty after her nights off, and in mid-January she and her children moved into the house that Charles had rented for them from his colleague. Until the move took place he stayed in the flat he'd rented, and the following day he moved back into his home; on the day after that he received Miriam home from Carrowbridge. All divorce proceedings were stopped, and the solicitors were paid off at a simply horrendous cost – for doing bugger-all, as Linda remarked.

She looked pale and she'd lost weight, but her basic strength of character came to her aid, the toughness gained by sixteen years of a difficult marriage and a responsible job. She thanked me for my help with the children over the New Year, and apologised for the disruption of my own plans; but there was a coolness about her, as if she was distanced from her colleagues. She may have felt humiliated in front of us all; she may have resented the fact that Charles had confided in me and enlisted my aid before he told her of his agonising decision; or maybe she just wanted to be left alone to lick her wounds, and we gave her the space to do just that.

The same applied to Dilly Fisher when she returned to part-time night duty in January. She had absolutely nothing to say to me, and Mrs Gresham did her best to avoid putting us both on together. All in all, the atmosphere at work was rather bleak.

And then, as if life was not sad enough, I lost dear old Peppercorn. I'd taken him in when I first moved to Chatsworth Road, because his elderly owner had died. He was then sixteen, an old gentleman resigned to his change of fortune, though he settled well with me and was now nearly twenty, a good age for a cat. There had been times when I'd shed tears into his fur and whispered thoughts that no human ear ever heard. When I'd woken up suddenly in the widowed bed and put out a hand to touch someone no longer there for me, my fingers had found the soft, warm, breathing body of Peppercorn, and he'd made a little chirruping sound of reassurance; he did a good job, and saved me burdening my daughters and friends.

But now it was time for him to go. Since Christmas he had lost weight and slept for most of the time; then his strength completely failed and he was too weak to stand; I spread a plastic sheet and wool blanket on one of the armchairs and laid him on it, stroking him from time to time and offering him drops of water on a spoon. He was not in pain, and I let the end come naturally; I left the gas fire on low all night, and in the morning Peppercorn was dead. At least we were alone, and I didn't have to deal with visits, phone calls, doctor, priest, undertaker and all the intrusions that attend a human death.

I put on my wellies and carried him outside. I got a spade from the shed and dug a hole near to where the Madonna lilies would bloom again in the summer. Pussage sat on the fence near to me and watched: how much did he understand? Cats have such wise faces.

But when it came to putting Peppercorn into the cold ground, I could not do it. I leaned upon the spade and gave way to copious tears that went on and on and would not stop. I had been dry-eyed at Tom's funeral, though Ruth, Emma and Joy had sobbed bitterly. Perhaps I was mourning for Tom again now, and for Paul and Mark and Dilly and all the sorrows of a sad world.

'What's to do, Shirley? What's up? Oh, I see. Yeah.' Brian Newhouse stood on the other side of the fence. He'd come to find out what I was doing in the garden on a cold January morning, and as soon as he saw he came round and took over the job, working quickly and silently. Within a few minutes Peppercorn was buried with dignity.

'You'd better go in and have a cup of tea with a drop of oh-be-joyful in it, Shirley,' said Brian, and produced a half bottle of brandy. I shook my head, but appreciated his unobtrusive kindness.

Later that day Martin called, and said what a blessing it was that I still had the other cat. Which was true, of course, but I missed old Peppercorn. He'd given a certain continuity to a period of transition in my life, and I was grateful.

Chapter Fourteen

On Trial

The day of the trial loomed nearer, became next Monday, then the day after tomorrow, and suddenly it was today, and pouring with rain. I put on my dark wool suit and boots, and carried a mackintosh. When Philip Crowne called for me at half past eight, we sat down in the living room while he said a prayer for Paul, Dilly, their families and all of us who were involved with the coming ordeal.

'Your evidence will probably count more for Paul than anybody else's, Shirley,' he told me. 'A professional woman like yourself, respected in the community, a regular churchgoer – you could make all the difference to the outcome.'

And then we got into his car and drove off to Manchester and the Crown Court. Our bags were searched as we went in and, herded together with other witnesses, many of whom I didn't know from Adam, we were duly instructed in court procedure. Any feelings of awe I may have had gave way in the course of the next two days to frustration and impatience to get on with what we'd come to do. Witnesses for the prosecution were called first, and it was Wednesday before I was summoned. We couldn't leave the building while the court was in session, neither were we allowed to sit in the public gallery until after we'd given our evidence. But at long last my moment came.

'Call Shirley Pierce.'

It was like going into a theatre. I was shown to the witness-stand, a raised, railed platform rather like a pulpit, from which I looked across to the twelve blurred faces of the jury in their snug little box. On the high bench above (the stage) sat the judge in his purple-edged robe and scarlet sash. He looked eighty if he was a day, but that could have been due to his wig and half-moon spectacles. On the floor below (the orchestra pit) was a long table at which sat the woman clerk of the court in a black gown, flanked by two younger women, and a girl who was the audio-typist, recording the proceedings word by word. On each side stood a barrister, begowned and bewigged, the prosecution and defence counsels; I immediately thought of Tweedledum and Tweedledee. At the back of the court was the public gallery (the auditorium), and in the middle was the dock (another stage) where Paul Meadows sat beside a police constable. We exchanged a smile and I gave him a little wave before I was called to order and handed the Bible on which to swear by Almighty God that the evidence I should give would be the truth, the whole truth, and nothing but the truth; an impossibility, as I now realise.

The counsel for the defence, Tweedledee, questioned me first, confirming my name and occupation and that I was a widow living at 50 Chatsworth Road, Marston. He was an oldish man with prominent teeth.

'Mrs Pierce, you describe yourself as a friend of the defendant, Paul Meadows?'

'Yes.'

And the questions and answers continued: where had I met him? How long had I known him?

'And so you befriended this young man, and he became a regular visitor?'

'Yes.' So far, so good.

'And did you feel able to cope with his mental condition?'

'Yes, I did.' I glanced up apologetically at Paul. 'I have a special feeling for him because of the damage he sustained at birth. As a midwife, I have strong views on safety in childbirth.'

'And do you consider that the defendant's mental and emotional problems are due to brain damage at birth?'

'Yes, I'm convinced of it.'

'There are some experts who take a different view, Mrs Pierce, but we will let that pass, as the medical evidence appears inconclusive on this matter.'

He glanced at the judge and prosecuting counsel as if half expecting some comment, but receiving none, he continued with his questions.

'Now, Mrs Pierce, did the defendant ever confide in you about his encounters with some other members of the public? I refer to brawls, fights and general disturbances. Did he tell you about these incidents?'

'Yes, he did. He came to me on several occasions needing first aid treatment for cuts and bruises, the result of persecution by gangs of youths – sometimes schoolchildren – who teased and tormented him.'

'How did they tease and torment him, Mrs Pierce?'

'They followed him in the street, shouting insults and obscenities. Their aim was to provoke him to lose his temper and retaliate, then they'd accuse him of attacking them for no reason. But there always *was* a reason. The mentally afflicted have always been a target for–'

'All right, Mrs Pierce, you've made your point. Now, why do you think Paul Meadows confided in you especially?'

'Because I understood him, and sympathised with his circumstances, as I've already said. We were friends, and he trusted me.'

'And did you advise him when he confided in you?'

'Yes, I always advised him to ignore such behaviour and to avoid confrontations with these ignorant louts. But sometimes it was very difficult for him to do that. His flat is in Boreham Road, near to Marston Comprehensive School.'

'Ah, yes, and we've heard that several incidents took place near to the school gates. I ask you, Mrs Pierce, did Meadows ever name Mark Fisher as one of the children who tormented him?'

I drew a long breath and swallowed. I looked up at the public gallery: Dilly Fisher sat there with her ex-husband.

'Yes, he did.' There was an audible inhalation in court. 'And what was your reaction when he told you this?' 'As usual, I advised him to ignore the boy, but it continued to happen, and in the end I spoke to Mark's mother who works with me at the Maternity Department of Marston General Hospital. I told her that I would complain to the headmaster if it continued.'

'And what was her reply?'

'She denied that her son had ever teased Paul.'

'And did you then complain to the headmaster?'

'No, because after the school summer holidays last year the trouble seemed to ease off, in fact Paul told me that Mark had not teased him again personally, though he suspected the boy of encouraging other children to do so.'

'Objection!' bellowed the counsel for the prosecution, but Tweedledee cut him short by telling me that the defendant's suspicions could not be accepted as evidence.

'Maybe not,' I said sharply, 'but I never knew Paul to lie.'

'Indeed? You always found him truthful, Mrs Pierce?'

'Yes, always.'

'And was his behaviour always good in your experience?'

269

'He had his moods, like the rest of us,' I conceded, 'but considering his circumstances, he behaved all right with me. We shared interests in common – music, plays – and we talked, you know.' It was difficult to find the right words.

'You were fond of him?'

'Haven't I already said so? I wouldn't have had him in the house otherwise.'

'Thank you, Mrs Pierce.' He turned to the judge. 'No further questions, m'lud.'

The judge nodded to the other barrister. 'Your witness.'

Tweedledee sat down and Tweedledum stood up. The prosecuting counsel was a younger man with dark hair beneath his ridiculous wig. His eyes were as cold as stones.

'So, Mrs Pierce, we have heard a very touching story of a kindly widow and a persecuted young man of low mentality,' he said with a supercilious smile. 'Now, I want you to tell the court what really attracted you to Paul Meadows when you met him at this – er – Shalom meeting last April?'

'I've already said that I befriended Paul because he seemed a lonely young man with pleasant manners and an interest in – in Christianity. And music,' I added, aware that I was being got at, and unsure of my ground.

'You say he was lonely. I note that you are a widow, living alone, Mrs Pierce. Would it be true to say that you too were lonely?'

I saw Paul regarding me intently, and I looked straight at my interrogator. 'No, I have a large circle of friends and colleagues. But it's true that I enjoyed Paul's company.'

270

'But this man is mentally below par, Mrs Pierce. We have heard a psychologist's report that puts his mental age at about twelve years.'

'I'd take issue with that,' I said coldly. 'Paul's appreciation of Italian classical music, for instance, is far ahead of mine, never mind a twelve-year-old child's.'

'Really? So you two used to sit listening enraptured to Monteverdi, Mrs Pierce?'

A minute ripple of amusement passed over the court, and I flushed angrily.

'And Vivaldi and Albinoni, yes,' I retorted.

'And what other activities did you indulge in?'

I took a deep breath to calm myself, aware that he was needling me to make me lose my cool and discredit my evidence.

'We watched television,' I began warily, and that's when Paul first shouted from the dock.

'Tell him how we watched Shakespeare, Shirley! Tell him how you gave Rosalind's speech from *As You Like It!*'

There was a gasp, and the police constable leapt from his seat, grabbing Paul's shoulder and warning him to be quiet.

'The defendant will keep silent in court,' pronounced the ancient judge, looking up from his scribbling pad. 'And I don't think we need to hear any more about his shared interests with this witness. Proceed with your next question, if you have one.'

'Thank you, m'lud.' The barrister turned to me with an actor's gesture, his black gown ballooning around him.

'Mrs Pierce, we have heard from other

witnesses about Meadows' frequent outbursts of temper, and a tendency to attack physically anybody he feels is making fun of him. Didn't you ever consider that you were taking a risk in entertaining a potentially violent man in your home – and alone?'

'No, never. He never attacked anybody who treated him in a civilised manner.'

'Oh, come now, Mrs Pierce, you must have been warned of the possibility that he might attack you as he had attacked others?'

I shrugged. 'A couple of people mentioned it.'

'And can you name those people?'

I didn't want to bring Martin's name in. 'Mr Crowne and – and Mrs Dilys Fisher. She's a colleague of mine, as I've said.'

Tweedledum smoothed down the two long white bands of his collar. 'Really, Mrs Pierce? You were actually warned by the poor woman whose schoolboy son was murdered by Meadows?' He looked significantly round the court and then at the jury before coming back to me. 'I put it to you, Mrs Pierce, that you experienced a certain sensation of power, a *frisson* of danger in the company of this retarded but not unattractive young man. What would you say to that suggestion, Mrs Pierce?'

'Objection, m'lud,' said Tweedledee. 'The question is irrelevant to the case. The witness is not on trial.'

'Objection sustained. Delete the question from the records,' ordered the judge.

Sustained maybe, and not recorded, but it had been said and heard, and I had no chance to reply. Looking back now with dreadful hindsight, that could have been the moment when some alert reporter in the public gallery first pricked up his ears.

Tweedledum was getting ready to come in for the kill. He pulled his gown around his shoulders, holding the edges in front with his thumbs sticking up in a typical lawyer's stance. He lowered his voice and assumed an expression of extreme gravity.

'So let me ask you, Mrs Pierce, how do you feel *now*, after the death of Mrs Fisher's only son at the hands of your – er – friend? *How* do you view the loss of this young life, a boy who has been described by his headmaster and other teachers as a very promising pupil?'

I drew another long breath, and remembered that I was on oath to speak the truth to the best of my ability.

'I am of course very sorry for Dilly – for Mrs Fisher and her family. But I still maintain that Paul was provoked beyond endurance.'

'Even though several children have stated that Mark was not involved in the incident that led to his murder by Meadows?'

'No – er, yes, I mean that Paul said he, I mean Mark, was standing near to the group of children who were taunting him, Paul, I mean – and egging them on.' My voice shook and my hands trembled as I spoke.

Tweedledum glanced up at the judge and then at the defence counsel before giving a dismissive shake of his head. 'I'm afraid that cannot be accepted as evidence, Mrs Pierce. Now, I have

273

just one more question to ask you, and it is this: was the defendant arrested at your home on October 31st last year?'

'Yes, he was.'

'And what did you say to the two police officers when they arrived at your home that evening, Mrs Pierce?'

'I – I was very shocked, and I said first of all that he wasn't there – was not in the house. But he called out from inside, and the officers came in and arrested him.'

'I see, Mrs Pierce. Thank you, that will be all.'

I stepped down, my heart pounding. I was trembling in every muscle, and felt that I had not served Paul well. I had conveyed nothing of his sensitivity, his appreciation of beauty and his capacity for friendship towards anybody who accepted him as a fellow human being and not some sort of sub-species.

Watching the rest of the day's proceedings from the gallery, I heard Philip Crowne testify about Paul's personality. He was asked if he had warned me to be careful.

'Mrs Pierce has been a good friend to Paul, sir, and genuinely did not realise the risk she was taking, I'm sure.'

'Not even after your own warning, Mr Crowne? Wouldn't you agree that was foolish, to say the least?'

'I'm here to give evidence about the defendant,' retorted Philip, never one to be awed by worldly traditions and trappings. 'He never attacked Mrs Pierce, and I have no reason to doubt her evidence. Or to try to discredit it,' he added with that extraordinary blend of humility and authority for which he was known.

He joined me in the gallery after stepping down, and I was glad of his presence. My head ached, and there was a strange tension in the atmosphere, odd whisperings and rustlings.

By the end of the afternoon all the evidence had been presented, all witnesses examined and cross-examined by the two barristers. There remained only the judge's summing-up and the jury's out-of-court deliberations before they brought in their verdict.

All this was postponed until the following day, and heaven only knew what it was costing the taxpayer. Was there really need for all this pomp and ceremony to decide on a retarded man's guilt or innocence, and then on what to do with him?

There seemed to be more bystanders than usual outside the court building as Philip and I left. Hurrying down the steps at the entrance, I heard my name called, and looking up I stared straight into the lens of a camera.

'Keep going, Shirley,' murmured Crowne. 'They're getting some pictures ready for the write-up in the *Manchester Evening News* tomorrow. This trial's going to attract a lot of publicity, but that needn't worry us. Just so long as they find him not technically guilty.'

When the court assembled the following morning the public gallery was packed to capacity. Sitting beside Philip and waiting for the summing-up to begin, I stared at the back of Paul's head and wondered about his future. They wouldn't send somebody like him to prison, would they? Would he end up in a secure psychiatric unit like Rampton? I thought he would be dreading the sentence, but I was wrong; he wasn't concerned with his future at all, but with his disillusionment in me, a steadily mounting resentment ever since I'd taken the witness stand and betrayed our friendship, as he saw it.

There was total silence when the judge began assessing the evidence received, much of it from witnesses who had testified about the character and lifestyle of the defendant.

'Here we have an unfortunate young man who, but for a tragic accident at birth, might have led a very different life. Witnesses of good standing have come forward to speak on his behalf, and we heard from a midwife who pleaded eloquently for a man she calls her friend, though he stands charged with a horrifying crime.'

That was as far as he got. There was a strangled shout and a scuffle in the dock: Paul's voice rang out across the court.

'Shirley! You didn't tell them how you loved me – how we loved each other on your settee, lots of times, and I held you in my arms and we had or-i-al sex! You never told them *that*, Shirley, you never–'

How long did it take him to utter those few words? How many seconds? I had scarcely registered what he'd said when two more police officers dashed to the aid of the one who was struggling with his charge, and it needed all their combined strength to overpower Paul, who fought with unbelievable ferocity. A howl of pain rose from one of the men who received a violent kick in the groin, and all hell broke loose in the court. The old judge banged his gavel on the bench while the woman clerk yelled for order, but the pandemonium continued until Paul had been handcuffed and dragged down to the cell below, still shouting his reproaches at me until he disappeared from sight and sound. Then the murmurings began in the public gallery.

'*What* was that?' – 'Did you hear what he said?' – 'Did he say *oral sex?*' – 'Some relationship!' – 'Watch it, she's there behind you' – Who?' – 'You know, the midwife!' – '*Wow!*'

It was going on all around us, and Philip Crowne stared at me in disbelief.

'Clear the court! Clear the court!' The clerk was standing up and brandishing papers while ushers ran to and fro. The door of the public gallery flew open, and we were all ordered to leave at once. I clung to Crowne's arm as we were pushed and shoved towards the exit, and all at once I saw Dilly Fisher's white face close to mine.

'So much for all your talk, Shirley Pierce,' she said in a low, tremulous tone, worse than any shout. 'May God forgive you.'

Bob Simmons was grinning, Mr Courtney raised his eyebrows, others simply gaped. A couple of reporters dashed past with their new mobile phones, just coming into use, and a whole posse of photographers was waiting outside.

Crowne shielded me with his arm as we hurried to his car, and until we were clear of the city traffic he drove in grim-faced silence; perhaps he was praying for the right words. As we reached

277

Marston he began to speak with grave urgency.

'This is going to be a testing time for you, Shirley, and my advice is to lay low. Don't say anything to anybody, don't give any interviews and be especially careful on the phone. You'll have to put your trust in the Lord's mercy, because only He knows the secrets of all hearts, and He alone can truly be the Judge. Ask for Him to–'

'Philip, it wasn't true what he said,' I interrupted, desperately pleading to be believed. 'I – we – never did anything like that. Just – there was only – kissing – that's all we ever–'

My words petered out against Crowne's incredulous silence. After all, I had testified that Paul Meadows never told a lie.

Outside 50 Chatsworth Road Crowne sighed and shook his head.

'Oh, Shirley, Shirley – what a silly woman you have been!'

Chapter Fifteen

Disgraced and Disowned

Once indoors I made a mug of tea, swallowed a couple of aspirins and went to lie down on the bed, drawing the curtains against the dull winter noon; but I could neither sleep nor read nor pray. The image of the courtroom remained fixed in my mind's eye, leaving no space for anything else. When the telephone rang, every nerve jangled.

'Hallo?'

'Philip Crowne here, Shirley. I thought you'd like to know that the trial's over.'

'Yes?' I waited in dread.

'Yes, my dear, it was completed in closed session, and the jury were out for less than half an hour.'

'And what did–?' I stood there holding my breath.

'It's more or less what I thought it would be. They brought in a verdict of manslaughter, on the grounds of his diminished responsibility and extenuating circumstances.'

'Manslaughter?'

'Yes, that means accidental killing, not murder. It won't bring the boy back to life again, but – are you still there, Shirley?'

'Yes, Philip, I'm sorry, I'm listening.'

'Paul is to be sent for two years to the secure wing at Carrowbridge, and then to be reviewed.'

'Carrowbridge?'

'Yes, it's separate from the main Psychiatric Unit, and it's good news, Shirley. He could have gone to Rampton, which would be much harsher.'

'Carrowbridge,' I repeated stupidly, thinking that Miriam King had just come out of the place.

'My dear Shirley, the Lord's ways are mysterious. It was probably that outburst from Paul today that convinced the jury, if they needed convincing, that he can't be considered a criminal, but neither can he be judged as normal. Anyway, that's the outcome, and I understand that it will be on *North West Tonight* after the six o'clock news. Now, Shirley, are you all right?'

'Yes, Philip, I'm fine,' I croaked. 'And thanks for letting me know.'

'Bless you. Above all put your trust in the Lord, my dear. Jesus is Lord, in this as in everything.'

Of course it was good news, but for the time being I was numbed by the day's events. When I could think clearly again, I would be thankful.

North West Tonight covered a city council rumpus and a hit-and-run driver who had killed a child; then against the exterior of the Crown Court a woman newsreader announced that Paul Meadows, an unemployed man of thirty-two, had been found guilty of the manslaughter of fourteen-year-old schoolboy Mark Fisher, and was to be confined in a mental health unit under secure conditions.

'There was a disruption in the court during the judge's summing-up, when the defendant became severely disturbed and shouted accusations at a woman witness in the public gallery,' she went on. 'He was quickly overpowered by police officers, and removed from the dock. The court was cleared and the hearing concluded in closed session.'

A school photograph of Mark was shown, and then a still picture of members of the public leaving the court. It included myself in sharply prominent focus, together with Crowne. And that was all.

I leaned back in the armchair and closed my eyes. I hadn't been named, and the trial was over. Was that the end of it?

Almost at once the telephone calls began, starting with the *Manchester Evening News*.

'Mrs Pierce?' asked a man's voice. 'Good evening, Mrs Pierce. Would it be convenient to send a reporter to interview you for our report on the Paul Meadows case in the *News* tomorrow?'

'No, no interviews,' I said quickly.

'But this is in your own interest, Mrs Pierce, a chance to put your own point of view in what could be a–'

'Sorry, but no. I have nothing to say.'

'We'd send a woman reporter, Mrs Pierce. We're sympathetic, you understand, and–'

'*No.*' I hung up, and almost at once it rang again. 'Mrs Pierce? Shirley Pierce?' asked another male voice, and this time it was from the Manchester offices of a national daily newspaper with the same request. I gave the same answer, but hateful suspicions began to surface, like bubbles on a fermenting brew. Those rustlings and mutterings in the public gallery following my cross-examination must have meant that somebody had sniffed out a salacious element in the tragedy, and made preparations to be ready for any developments. And Paul had supplied it in good measure: *oral sex*.

I shuddered. Why had he said that, or rather shouted it from the dock? Where had he ever heard or read about it? In St Botolph's? In some pornographic magazine? He couldn't even pronounce it, and had given it three syllables, or-i-al. He'd also said that we'd loved each other, and that he'd held me in his arms. We'd embraced, certainly, many a time, at Shalom meetings and at my home. We had sat with arms entwined on the sofa – he'd called it the settee –

and he had buried his face against the dress material covering my breasts, and had sighed with pleasure.

And we had kissed each other's lips, that evening of *As You Like It*. It had been a moment of special closeness that I had deliberately allowed him, his mouth upon mine. *Oral contact*.

I gasped, for there, surely, must be the explanation. In Paul's limited experience, *that* was oral sex; he could have no knowledge of the further explorations made by the sexually adventurous, which would be as unknown to him as to my parents' generation. (Though how could I be sure of that? What after all did I know about other people and what they got up to behind closed doors?)

I began to understand that for Paul the sweetness of our kiss that night had sealed the love between a man and a woman; but my words from the witness stand had reduced it to mere pity on my part. I had cut him to the heart, wounding him more deeply than anything else said at the trial.

And he had hit back. The three struggling policemen had caught the blows and kicks, but the flying words had found their mark and struck me down.

The phone rang again, and I refused to speak to another national daily; when a notorious Sunday newspaper came on, I took the receiver off the hook.

Then the doorbell rang, and I cried out, 'Who is it?' When Martin answered, I opened the door and practically threw myself into his arms.

'Oh, Martin, Martin, thank God you're here!'

He held me close and soothed me, though of course he was mystified.

'What is it, darling? What's the matter?'

'Did you see the news, Martin? And *North West Tonight?*'

'Only the headlines on the radio at six o'clock – why, was there something about this wretched trial? Has he been sentenced? I hope so.'

'Two years at Carrowbridge – the security wing.'

'Thank heaven for that, and let's hope he stays there. But why are you so upset, Shirley dear? Is it because you gave evidence against him?'

'No, Martin, *for* him,' I groaned. 'But he turned on me in the court today, in the middle of the judge's summing-up, and he accused me – oh, Martin, it was a nightmare.'

I clung to him and sobbed in his arms, willing him to make me feel safe.

'Oh, you poor little darling! But didn't I tell you over and over again not to have anything more to do with him? You just wouldn't listen, and you'll never know how much I worried about you having him round here when you were alone. I didn't even like you visiting that remand centre week after week, as I'm sure you realised.'

'I know, Martin, I know. I've been a silly woman, but I meant it for the best,' I said despairingly.

'All right, all right, Shirley dear, he won't trouble you any more now, though I'd be happier if he was in Rampton. Don't cry, darling, it's over and done with now. Sssh, ssh,' he whispered, stroking my hair, kissing my forehead. 'All over now, darling.'

I wanted to believe him, to let him convince me that we could now look forward to a shared future in which I would be happy to heed his wishes and be safe in his care. That night I went to bed in a more hopeful mood, taking a mogadon tablet to ensure sleep; it didn't protect me from the lurking terror that comes in the strange disguises of nightmare. I wandered barefoot along the main corridor of Maternity, looking for my shoes; I held a baby to my breast, and found that it had grown into a man; Pussage sat watching me, wearing spectacles and a lawyer's wig. I awoke with a cry, and reached for the bedside lamp: it was just after six. I reached for my prayer-book, but could not focus on the readings for the day, so took refuge in reciting the words of set prayers, *Our Father* and *Hail Mary*, reassuring in their familiarity, and I walked to church for the weekday Mass at nine. Exchanging smiles and good-mornings with the little group of mainly elderly worshippers made me feel blessedly normal, and the brisk walk gave me a good appetite for porridge, a boiled egg, toast and coffee.

The condemned woman ate a hearty breakfast.

Afterwards I set out on the bicycle with my shopping-bag in the basket; it was cold but the sky was clear, and spring seemed not too far away. In three weeks' time we would be into March, and the daffodils would be shooting up.

My first stop was the supermarket, and it was there in the magazine section that I first saw the newspapers. At least it wasn't in Prickett's

284

Newsagents, where Cyril and Sandra knew me.

It took me a while to understand the bold, black headings. The letters jumbled into each other, and only gradually unscrambled themselves to spell out messages that burned on my retina. I stood there in front of them, wanting to turn away but mesmerised to the spot, unable to move. Not every paper featured the Paul Meadows case on the front page, but two tabloids had banner headlines. One said:

SECRET LIFE OF RESPECTED MIDWIFE?
Dramatic Accusation from Dock

Below this was a photograph of me leaving the court and looking straight at the camera, with Philip Crowne behind me. There was a school photograph of Mark Fisher, and a blurred picture of Paul Meadows taken from some group photograph and blown up.

The other tabloid divided its front page between the latest Princess Diana story and the Meadows trial:

SHOCK REVELATIONS IN COURT

There was the same picture of me, and the beginning of the story beneath it. I leaned forward to read it, and one short paragraph stood out as if highlighted.

'...and alleged that he had had an intimate relationship with her, including oral sex. At this point he was overpowered by court officials and...' Here the reader was asked to turn to page 2, column 1.

Somehow I got myself out of the supermarket and cycled home without buying anything. I had to hide my face from the world that would read those newspapers today. Those headlines would be seen everywhere, in London, in Birmingham, in Shrewsbury and every town and village in the United Kingdom. My name would be a byword, a joke in pubs and clubs, an object of scorn and contempt. I wanted to dig a hole and bury myself, never to face family and friends again. When I thought of my parents I groaned aloud, but my mind reeled away altogether from the image of my daughters, and what their reactions would be. I decided to write to them both straight away, explaining how this had come about, and begging their forgiveness for the pain and embarrassment I'd caused them through my stupidity.

And that was how I spent most of that black Friday, sitting beside the gas fire with Pussage on the rug. I composed a draft of a letter in pencil, and then wrote it out in carefully chosen words to each daughter; by mid-afternoon the letters were in envelopes, but I had no stamps and was faced with getting them to the post office.

When the phone rang I thought it would be Martin, but it was Father O'Flynn.

'Well now, Shirley, how are ye?' His Irish brogue was overlaid with half a lifetime of Lancashire. 'I've seen in the paper about this business in the law court, and I guessed ye might be feelin' a bit down.'

'You could say that, Father,' I replied miserably, though his tone warmed me; it was the first ray of light in the dark.

'Is anybody with ye, Shirley? Would ye like me to come over and have a little chat, now?'

'I don't really want to see anybody, Father.'

'Ah, well now, shuttin' yeself away won't do any good, y'see. Put the kettle on, and I'll be over in about ten minutes.'

I saw a diffcrent side to my parish priest that day; he arrived all smiles and with a story about one of our older parishioners.

'Did ye hear about poor Eddie Taggart, Shirley? He had a big win on the horses, a real jackpot it was, and didn't he tell Bridie he'd buy her whatever she wanted – and all she asked was to go on Father Halloran's pilgrimage to Fatima in May. And isn't Eddie terrified o' flyin'! Bridie's over the moon, but poor old Eddie's tremblin' in his shoes – and he won't see a bar the whole time because they're stayin' at a dry hotel – old Father Halloran frowns somethin' terrible on the drink!'

His chuckles eased the tension a little, and I even managed a sympathetic smile for Eddie.

'Come on, Shirley, we've seen a few nine day wonders in our time, and seen 'em forgotten when the next one came along.' He sat comfortably in the armchair, sipping his tea. 'Now, if ye want to talk about it, I'm listenin', and if ye want to make your confession, I'll hear it. Or not, as ye please. Y'see, Shirley, ye won't be able to tell me anythin' I haven't heard before.'

I heard myself responding sadly to his kindness. 'Father, I've done so many worse things in my life. I wasn't a good wife, and I was a rotten stepmother. But I only intended good to Paul

Meadows, and look at all the damage I've done.'

'Ah, Shirley, isn't it always the way? Many a time we get off scot-free after the really bad sins o' the heart that only God knows about – but it's the foolish things done with the best of intentions that get us hanged.'

'And this is a public execution,' I said bitterly. 'Paul Meadows was tried in a court of law before a judge and jury, but I'm condemned without a trial.'

'But the Lord hasn't left ye to bear it all on your own, Shirley. Now, then, what I want ye to do is come to church as usual and take the Sacrament, just as ye did this mornin', right? Don't stay away at the time ye need it most. Take advantage of it, and give thanks to God.'

I promised that I'd come to Mass on Sunday as usual.

'Good girl. Now, bow your head for the Lord's blessin'.'

He said the time-honoured words, and I made the sign of the Cross with him. On the doorstep he shook my hand warmly, assured me of his prayers and asked me to remember him in mine. At that moment Lilian Newhouse appeared with a bottle wrapped in red tissue paper.

'Looks promisin',' remarked Father O'Flynn as he left.

'Hi, Shirley love, we thought this might help keep your spirits up. We don't believe a word of that rubbish in the papers, Brian and me.' She thrust the bottle at me, revealing the label of a good quality French brandy.

'Oh, Lilian, you're too good–'

'No, it's you who's been too good to that daft bugger – all you did for him, and this is how he pays you back!' she said indignantly, though I wondered what Brian really thought. 'D'you want anything from the shops, love?'

'Oh, Lilian, will you post these letters for me? I want them to go today by first-class mail.'

'Sure thing. No, don't be daft, I don't want any money.'

As soon as she'd left, the doorbell rang again, and it still wasn't Martin, but how welcome was the face of my friend Linda Grierson! She came straight in and gave me a bear-hug.

'Shirley dear – oh, Shirley, you poor old love. I just had to come over to see you.'

She had brought a pot-plant, a flowering azalea full of pink and white blooms.

'We're just so sorry. Shirley. The – er – papers arrived on the ward this morning before we went off duty, and the patients were – anyway, people who know you judge you on how you treat them, not on what they might read in the gutter press. Oh, before I forget, Bernie sent you this.'

It was a little plastic piety card, with a picture of Christ on the Cross and his Mother and the apostle John at the foot. It was to remain in my pocket for weeks to come, a reminder of the warmth of a friend's love.

'It'll be a nine day wonder, Shirley,' said Linda, echoing Father O'Flynn. 'It'll blow over in time, and you can weather the storm. If I can survive, so can you.'

'I was certainly worried about you,' I told her. 'How are you getting on in this other house?

289

Have the children settled in?'

'Yes, it's nice and handy for their schools. Quite cosy without being too cramped for the four of us. You'll have to come and see us.'

Not the five of us any more. She hugged me again. 'God knows what I would have done without you, Shirley, and I'm sorry I've been a bit off lately, especially after all you did for me at the New Year. It must have messed up all your own plans, and I never thanked you properly. I'm sorry, love, I really am.'

'So was I – for you, I mean. And for Charles. He must have had an awful Christmas, poor devil, knowing what he was going to have to tell you. I've never seen a man so torn.'

'Yeah, poor old Charles. And she's really better, I believe – people have seen them out together and didn't recognise her, she's so much changed for the better. Whoever would have thought it?' She stopped suddenly, and I saw the pain in her eyes.

I shook my head and put on a broad accent. 'Ee, lass, it's been a reet to-do fur thee and me, a'n't it?'

'Kid, it's been a bugger up the backside, and no mistake.'

'Oh, *Linda!*' And of course we both grinned at this coarse summing-up of our misfortunes. She brought me such relief and comfort. There were no reproofs, no reservations, and mercifully no advice: just the solidarity of friendship.

'Shirley, I can't stay, I'm on again tonight – but I'll be in touch.'

'Give my love to them all,' I said tremulously.

'Say I'm surviving.'

After she'd gone I realised that she hadn't once asked about the truth of the reports. Her visit, following on Father O'Flynn and Lilian, built up my courage before the next onslaught of body-blows. And they came thick and fast.

I still hadn't heard from Martin, and was wondering whether to call him when the phone rang. It was my brother Edward, calling from his home in Kent. He came straight to the point.

'What the hell is this all about, Shirley? I simply couldn't believe my eyes when I saw the paper this morning. What's going on?'

I told him as well as I could. We didn't write very often, and he'd never heard Paul Meadows' name. I'd told him about my unofficial engagement to Martin Hayes when we'd exchanged Christmas cards.

'It sounds as if you've been incredibly indiscreet, to say the least, and you might have thought a bit more about your family. I'm not letting on to anybody round here that you're my sister, for the sake of the kids – the grand-children.'

'It's a good thing you live so far away, and have a different name,' I said, chilled by his severity.

'What does your fiancé think about it?'

'Martin? Oh, he's been wonderful, very kind and understanding,' I said, thinking of last night when we had talked of our future.

'Hm. Well, I'm afraid they're not so happy at Shrewsbury. I had a call from Dad today, he phoned me at work, and says that Mum's in a pretty bad state over it.'

'Oh, my God! Edward, how *awful,*' I wailed, stricken by remorse. 'I'll ring them straight away.'

'No, don't – not yet. Give the poor old souls a chance to calm down a bit first. Dad's heart isn't too good, and Mum's probably more worried over him than anything. It's one hell of a shock at their age.'

'But Edward, I'll *have* to tell them there's no truth at all in what's in the papers.'

'So you may say, Shirley, but there must be *some* grounds for that chap saying what he did. And you went out of your way to say that he never told a lie. Talk about hoist with your own petard – unfortunate, to say the least.'

'Yes, but–' I floundered, desperately trying to think of a way to convince my brother, but he was genuinely shocked. And unbelieving.

'The trouble with you, Shirley, is that you think we were all born yesterday.'

'That's not true, Edward, I *don't* think that. Please believe me, I'm terribly sorry about everything. I've been a silly woman, I know that, but I never did what he said, but – oh, Edward–' I choked on my own words.

'Well, well, there's no point in crying over spilt milk now,' he said with a slight lessening of condemnation in his voice. 'Knowing you, I'm inclined to believe you're probably the victim of your own foolishness, but don't expect other people to be as sympathetic as I am.'

There was a pause while I sniffed back tears and he cleared his throat. 'Look, I'll put in a good word for you with Mum and Dad, but give them time to get over the first shock before you contact them, right?'

I swallowed. 'Thank you, Edward. I do appreciate that.'

'Yes, well, all right, then. Take care of yourself, because you're in for a rough ride, especially with Ruth and Emma, I'd guess. I'll be in touch, then.'

'Goodbye, Edward. Give my love to Sylvia.'

'Will do. It hasn't been very pleasant for her, either. Bye.'

When he rang off I realised how cold I felt, especially my hands and feet, in spite of the warmth of the room. I'd eaten nothing since breakfast, and felt both empty and nauseated at the same time. I was about to make tea and add a drop of Lilian's oh-be-joyful to warm me, but on my way to the kitchen the telephone rang again. Martin? I picked up the receiver.

'Shirley? Hallo! Olive Gresham here.'

'Pardon?'

'Mrs Gresham, Shirley. Don't say you've forgotten who I am!'

'Oh, Mrs Gresham, of course, yes. I'm sorry, there's been so many things to – er–'

'I'm sure it's a very difficult time for you, Shirley, and that's why I feel I should come to see you. We need to have a chat about a few things. Would some time this weekend be all right?'

'That's very good of you, Mrs Gresham. Any time, really. I'll be here.'

'Good. So what about tomorrow afternoon at about two? Would that be all right for you, a Saturday afternoon?'

'Yes, er – yes, I should think so. It's good of you, Mrs Gresham,' I said again, grateful to her for calling me and being nice. I didn't like putting the phone down to be left alone with the thoughts of my parents and my brother.

And my daughters. My beloved Emma. I must speak to her, I must hear her voice. As soon as Mrs Gresham had rung off I made a mug of tea and added a good slug of brandy. I took it to the telephone and sat down to dial the number of Emma's flat.

A girl's voice answered, not Emma. 'Hallo.'

'Hallo,' I repeated, trying to sound bright and businesslike. 'Is Emma there?'

'Who's speaking, please?'

I hesitated. *Suppose she didn't want to speak to me.* 'T-tell her it's Rosemary Stark,' I said, naming a girl Emma had known at school, then waited for what seemed an age while the receiver shook in my hand and I took a gulp of the fortified tea.

Then 'Hallo'. And this time it was my daughter. 'Emma dear—'

'That's not Rosie Stark! Is it you, Mother?'

'Yes, Emma, it's your Mum. Listen to me, please, dear, I have to ex—'

'I'm sorry, but I can't speak to you. I don't want to hear anything.'

'Emma, please listen to me—'

'No, I won't! I *can't!*' I realised to my horror that she was crying. 'I couldn't believe it, I just *couldn't!* How do you think I can face my friends knowing *that?* It's a nightmare – oh!'

I heard her sobbing while the other girl murmured in the background.

I was crying, too. 'Emma – oh, my little Emma.'

'Don't you little Emma me!' she retorted with the heartless indignation of the young. 'Danilo says he suspected it all along, and we actually had a *row* about it – and he was right all the time – how do you think that makes me feel?'

And that was all. The telephone crashed down at the other end, leaving me standing there holding the receiver and whimpering. Not crying, but making little moans and whinges like a wounded animal. Animals don't cry, and this pain was beyond tears.

There had still been no word from Martin, and at last, having reasonably composed myself, I decided to take the plunge and dial his number. When there was no reply, I thought he was probably at Laura's, and I wasn't going to call him there. I disconnected the phone, had a hot bath and took two mogadon tablets with a large brandy – the label on the chemists' bottle warns against taking alcohol – and went to bed, where I must have virtually passed out. At least I had a few hours of oblivion.

Saturday dawned, bringing headache and a numbness of my faculties that was preferable to the raw pain of conscious thought. I took two aspirins with a mug of tea, and decided to stay where I was. There seemed to be no point in getting up if I wasn't going out, and Mrs Gresham wasn't calling till the afternoon, so I left the curtains drawn and buried my head under the duvet.

But sleep refused to be recalled. Pussage was walking all over me, mewing for his breakfast, and it seemed sensible to try to eat something myself.

A glance in the mirror gave me no joy; I went downstairs, switched on the gas fire and Radio 4, and put two slices of bread in the toaster.

Plop-plop-plop: the impact of mail on the doormat reminded me that both Emma and Ruth would be receiving their letters about now. Would they pay any attention to my pleas? Would Emma be moved to mercy? It would be a very long time before I'd dare to dial her number again, but I felt I had to ring Ruth, if only to find out the worst. No doubt she too would be shocked and upset, but she had the consolation of her family, and none of her friends need know that the Mrs Pierce in the papers was her mother. Yes, I'd have to phone her when I'd plucked up enough courage.

Pulling my dressing-gown around me, I went to pick up the mail. Under the circulars and charity appeals was a letter with a first-class stamp, post-marked Manchester; I did not recognise the firm black handwriting. I opened it, and the type-written letter inside was brief and to the point: no room for any kind of misunderstanding here.

To Mrs S. Pierce.

I have to inform you that there is to be no further contact between yourself and my father-in-law, Mr Martin Hayes, who has suffered a severe emotional shock and possible heart seizure. He is currently under the care of my wife Dr Goodson at our home.

As Mr Hayes' condition is a direct result of recent press reports concerning yourself, I have to inform you further that any attempt by you to contact him, either verbally or in writing or through a third party, will result in legal action being taken against you.

Victor M. Goodson

It would have been funny if it had not been one more indication of my descent to the rock-bottom of disgrace and notoriety. After the agony of Emma's rebuke I hardly cared about a prat like Goodson, though I wondered how much Martin knew about this. Had it been sent with his knowledge and consent? I tried to tell myself that he would have stood up for me, but after rereading it twice, the implications were all too clear; the message came over with absolute clarity

Our engagement was off. The Goodsons clearly believed me guilty of carrying on a sexual relationship with a mentally subnormal man, and initiating him into all kinds of disgusting practices. To them I must be the equivalent of a child-molester, and they wanted Martin to have nothing more to do with such a pervert.

And he was carrying out their wishes. It was all over.

I went to the kitchen to plug in the kettle and make yet more tea. I sat down while it boiled, staring at the wall and trying to take in the new situation. My whole future would have to be readjusted. There would be no wedding, no move to Wilmot Avenue. I would remain a widow living here at 50 Chatsworth Road and working nights at the Maternity Department of Marston General for another dozen years, until I was sixty, maybe even longer.

It was ten o'clock; time for me to take the bull by the horns and call Ruth. I got Richard.

'Yes?' He sounded terse.

'Richard – good morning. It's Shirley here.'

'I was afraid it might be. Have you the slightest idea of the trouble you've caused?'

Oh, no. Was I to be totally rejected here as well?

'Please, Richard, believe me, I'm suffering, too.'

'Maybe you are, but in your case it's self-inflicted. Had you no thought at all for *us* when you took up with that deranged man?'

'Please tell me, how is Ruth?'

'Quite frankly I'm surprised you've got the nerve to ask about Ruth, after what you've done. If you really want to know, she's in bed, and I've had to get the doctor out to her.'

'Oh, *no!*'

'Oh, *yes*. I've hardly slept because she's cried half the night, and of course the children are thoroughly unsettled, thanks to–'

'Will you please tell her I called, Richard, and say I'm very, very sorry about all this. I love her–'

'Oh, come off it, that sounds just like the kind of hypocrisy that's always put me off your so-called religion. Anyway. I haven't time to stand here and–'

This time it was I who hung up. If I couldn't speak to my daughter there was no point in listening to the verbal posturings of my son-in-law. And I hadn't even asked if my letter had arrived. As with Emma, time would be needed for Ruth to calm down and either forgive me or not. Meanwhile I had to leave both of them alone.

It must have been after this particular kick in

the stomach that I began to discover a small up-surge of courage against the forces arrayed against me. I washed, dressed, lunched on scrambled eggs and put on a good face for Mrs Gresham when she rang the doorbell on the dot of two.

'Hallo, Shirley, how are you?' I felt her eyes upon me as I opened the door to her.

'It's very nice to see you, Mrs Gresham.' She came in and put her black handbag down beside the armchair I offered her.

'Thank you. Let me start by saying how sorry I am – how sorry we all are about this whole business.'

'I'm sorry, too, Mrs Gresham. I had no idea there'd be this kind of publicity, and the story in the papers is quite untrue, you know.'

She leaned towards me, and I saw the genuine concern in her brown eyes. 'Yes, well, that's the reason I'm here, Shirley. I wanted to see you and tell you before you get the official letter on Monday.'

Every muscle in my body seemed to stiffen at hearing these words, and I knew what I should have guessed earlier. 'Official letter, Mrs Gresham? Do you mean I'm being sacked?'

'No, not dismissed from the Marston Health Authority, just suspended from duty while the management examines your contract.'

'I see.' I felt my face flame. 'It's Hawke, isn't it? He's got me over a barrel, hasn't he? It's just the excuse he wanted – isn't that right, Mrs Gresham?'

She shifted in the armchair. 'No, Shirley, this isn't just Mr Hawke, and it isn't just the Health

Authority. This will have to be looked into by the United Kingdom Central Council for Nurses and Midwives, that's the body which deals with serious disciplinary procedures – and the Royal College of Midwives will have a say as well, as you're a member. Meanwhile you'll be suspended on full pay.'

'But I haven't been guilty of any professional misconduct, Mrs Gresham!' I protested, raising my voice. 'Have there been any complaints about my midwifery practice? Has any mother or baby been harmed by my negligence?'

'No, Shirley, of course not, but you've been involved in this awful trial–'

'*I* wasn't on trial, I was a witness, more's the pity. The allegations made about me by Paul Meadows were completely untrue. I've already been through hell over this publicity, and so have my daughters and parents, just because I've been a silly woman. But don't accuse me of misconduct or negligence, because–'

'I'm not accusing you, Shirley!' she said, also raising her voice. 'But there has to be an inquiry after something like this, surely you must see that. And the fact is, my dear, you haven't helped matters by having such a – a belligerent attitude towards authority. You've put people's backs up, and you were warned that it would count against you in the event of any trouble.'

'Mrs Gresham, this isn't fair, and I'll fight it. I'll–'

She looked at me regretfully, and didn't need to say anything. We both knew that in my present circumstances, I couldn't fight my way out of a paper bag.

'Listen, Shirley, you'll get a fair hearing, I promise. I'll represent you myself at the UKCC inquiry, and you'll get a good testimonial from the authority.'

'Not from Hawke, I won't.'

'Maybe not, because you've gone out of your way to antagonise him. Anyway, Shirley, I've said what I came to say, which was to prepare you for this letter. I couldn't just let it explode like a bomb through your door.'

'And I've had a few of those lately, Mrs Gresham.'

'Yes, I should imagine so.' She sighed and picked up her handbag. 'But you're a survivor, Shirley, and I believe you'll come through it. Your colleagues seem to be rock-solidly behind you.'

'Except for poor Dilly Fisher.'

'Yes, poor Mrs Fisher, she's the one to be pitied the most, and never let us forget that, Shirley. It's the worst thing that can happen to any woman, to lose a child. Even so, you can hardly be held responsible for what happened to her son.'

There was no reply to that, and I simply thanked her again. 'It was good of you to come and tell me yourself, Mrs Gresham, especially on your weekend off.'

'I couldn't do otherwise, could I? She smiled as she shook my hand. 'It won't be easy to find a replacement for you on nights.'

'Nobody's indispensable,' I remarked drily, thinking that she'd probably been reminded of that already by the management. I could picture William Hawke rubbing his hands together in satisfaction at my downfall.

As I let the midwifery supervisor out of the front door, I saw June Tippett going past the house pushing the pram with Mandy and the toddler trotting along on each side. She looked towards me with a widening of her eyes that held more of curiosity than compassion. What did she and all the other mothers I'd looked after make of this nine day wonder surrounding Sister Pierce?

And what did Martin really think about me? And what did *I* feel about him? How much of a blow was it that I had lost the man who was to have become my second husband later in the year? Facing the fact of his rejection, I found that compared to the searing pain of my daughters' shock and anger, Martin counted for very little. Indeed, I now discovered a certain liberation in the ending of an engagement to a man I had never truly loved.

Somewhere deep down in my troubled psyche there was a tiny exhalation of relief.

Chapter Sixteen

Reconciliation

'That you, Shirley? Dad here. Sorry we haven't rung before, but Edward said we'd best leave it till the dust had settled a bit.'

'Oh, *Dad*, I'm just so glad to hear you, you

don't know! How's Mum? Is she feeling any better yet?'

'She's not too bad, but we've both been worried about you, stands to reason, and this evening I says to her, "Never mind what Edward says, I'm going to ring our Shirley". So how's it going with you, then?'

'I'm all right, Dad, there's no need to worry about me.' I forced myself to speak steadily, without any tearful faltering. 'The worst part of this is the trouble I've caused to – to my family, you and Mum and the girls and Edward. That's what I'm sorriest about.'

'I came through Dunkirk and the Normandy landings, don't forget, girl. Takes more'n a load o' garbage in a newspaper to throw me off course. But are you really all right, Shirley? I was afraid you might've lost your job.'

'Well, I still might have, Dad. I'm to be suspended on full pay for the time being. We'll just have to wait and see.'

'H'm, that doesn't sound so good. But all this court business is nothing to do with your work, is it?'

'Nothing whatever. And if you and Mum were wondering about what he – what was said in court, well, it wasn't true, Dad. I mean it just wasn't true what he said.'

'We didn't think it was, Shirley. You were just a – a–'

'A silly woman, Dad.'

He gave a non-committal grunt. 'Well, never mind, as long as you're all right. When will you know about your job?'

'I honestly don't know. There's got to be an inquiry. It could go on for weeks.'

'Uh-huh. Have you spoken to the girls?'

'Yes. Not good, I'm afraid, Dad. They're very upset.' I heard the break in my voice, and coughed.

'Yeah, well, they're young, aren't they? They'll come round.'

'I hope so.'

'D'you want to speak to your mother?'

'If she wants to, yes, I'd love to have a word with her.'

My mother's subdued little voice came on the line, giving me another twist of the knife. I could picture her face, creased with anxiety and bewilderment at something so alien to her experience.

'And what about your nice Mr Hayes – Martin – is he standing by you, Shirley?'

'No, Mum, that's all over.'

'Oh, dear. That's a pity.'

'It doesn't matter. I'm much more concerned for you and Dad.'

There was a pause, and I heard her take a breath. 'Would it be a help if you were to come and stay with us for a bit, Shirley? Get away from all the gossip and – everything?

I closed my eyes as I replied. 'That's very, very good of you, Mum, and I'm grateful, but no, I have to stay here and take each day as it comes. I'm fine, honestly. I – I'm going to church tomorrow, and my friends are wonderful. Look, Mum, I'll have to go now, but thank you so much. God bless you both.'

I rang off just before my voice gave out. Edward and I had underestimated the stamina of our parents: the old can be so much more resilient than the young.

On Sunday morning I kept my promise to Father O'Flynn and went to the eleven o'clock Mass, keeping my eyes down as I walked up the aisle and took my usual place three rows from the front. I knelt down to give thanks for being there.

After taking the Sacrament I returned to my place and knelt again. As always during Communion the choir sang a hymn, and the words from Isaiah floated across the church.

Do not be afraid, for I have redeemed you;
I have called you by your name: you are Mine.

When you walk through the waters I'll be with
  you;
You will never sink beneath the waves.
Do not be afraid...

When the fire is burning all around you,
You will never be consumed by the flames.
Do not be afraid...

I had heard and sung these words many times before, but now they came to me with a new conviction; these ancient assurances are only truly understood when they are most needed. Father O'Flynn had been right to advise me to take what was on offer.

On my way out a hand was laid on my arm, and

I turned to see old Mrs Rogers looking me full in the face.

'You were so good to my son and daughter-in-law the night they lost their baby,' she said. 'I was thankful that you were there to look after them.'

Of course. This old lady was the other grand-mother of little stillborn Joanna. I took her hand and pressed it. 'Thank you very much, Mrs Rogers,' was all I could say.

Others were passing us, shaking hands with Father O'Flynn on their way out of church.

'Morning, Mrs Pierce' – 'Hallo, Shirley!' – 'Hi!' – 'Nice to see you, Mrs Pierce'.

I had to make a hurried exit to hide my tears, but they were grateful tears, springing from a deep thankfulness for all the blessings I'd received that morning.

Monday's post brought the 'suspension from em-ployment forthwith,' duly signed by W. Hawke; being forewarned was a help, saving me another nasty jolt. There were also *Thinking of You* cards from Pearl Amos and Sue Weldon (hers included Jim Digweed), and some of the day staff, which I put in the front window. But there was nothing from London. Or Birmingham.

Going to church had been the first step: now I had to go shopping. Cycling around Marston shopping centre, I encountered a few blank stares, raised eyebrows and the usual smiles and hallos from familiar faces. It was in the super-market that I was pulled up short on overhearing a woman pointing me out to her companion.

'You'd wonder how she's got the nerve to show her face, wouldn't you?'

My heart began to thump, and my hands gripped the supermarket trolley. I lowered my head as I passed a knot of shoppers, and was tempted to make a quick exit, abandoning the trolley in the aisle. But I summoned up my courage, raised my head, finished the shopping and stood at the check-out where the girl cashier's mechanical 'Thank you, goodbye!' was a positive comfort. It was a hurdle cleared, and nerved me for the next stop which was the chemist's. Here I got a cheery greeting from the enormous lady clutching her podgy baby and taking up most of the room at the counter.

'Hallo, Sister Pierce!'

I stared back at her. 'Marjorie Maybury, what a nice surprise! And hasn't that lovely boy of yours *grown!*' Baby Gordon Maybury was now six months old and dribbling with his first tooth. His mother smiled fondly.

'Yes, my Ken's that proud of him, Sister – took him into work last week to show them in the office,' she said. 'Yes, he *did*, didn't he, my little treasure!'

'Bub-bub-bub-bub-bub!' answered Gordon with a wet smile.

'I tell everybody how wonderful you were the night he was born,' beamed Marjorie, turning to the white-overalled girl assistant. 'Nothing was too much trouble for them, they even got the operating theatre ready in case I needed a Caesarean!'

'Did they really?' The assistant was impressed.

'Oh, yes, they don't take any chances at Marston General, we had marvellous treatment – didn't we, my little pet? You're Daddy's little wonder-boy, that's what you are!'

Dear Marjorie Maybury, so absorbed with her darling son that she had probably not even heard about the trial and the scandal that now raged around me. May I be forgiven for ever joking about her size and baby Gordon's triumph over technology.

When I got home the telephone was ringing.

'Shirley, is this true?' demanded Linda.

'Is what true?'

'That you've been suspended from duty.'

''Fraid so, love. Mrs Gresham came over on Saturday afternoon to warn me.'

'Bloody hell! They can't do this!'

'They can and they have, Linda. There's to be a disciplinary hearing by the UKCC as well as the Marston Health Authority. Mrs Gresham says she's fairly hopeful for me.'

'You're not going to take this lying down, are you, Shirley?'

'Linda dear, I'm down already, so I'm not really in a position to argue.'

I heard her muttering under her breath, and then she said, 'Maybe *you're* not, Shirley Pierce, but there are those with other ideas.'

'What do you mean?'

'You just wait and see,' she said grimly, and rang off.

Later that day I was called by the *Manchester*

Evening News.

'Good afternoon, Sister Pierce,' said a polite female voice. 'We're reporting on your suspension by the Marston Health Authority, and we'd like to know if you have anything to say about it.'

'Only that I haven't been accused of anything to do with my work,' I replied, wondering who'd told them.

'Thank you. May I ask what is your opinion of the Health Authority?'

'No, I have no comment. Nothing else to say.'

Nevertheless I bought Tuesday's paper as soon as it was on sale. There was a small headline on the front page, MIDWIFE SUSPENDED, and 'see page 5'.

I opened it, and there on page 5 was the now familiar photograph taken outside the Crown Court, and under a heading, SHE GOES, WE ALL GO, was the report. My mouth fell open as I read.

Midwives on night duty at Marston General Hospital are up in arms over the suspension of Sister Shirley Pierce, following allegations made about her by recently convicted Paul Meadows, now serving a two-year sentence for manslaughter.

Mr William Hawke, Departmental Manager for Obstetrics and Gynaecology at the hospital, said that the suspension was a regrettable necessity after the detrimental publicity surrounding Mrs Pierce's association with the Meadows trial. 'We have to put the interests of the patients first,' he told the *News*. 'Women booked to have their babies here might well take exception to her presence at such a critical time in their lives. Naturally we are all extremely sorry about the step we have had to take.'

Then came the real bombshell, the bit that took my breath away.

However, it appears that her colleagues have rallied to the defence of Sister Pierce, and an ultimatum has been handed in to the Marston Health Authority by five members of the night staff who have threatened to resign their posts as from Saturday of this week if Sister Pierce has not been reinstated by then.

Sister Linda Grierson told the *News* that the suspension was 'grossly unfair,' and Dr Lance Penrose, obstetric registrar, said that to remove Sister Pierce from her highly responsible post would be 'crazy'. Mrs Pierce herself declined to comment apart from reaffirming that she had not committed any professional misdemeanour.

It was true: Sisters Grierson, McCann and Amos, staff midwife Weldon and nursing auxiliary Sandra Nunn had put their careers on the line for me, which was terrifying. Suppose their gamble didn't come off?

My telephone began to ring at all hours, and one of the callers was Howard Grierson, of all people, with a somewhat mystifying message.

'I'd like to express my support for your reinstatement, Sister Pierce. We on the council feel that the hospital management has acted high-handedly, and I've had a word with Councillor Crowne about adding out protest to that of the midwives.'

I didn't know quite how to react to this, from a man who on our last stormy encounter had called me a home wrecker.

'Why, thank you, Mr Grierson.'

'Yes, well, I wanted to let you know that we're behind you, Sister Pierce. Phil Crowne agrees with me that, er – you did as you thought best at the time.'

Curiouser and curiouser. What exactly was he getting at?

'I appreciate your support, Mr Grierson.'

'Ah, yes, well – I appreciate what you did for my children, Sister Pierce. My little girl told me all about your kindness over the New Year.'

'Mrs McCann and I only did what any friend of Linda's would have done.'

'Er – maybe so, but the way I look at it, Sister Pierce, is that one good turn deserves another.'

Had the man been drinking, I wondered.

A council-of-war was held at 50 Chatsworth Road on Wednesday evening, before my colleagues went on duty.

'Mrs Gresham will take midwives from day duty to replace you,' I warned them.

'No, she won't,' replied Linda at once. 'The day staff have flatly refused to cover.'

'Then she'll take on agency staff.'

'Come off it, Shirley, you know very well that agency staff couldn't take over and run a Unit like ours. And don't underestimate Mrs Gresham. Hawke may think he's got her in his pocket, but that's where he's mistaken. She's on our side, playing him along.'

'Sure and she's good at it,' added Bernie. 'She doesn't come right out and oppose him, she just sits there watchin' him headin' for a brick wall. At speed.'

We giggled, though I was far from happy about the risk they were taking.

'Have you heard about Madge's petition?' Pearl asked me.

'You mean Madge the ward clerk?'

'Yes, she's inviting ex-patients to come in and sign a petition for your reinstatement.'

'Is she? Oh, bless her!' I cried. 'It's hardly three months since she lost her little granddaughter.' The memory of that sorrowful night flooded back to me, and I shook my head. 'Though I can't see a lot of mums turning out to sign, can you? Especially in this miserable weather.'

'And half o' them live out at Cockshott, any-way,' added Bernie. 'Never mind, it's a lovely gesture on Madge's part, and ye never know, she might get more'n we think.'

'If she gets a few hundred, it'll be something to show to the inquiry,' said Sue Weldon with a kind look, though I was full of fear that my colleagues might lose their jobs just because of me. I wasn't worth it, a woman held in contempt by people like the Goodsons, my brother Edward and – but the thought of my daughters was too painful to dwell on.

And then something totally unforeseen happened, which put a new perspective on everything. Even thoughts of Ruth and Emma were temporarily displaced when I answered the door on Thursday afternoon and saw the woman standing there, pale-faced, though her nose was reddened by the cold; she regarded me warily with eyes that were even more like Tom's now that she had reached middle age.

'Hallo, Shirley,' she said.

'*Joy.*'

For she was Tom's eldest daughter, last seen at his funeral just four years ago, and the very last person I expected to see now.

'I read about that trial in the papers last week, and wondered if you still wanted to meet again,' she said, coming straight to the point.

So after ignoring my overture of nearly six months ago, she had now come to gloat over my misfortune. Fair enough. I opened the door to her.

'Come in.'

'Thank you.' She followed me into the living room, putting down a canvas overnight bag and handing me a bunch of daffodils in bud. 'I bought these outside Manchester Piccadilly Station. Thought they looked cheerful on a day like this. Or will do, when they come out.'

'Thank you. I'll put them in water,' I said mechanically. 'Give me your coat, and take a seat. I expect you'd like a cup of tea.'

'Yes, please, that would be nice.' She sat down in the same armchair that Mrs Gresham had used, and warmed her hands at the gas fire while

I went out to the kitchen, my head whirling with contradictory thoughts. I had so much wanted to contact her last summer, and she had refused. Now that I was in trouble, she had reappeared. What was her game? And how should I react?'

She looked up when I carried in the tea tray. 'How are Ruth and Emma?'

'Ruth's happily married with two children, and lives near Birmingham. Emma works for a publishing house in London.' I poured out two cups and handed her one. 'How are Jade and the boys?'

'Jade's married with two children, Alistair's in his first year at University, and Leigh's unemployed and living with a girl who's got a young child. Not his. Thanks.' She took the cup, waving away the sugar bowl.

We were like two cats circling around each other, sizing each other up. There had to be a good reason why she had decided to turn up now, of all times.

'How far have you come today, Joy?'

'From Farnborough, in Hampshire. I live there.'

'Quite a distance, then.'

'Bus to the station, train to Waterloo, tube to Euston, Inter-City to Manchester Piccadilly, suburban line to Marston.'

My God, I thought, what a journey. She must have really wanted to see me. While she drank her tea I took in the details of her appearance. She was thinner, with a network of lines around her eyes and mouth, and her hair was greyer than mine. How old would she be? Forty-four, yet she looked nearer fifty.

'So, Joy,' I said at last. 'You and Andrew are on your own now, then?'

'No, there's only me. Andrew left last July. We're getting divorced.'

'*What?*' I stared in disbelief, and she nodded.

'Oh, Joy, I didn't know – I'm sorry, I had no idea. After all that time,' I floundered, unable to find the right words.

'Twenty-four years,' she said flatly. 'And it all counts for nothing with him now that he's found the real love of his life. She's a singer.'

'I just can't take it in,' I said helplessly.

'Neither could I, but it's true. According to him, our marriage was a mistake from the start. I trapped him into it by getting myself pregnant, if you remember.' She gave a mirthless imitation of a laugh.

'Oh, Joy.' How inappropriate the word sounded. 'That's terribly unfair of Andrew. If anybody was to blame for you becoming pregnant – apart from *him*, I mean – it was *me*. All that upset at the time, and you being turned out of your home – oh, *God*.'

I found myself pacing up and down the room, clasping and unclasping my hands.

'Joy, this is such a shock. I'd always thought that yours was a happy marriage, even if it *did* have that bad start – and that was *my* fault. Your life was turned upside-down, and all because I was pregnant by your father and he had to marry me. And I turned you out of your home, that's why the same thing happened to you, and then you made a bad marriage.'

She was clearly surprised by the effect of her news, and slowly shook her head.

'No, Shirley, that's not altogether true. We *were* happy, Andrew and I, and our marriage wasn't bad. He always had a bit of a roving eye, but I knew I came first with him, that is until last year, when–'

But I needed to exorcise the past, to confess to the bitter remorse that had haunted me for so long.

'No, Joy, you've come all this way, and you must hear me out. Your father always blamed me for making him choose between us, and if I hadn't been expecting Ruth, he might well have chosen you. He never forgave me for it, and that's why I found it so hard to forgive *you*. And now it's all too late – oh, poor Tom!'

There was a long silence, though the words continued to hang in the air like a vapour; like the shadow that had hung over my marriage, and all because of my unforgiving attitude towards his daughter. The confession had been made, and now it was her turn to speak.

'It would have meant a lot to Daddy if we could have been friends,' she said at last. 'But it wasn't all your fault, Shirley, we were both young and immature. I resented you for taking my mother's place, and you resented me for being there between you and Daddy, turning a young wife into a stepmother.'

I nodded miserably. Resentment was a mild word for what I'd felt towards this woman. It had poisoned the air. She drew a deep breath, and went on talking.

'It's a funny thing, but when I got your message through Jo Greene I almost panicked, you know. I was in the first shock of Andrew leaving me, and I didn't want you to know about it. It was pride, I suppose, I couldn't bear you to know that my marriage had failed, and I asked Jo not to tell you or anybody in Marston. Then last week when I read about that awful trial and realised it was you, my first reaction was to say, "Serve her right!" – but then I couldn't get it out of my mind, and I thought about your note last year and, well, I felt that perhaps now was the time to look you up again, now that we're both older and wiser.'

I simply did not know what to say, and came out with the question, 'You say this – this other woman's a singer?'

'Yes. Andrew's in the local operatic society, that's where he met her. They'd been seeing each other for two years, it turned out, and were waiting until Alistair went to University, so that all the kids would have left home when the marriage broke up, and they wouldn't be too upset by it, so he said. Never mind about *me* being upset, and all on my own!'

'So how have they taken it?' I asked gently.

Her mouth hardened a little. 'They haven't been particularly comforting, actually. Jade has stayed in touch with Andrew, but she always was her daddy's girl. I wouldn't mind, only the new lady-love goes with him on his visits to Jade and her husband, and they take the children out together – she's taking my place with my own grandchildren, and that's something I find hard to cope with.'

'Good God, so would I! And what about the boys?'

317

'They say they don't want to take sides, which is fair enough, though I know Leigh touches his father for money, which is such a great mistake. That boy needs a firm hand, and all he's getting is a thoroughly bad example. Alistair's having a great time at University, and has made a whole new circle of friends. Oh, Shirley, I've never felt so alone – so lost.'

What could I do but put my arm around her and try to give what comfort I could; I told her about Linda Grierson, another woman with three children, though younger than Joy's, and also feeling lost at the collapse of her hopes of a future with Charles King.

'She should go back to her husband, give him another chance, make a new start,' Joy said emphatically. 'If only *I* could!'

'Come on, I'll make another cup of tea and put a drop of oh-be-joyful in it!' I laughed, but she turned round to face me squarely.

'Here we both are, Shirley, a quarter of a century on from our first meeting, and we've both known trouble. There's no point in being enemies now, is there?'

Enemies. For that is what we had been. I swallowed, knowing that a great deal hung upon my next move.

'How long are you staying in Marston?' I asked.

'Till about the weekend. I might as well look up some old friends while I'm here.'

'Where are you staying?'

'I've booked a room at the Irving Arms.'

'Stay here, Joy.'

'*Here?* With you, Shirley? Are you sure?'

'Yes. You're Tom's daughter, just as much as Ruth and Emma, and long before they were born. Tom would have loved to think of you staying with me. And I want you to.'

That was the moment when we held out our arms to each other, and I can't ever describe the relief contained in that embrace, and the inner peace that washed over me. Our tears flowed and mingled in a healing stream that carried away the hurt and pain of years. Even the trial and its damaging aftermath, the estrangement from my daughters, was less important, at that moment, than this merciful deliverance from the past.

'Oh, Joy, forgive me for all those years when we should have been friends, and Tom could have been happy with both of us – though it's too late for that now, too late,' I mourned.

'But we shall be friends *now*, Shirley, it's not too late for us. Don't let's look back.'

And friends we were, and are, and shall remain. A burden was lifted, a shadow fled away for ever. My stepdaughter had returned, miraculously changed into a friend to console me for the rift with my own daughters. Philip Crowne would say it was God's timing.

We talked endlessly for the rest of that day, and she heard all about the situation with Ruth and Emma. 'I've shamed them, and they're badly hurt, they've lost all respect for me,' I told her sorrowfully. 'They can't bear to speak to me, not even on the phone. It could be permanent, I don't know – it's absolute agony, Joy.'

She held my hand and gave sensible comfort. 'Ah, that's young people for you, Shirley. Give

319

them time to get over the shock of discovering that you're human, and they'll come round.'

I asked her if she would stay over the weekend and give me support on Saturday, when my colleagues would find out if their ultimatum had worked, whether Hawke and the management would cave in to the night staff or call their bluff and accept their resignations. If the latter, then my duty was clear: for the sake of women in need of a midwife I'd have to hand in my own resignation and order the others to withdraw theirs. I told all this to Joy, and she promised to stay to see it through with me.

Saturday arrived, and Linda telephoned in the morning, sounding excited.

'Shirley, can you be here for two o'clock?'

'Where? Oh, Linda, not the hospital, I don't think I could face it, love.'

'Come on, Shirley, pull your socks up! You'll find a *lot* of friends here, I promise.'

'Linda, if your jobs are threatened, I shall res–'

'Look, put your uniform on, smarten up, and get yourself over here for two o'clock, OK?'

I had no choice. After all my friends had done on my behalf, I had to be there to hear the outcome. Joy said she'd accompany me, which was just as well, because I was literally shaking as we approached the hospital gates and turned towards the Maternity Unit.

And what I saw took my breath away.

There at the entrance was an enormous crowd of mothers and babies, toddlers and older children. They thronged the ambulance bay, and began to cheer as I walked towards them on Joy's arm. Madge the ward clerk was jumping up and down, waving a great bundle of sheets of paper.

'*Three thousand signatures*, Sister Pierce!' she shouted.

And so there were, names from years back, and a separate stack from Cockshott, where a couple of enterprising mums had taken the petition from house to house and from pub to pub; heaven only knew who some of those signatories were. Linda, Bernie, Pearl, Sue and Sandra were there with good support from other staff from night and day duty; and the reporters from the *Manchester Evening News* found themselves shoulder to shoulder with both BBC and Granada TV cameras ready to record the scene for regional news slots.

And there to hand in the petition was Councillor Howard Grierson.

'It should be Madge, of course, she's done all the slogging, but we thought Hawke might just ignore her,' hissed Linda in my ear.

'Did *you* ask him to come here?' I asked incredulously.

'No, the artful devil says he's here to represent the Marston Metropolitan Borough Council, and it's due to him that the TV cameras are here; so we mustn't look a gift horse in the mouth, even though he'll take all the glory for our hard work. Never mind, here's Mrs Gresham to receive the petition. Smile, everybody, and cheer – you'll be on TV tonight!'

I bestowed a radiant smile on Mr Hawke who was lurking unhappily behind the Supervisor as she accepted the wodge of paper from Grierson and made her short rehearsed speech.

'And I am very happy indeed to announce the reinstatement of Sister Pierce as from Sunday night–' She had to pause for the outbreak of loud cheering and clapping that followed this statement, and Grierson hastily shoved himself between Linda and me, a hefty arm flung round each as the cameras moved in. His motive for supporting me was now evident, though judging by Linda's face, he was in for a long haul yet.

'You'll get an OBE for this, Councillor Grierson,' she muttered out of the corner of her mouth, and his eyes lit up in happy surprise until she explained, 'Other Buggers' Efforts'.

And then it was hugs and handshakes all round as I walked among the mothers who'd supported me, especially those from Cockshott, the ones I'd been inclined to dismiss all too often in the past. Can any good thing come out of Nazareth? asked the cynical Nathanael, and I had asked the same about Cockshott, and like him had got my answer. I was humbled by these underprivileged women who had not condemned me out of hand as some others had done, but had come to my aid. Perhaps they'd felt they should support me when I turned out to be no better than they were: I was their sister in more ways than one.

And as for my colleagues, what congratulations were exchanged, what loving thanks! They were on the crest of a wave, having successfully defied the Marston Health Authority in their loyalty to one unlucky member. I was proud to introduce my stepdaughter to them – much to their surprise, because of course they knew my history. Linda shook Joy's hand warmly.

'This is a great day for Shirley!' she enthused. 'Mr Hawke – that's him skulking over there – says the night staff are a law unto themselves, and he's quite right, because we *are*. All for one, and one for all!'

Chapter Seventeen

Older and Wiser

Yes, it's easy to be wise with hindsight, and looking back now from a distance of ten – no, it's eleven years now since it all happened – I can see a kind of inevitability about those events which touched so many lives. I'm wiser now – well, I should be, I'm approaching retirement, and in another ten years I'll be old. The fires of life have died down or, as cynics might say, the oestrogen levels have dropped, which makes life simpler, and you can call that wisdom if you like. Older and wiser.

The one who suffered the most, of course, was Dilly Fisher. The fact that Mark wasn't a very nice boy is neither here nor there; he was her son, the child of her womb, and she loved him. His death was an irreplaceable loss, though her daughter's marriage four years ago has brought her two little grandsons, Michael and Matthew; I'm sure she gets more pleasure from being a grandmother than she had when struggling with two selfish teenagers.

Mind you, that's not Dilly's only consolation nowadays, for she has remarried. Yes! When Martin Hayes recovered from the shock of the Paul Meadows trial, he began to attend Moor End Methodist church, and the next thing we heard was that he was giving Dilly a lift to and from the Sunday morning service; then he began to stay to Sunday lunch. It's funny to think that it was I who drew them together in a common disavowal of all that I stood for, the fact that they had both been deceived in me; but as their attachment grew, my image faded, and they discovered a new fulfilment in each other. It's not so surprising, is it? They were both lonely, he needed gentle female companionship, while she had long dreamed of being looked after and cherished instead of wearing herself out on night duty. Now she stays at home and spends her days and nights making a grateful husband happy, and he looks on Michael and Matthew as his own grandchildren, just as much as Laura and Victor's family. Which has led to a degree of coolness on the Goodson's side, or so I've heard.

Linda did not at once respond to Howard's eager expectation that she would return to him. She stayed in the house that Charles King had rented for her and the children for the full six months, and then quietly moved back into the matrimonial home. Howard said it was the children that brought them back together, but there was also the fact that time was up, and the owner needed his house. So Charles's marriage to Miriam was saved, and so was Linda's to Howard, though things are very different in the Grierson household these days; Linda went back on her own terms and, after all he'd been through, Howard was more than willing to abide by them. The boys have grown up and left home, Simon's engaged and Andrew has a live-in girlfriend; Cathy's at the Metro University, as they now call the old Technical College, and Linda applied for and got the post of Senior Clinical Midwife on the Delivery Unit, so she's not on nights any more. It gives her more time for a social life, and she's become secretary of the Marston Local History Society, attending the lectures and outings that she helps to organise.

On the odd occasions that I bump into Charles King, he usually gives me a smile, but he has a burdened look, a look such as you see on the faces of parents who have to cope with a handicapped child year after year. They say he's as surly as ever at the Path Lab, especially when he gets called out at night – yet I like to think that he had that passionate affair, even though it had to end. And I know that Linda does not in her heart of hearts regret it.

Grierson's dreams of a Parliamentary career may have come to nothing, but another councillor took up the challenge, and became MP for Marston. Everybody agrees that he's the best we've had for decades. You know who I mean, don't you? Philip Crowne, of course! His work with homeless young people led to his involvement with undercover police activity in exposing a series of paedophile rings, resulting in several convictions. I don't know who first came up with the idea that he should run for Parliament, but in 1997 it was announced that he would stand as an Independent candidate in the general election. He did better than expected: the Labour woman got in, with the Liberal Democrat coming second, only a few hundred votes ahead of Crowne, who beat the Conservative into fourth place. It was a valuable experience for him, and in 2001 he stood again, this time as Lib-Dem, and didn't we all cheer on election night when he beat Labour by a whisker and was declared the winner, Philip Crowne, MP! He's already proved his worth in the House, and there are those who'd like him to lead the party at some future time. God knows that place needs all the men of principle it can get. The only regret is that Shalom didn't survive without his on-the-spot leadership, though the good influence of the movement still lives on in Marston.

It took quite a while for my daughters to come to terms with my fall from grace, and when they finally got round to it I had to keep my emotions firmly under control. There were no dramatic scenes of reconciliation, and neither of them actually mentioned the scandal. Ruth just lifted up the phone one day and said it seemed ages since we'd had a chat, and that Helen kept asking for Nana Pierce. So on my next nights off I went to Steephill again, and soon got back into Richard's good books with some late night and early morning baby-minding. I did happen to know that an old school friend of Ruth's had sent her the local paper with the pictures and write-up of the petition being handed in at Maternity, though Ruth didn't mention it; I suppose she thought the less said, the better. Helen's now at senior school and does all sorts of extras, like ballet and tap-dancing, and has an adopted pony at the riding stables; Tim's a lively little lad, due to go up to the Comprehensive next September, and says he wants to be a footballer.

Emma also resumed contact as if nothing had happened. She just rang one day out of the blue to say that she'd finished with Danilo, and I nearly wept for joy at hearing her voice, though I managed to stay calm. She asked if she could come home for a weekend and bring this terribly sweet guy who was with BBC Radio 4 and did fabulous interviews, clearly a future Jeremy Paxman or John Humphries. So up they came, and I took to Greg on sight. Their courtship was rather stormy – they got engaged, but Emma broke it off and went around with another couple of Romeos before hurtling back to Greg with such penitent passion that the next thing was that she was pregnant, and a hastily arranged wedding took place at a Marylebone registry office. She looked so sweet in a pale blue Regency style gown, the sort they wear in those Jane Austen costume dramas, with very high waists that make them look about four months anyway. Little Louise is a darling, of course, and now has a brother, Oliver, though as they live in London I don't see as much of them as I'd like; perhaps when I'm retired it will be easier.

I'll tell you who I *do* see, though. My stepdaughter Joy moved back to Marston, and asked me if I'd like to go on holiday with her the following year. There seemed to be no reason why not, so we booked a week at a little guest house in the Yorkshire dales, and found that we loved every minute of our walks, talks, evenings at the local pub and the pleasure of each other's company – whoever would have thought it? In the course of our rambles we came across a nicely laid out caravan site at one end of a sheltered valley, and one of them was for sale. We both immediately had the same idea: why not pool our resources and buy it? And we did. It means that we have a permanent holiday retreat to which we can go at any time, and we also rent it out to people we know like Sue and Jim Digweed and their children, and other Maternity staff. Joy's son Alistair has stayed in it with his partner, and Lilian Newhouse spent a week there with her sister – that was after Brian got married to a divorced woman with two children.

Joy and I have grown as close as sisters, and I was her sponsor when she was received into the congregation of St Antony's. I find that the consolations of the church are my greatest support, though poor Father O'Flynn isn't quite the jolly Friar Tuck that he used to be. Like so many other good-living, dedicated priests of the church, he has had to bear the shame of the scandals in recent years, the number of priests who have abused children entrusted to their care, with the result that the great majority of blameless ones now live in a blame culture.

'I feel the eyes watchin' to see if I so much as pat a child on the head, Shirley,' he tells me sadly. 'And the ears listenin' when I talk to the kids about what they did at school – all the things I like to laugh and joke about with 'em.' He sighs and shakes his balding head. 'God knows I'd die before harmin' a hair o' their heads, but I have to be on me guard all the time, and that's not good for a priest who's supposed to be a father of his flock, now is it?'

Dear Father O'Flynn, at least he can confide in me, knowing that I'll understand, but the easy friendliness has gone out of his eyes, replaced by wariness in case he lets slip a careless witticism or makes a gesture (like putting an arm around a weeping child) that could be misconstrued.

'It's what God sees in you that counts, Father, and not what people think they see,' I try to assure him, but we both know that this damaging episode in the history of the Roman Catholic church is no mere nine day wonder, as my own ordeal was.

All right, so now I must come to it, the bit I've been putting off and which you've been waiting to hear. What of Paul Meadows? After all, he was the pivot on which my fortunes turned, the cause of my losing a prospective husband, making headlines in the tabloids, alienating my daughters and coming close to ruining my career.

I continued to be bothered by the way I'd abandoned him, especially when Philip Crowne told me that he'd been sent temporarily to the hospital wing of Strangeways Prison because there was currently no vacancy at Carrowbridge for a patient of his category, an unstable character of low mentality who had actually killed somebody. Crowne had managed to get to see him, and reported that he was being quite kindly treated and had made a friend of another inmate, just as he'd done at St Botolph's.

In the April, ten weeks after sentencing, he was transferred to Carrowbridge and placed in Block D, the separate secure wing with its locked doors and high barred windows. Here the inmates were not prisoners but patients under the care of bearded Dr Czerninski and his team, who held group discussions and counselling sessions with all sorts of therapeutic activities, from sketching and clay modelling to expressing themselves through dance and drama.

I knew that I had to go and see Paul, if only once. Even if he rejected me, and shouted accusations of betrayal and treachery, so that I'd be asked to leave. And if the truth be told, I needed to see him to find out how he was doing: was he halfway happy, or did he lead a wretched existence in captivity? I had to know, and that meant going to see for myself.

I was shown into the community room of Block D, and at once picked out Paul who was sitting in an armchair talking to a pasty-faced man whose features seemed permanently set in a downcast mould. Paul was neatly dressed in corduroys and a clean blue sweatshirt, his hair was brushed, his shoes polished, and he seemed perfectly relaxed.

A few other men were talking, reading, sketching or staring into space, and the air smelled of mixed cigarette smoke and freshener spray. Two uniformed nurses, a man and a woman, kept an informal watch.

'Visitor for you, Paul,' said my escort, and I stepped forward, putting on a smile. As soon as he saw me his face lit up.

'Shirley! Long time no see! How are you?'

'Oh, Paul – how are *you*?' We shook hands, and I sat down.

'Fine, except that I've been rather busy lately. It's Dr Czerninski's round tomorrow, and I've just been telling Leonard here what to expect.'

His companion glanced nervously at me, and I smiled.

'Leonard came in on Monday evening, and he's just getting to know us,' Paul explained, leaning towards me confidentially, though his voice was loud enough for everybody in the room to hear. 'I think he's going to need quite a lot of help, actually. They haven't sorted out his medication yet.'

The male nurse strolled over and winked at him. 'OK, Paul, keep it down a bit, mate. And don't forget the quiz tonight. Try to get 'em out of the TV lounge, will you? It's time that lot learned to use their grey cells.'

'Sure, see what I can do, mate,' answered Paul with a conspiratorial grin, and I could see how thrilled he was at being given this apparent equality with the staff. The nurse gave me a meaningful look.

'Is the lady a friend?' he inquired casually.

'Oh, yes, this is Shirley Pierce. She's a midwife at Marston General Hospital, and I met her at Shalom – you remember what I was saying at the discussion group, don't you?'

'Oh, yes. Oh – *yes*.' The man's eyes met mine in a gleam of recognition. 'Pleased to meet you, Shirley. Nice for Paul to have a visitor.'

He tactfully turned his attention to Leonard, but I guessed he'd have an interesting tit-bit to share with his colleague. *See that woman over there with Paul? That's HER.*

Well, what of it? Paul was obviously well settled here and liked, in fact he was probably a useful buffer between the staff and the disturbed, unhappy newcomers to Block D. Always ready to meet and talk to new friends, his outgoing nature responded to all sorts and conditions of men and women and, in a controlled environment like this, he was protected from the sort of tormenting he'd received out in the real world. As I'd testified on the witness stand, Paul Meadows posed no danger to anybody who treated him half decently.

I stayed half an hour, during which time he did almost all the talking, recounting the life histories of other patients and explaining the various activities on the daily timetable. He was as happy as at any time that I'd known him. When my time was up, I did not give him a hug but settled for a warm handshake, gripping his hand in both of mine. There was no 'Shalom!'

And after two years, what happened then? What *does* society do with men like Paul? There is no satisfactory answer. He was transferred to Clive

Woolton Court, a block of flats designed for the partial shelter of people with mental and social problems, unemployable for one reason or another, but theoretically able to take care of themselves under the supervision of a team of wardens. Thank heaven it isn't in Manchester, but near Fleetwood, so his sister can visit him from time to time, his father now being dead. I shall probably never see him again (though who knows?), but I will never forget him: there will always be a troubled place for him, and my betrayal of his innocent love in my memory.

And I shall be forever haunted by the possibility that somewhere there is a damaged life making his or her way through this cruel world because of my delay or misjudgement as a midwife. That thought haunts us all.

As for me, I'm in much the same situation as I was when this all began – still on night duty at Marston General. It gets busier all the time, and the number of deliveries increases every year; but the staff, that band of sisters, is as closely knit as it ever was.

With examinations coming up, there are no student midwives on night duty at present, which means I'll have this next delivery all to myself, a rare treat. The patient's a nice woman, and I remember her from when she was in having her first baby, a girl. Her husband's at her side, and they've put their trust in me; a woman in the agony of labour doesn't ask for a character reference from her midwife.

'It won't be long now,' I tell them with a smile,

pulling on the gown and gloves. No matter how many times you see it, it's always a new miracle, this entry into the world of another soul, a new human being with maybe seventy or eighty years or more of life ahead.

She's in second stage now, and the vertex is advancing well. I feel the familiar exhilaration as the moment approaches.

'All right, love, you're doing fine, nearly there now. Can you give just one more push for me? Good girl, that's right – and another – good, now pant in and out, in and out like a puppy-dog, that's the way – oh, there now, *look*, both of you, you've got a little boy, a son! Isn't that wonderful? Yes, love, he's all right, he's fine, in fact he's gorgeous – look at him!'

I clamp and sever the cord, then hold the slippery, squalling newborn infant up before their awestruck faces.

'There he is, love – our baby,' breathes the husband, but his words are drowned by the piercing yells that fill the delivery room. I wrap a towel round the squirming pink body and hand him to his mother who holds out her arms for him.

'Listen to him!' I say, as flushed and triumphant as if I'd given birth to him myself. 'Isn't that the most beautiful sound in all the world?'

The publishers hope that this book has given you enjoyable reading. Large Print Books are especially designed to be as easy to see and hold as possible. If you wish a complete list of our books please ask at your local library or write directly to:

Magna Large Print Books
Magna House, Long Preston,
Skipton, North Yorkshire.
BD23 4ND

This Large Print Book for the partially sighted, who cannot read normal print, is published under the auspices of

THE ULVERSCROFT FOUNDATION